THESE DEAD PROMISES

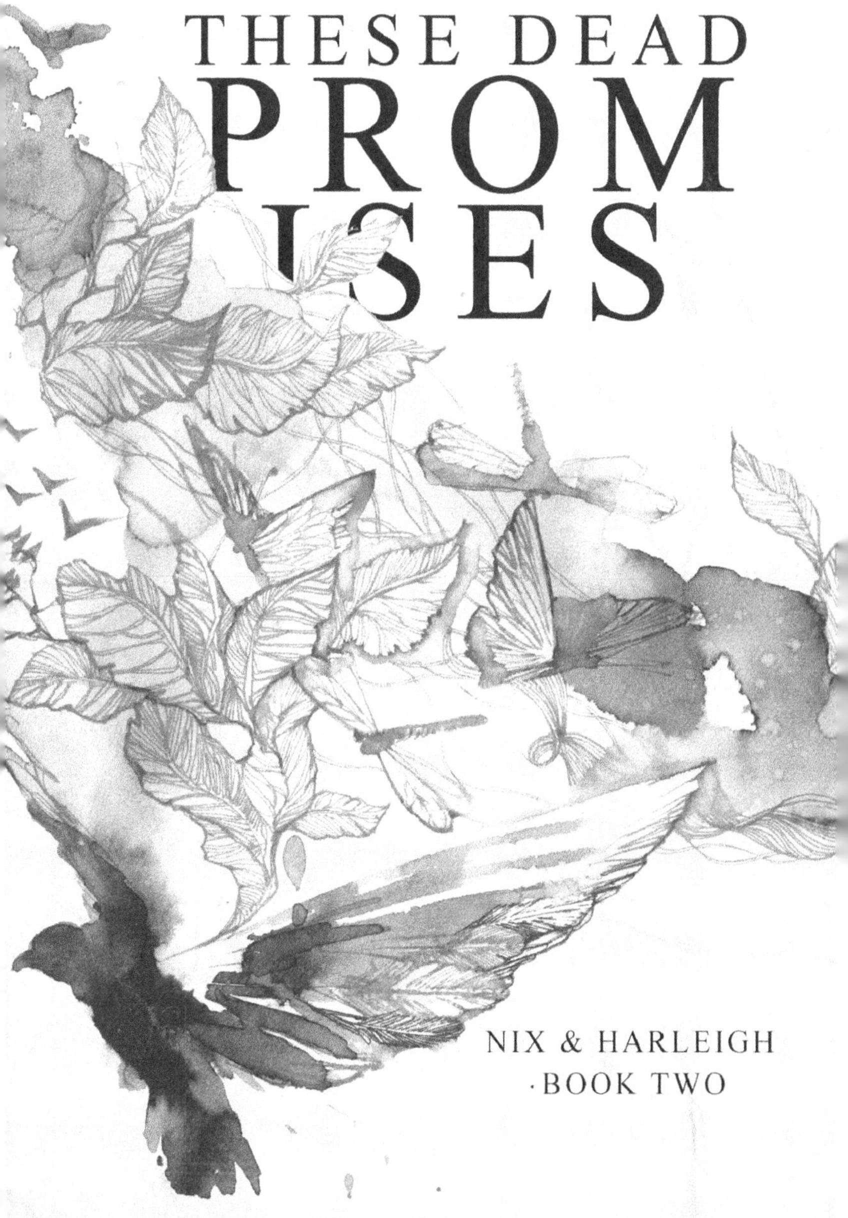

NIX & HARLEIGH
·BOOK TWO

THESE DEAD PROMISES
SPECIAL EDITION

NIX & HARLEIGH BOOK TWO

L A COTTON

Published by Delesty Books

THESE DEAD PROMISES
Nix & Harleigh Book Two

Edited by Andrea M. Long
Proofread by Sisters Get Lit.erary Author Services
Cover Designed by Lianne Cotton

DARLING HILL

These Dark Hearts
A Nix & Harleigh Prequel

These Dirty Lies
Nix & Harleigh Book One

These Dead Promises
Nix & Harleigh Book Two

HARLEIGH

"So, girls," Michael said across the table. "What did you both get up to yesterday?"

Celeste shot me a startled look, clearing her throat and grabbing her glass of water.

"Uh, we… Miles… and—"

"Didn't you say you were hanging out with Mulligan and Miller?" A smug smirk played on Max's face, and I tightened my grip on my fork a little, wishing I could stab it in *his* hand.

"Uh, yes. Yeah. We uh… we stayed over at Miles's."

"You did, huh?" Michael frowned. "Well I hope you slept in one of the guest rooms, Celeste."

"Daddy!" Her cheeks flamed as she dipped her eyes and focused on her plate.

"I always did like Miles," Sabrina said, helping herself to another glass of wine. "But he's a little bit… what's the word… dimwitted."

"Mom." Celeste balked, her eyes snapping to her mom. "Miles isn't dimwitted. He's… nice."

"Nice, yes. But his parents are concerned he won't get the grades required for Columbia."

"I've already told you, I'm not sure I want to even apply to Columbia."

"Now, sweetheart, don't be so hasty." Michael sat back in his chair, surveying the three of us. His children. Two he wanted. One he didn't.

When Celeste had woken me earlier, informing me they were back from their trip and wanted us to eat together, I'd almost laughed in her face. We rarely ate together. Not after those early days, when I'd first arrived and they'd tried to coax me out of my room for dinner.

Since I'd returned from Albany Hills, I could count on one hand how many times we'd eaten as a *family*. So color me suspicious that they chose today of all days.

Besides, the last thing I wanted to do was sit around and play happy family knowing Michael had made sure to drive a wedge so deep between me and Nix that there was no coming back from it.

My eyes flickered to Max and his smirk grew, only fueling the fire in my chest. "You and Miller are getting close, huh?"

I narrowed my eyes, wondering where the hell he was going with this. It was a game, that much I knew. But what was his end goal?

And why hadn't he told his parents yet of his suspicions about me and Nix?

"Harleigh," Michael said, and I blinked over at him. "Is that true?"

"I… we're friends." My brows crinkled, anger pulsing inside me, making it difficult to concentrate.

"After our conversation, I got the distinct impression you weren't."

"It probably isn't a good idea for the two of you to—"

"Sabrina." My father shook his head, patting her hand.

"At least she's hooking up with Miller and not that kid from across the reservoir. What's his name again? Wild? Wiler? Wilder." Max grinned triumphantly. "That's the one, Phoenix Wilder." He sat back as if he'd pulled the pin on a grenade and intended on watching it detonate.

A ripple went through the room as Celeste stared wide-eyed at me and I glared at Max. I didn't think I'd ever hated anyone more than I hated him in that moment. And for someone who harbored a lot of hatred in her heart, that was saying something.

Michael cleared his throat, muttering, "Max, that's enough"

"Sorry, Dad. I know you don't like talking about—"

He slammed his hand down, making the glassware clatter. "I said, that's enough."

"Harleigh knows better, don't you?" Sabrina said, concern and something akin to disgust glittering in her eyes. "She understands that she left that life behind when she came here."

My heart sank.

They would never accept Nix.

They would never accept me hanging around in The Row and clinging onto my past.

Michael watched me, his eyes boring into mine. He didn't say anything, but that only made it worse. The tension crackling around us.

Harleigh?" Sabrina repeated, and I blinked over at her.

"Y-yes."

It wasn't an answer to her question, but she read it as one, and I didn't correct her.

"Good." She gave me a curt, dismissive nod, as if that was that. As if it wasn't worth talking about because it wasn't even possible that I would ever try to rebuild bridges with Nix or anyone from my past now that I lived here. I had this nice shiny life in Old Darling Hill. What more could I possibly need?

My skin felt too tight, the air too thin as I shifted uncomfortably in my chair. I knew dinner with them was a bad idea.

Anger bubbled inside me: hot, fiery anger. I was burning up, sweat trickling down my spine as I sat there and tried to rein in my emotions.

Celeste tried to catch my attention, but I ignored her, my gaze wholly fixed on Michael.

My father.

The man who had cast me and Mom aside like we were nothing more than dirt on his shoe. I still didn't understand his true motivation for coming for me that day. Did he think it would place him as my savior? Or was it years of guilt that had brought him to the police station that morning?

Time might have smoothed the cracks, eased some of that betrayal. But now I knew the truth—now I knew he was responsible for keeping Nix away from me—there would be no forgiveness. It had only reaffirmed what in my heart I knew to be true. Michael Rowe was a cold, selfish, heartless man.

And one day, I would find a way to ruin his perfect life, the way he'd ruined mine.

"Oh my God," Celeste whispered as we reached the roof terrace. "That was…"

"Yeah." A heavy sigh left my lips as I flopped down into the rattan egg chair. Celeste sat on the small cube and gave me a weak smile.

"What are you going to do? About… you know."

"I don't know." I clutched my cell phone, staring at the blank screen. Nix had already texted me. Twice to be exact. He wanted to see me tonight. But Max knew.

Somehow Max knew.

And I didn't doubt he was going to lord it over me and use it to his own ends.

My cell vibrated, startling me, and sending my heart into a downward spiral.

"Is it…?" My eyes collided with Celeste's and I nodded. "Well," she urged. "What does it say?"

I read Nix's text, blood roaring between my ears. "Can I see you tonight?"

"Yes. Say yes."

"I-I can't."

"What?" She frowned. "Of course you can."

"It's too risky. I need to think…" I needed to catch my breath.

Last night had been like all my dreams come true. Being with Nix, feeling his weight on top of me, him moving inside me… I would never forget how amazing it felt. But if Max knew, if he had proof and told Michael, I couldn't risk it. Not yet.

"Harleigh, it'll be okay."

"Will it?" My heart cracked. "He… he threatened Nix, Celeste. He lied to both of us. Do you have any idea what that did to me?"

Thinking Nix had abandoned me had ruined me. Wrecked me in a way even I hadn't expected. Losing my mom didn't come close to what it felt like to lose Nix. In a world where I'd never quite fit in, he was my anchor. My North Star. Losing that had been like losing a part of myself. A vital piece of my heart. Without it, I'd felt lost. Drowning in darkness.

"Harleigh?"

Jerking out of the maudlin thoughts, I forced a weak smile. "Sorry."

"You could say you're going out with me, Miles, and Nate."

"I don't want to use Nate like that, it isn't fair."

"Yeah, it's a bit awkward."

"What?"

"Well…" She bit her lip. "I'm pretty sure he likes you."

My heart sank. "No he doesn't." But the words were like ash on my tongue because I had sensed something earlier when he'd given me a ride home.

"Don't worry. He knows you belong to Nix."

Nix.

Just the sound of his name made my heart swell. But it frayed around the edges, straining with all the pain we'd endured.

All because of *him*.

My father.

Anger rose inside of me, an unrelenting tsunami, gathering speed and strength. My fingers curled into a fist.

"Harleigh…" Celeste said softly. "You're growling."

"I'm…" She was right. A low keening sound rumbled in my chest.

"You're angry."

"Angry doesn't even begin to cover what I feel toward him." My body vibrated with restless energy.

"We should get out of here. Come on." She held out her hand and I stared at it like it was contagious. "You need a distraction. Sitting here stewing on things isn't going to help anything."

"Where will we go?"

"Does it matter?" Her brow quirked up.

"Fine." I stood. "But we should probably avoid your dad and Max."

Because I felt… *wrong*.

I felt like I might explode at any second and do something stupid.

Concern flashed in Celeste's eyes but she schooled her expression. "I have an idea. Do you trust me?"

"You know I do." She was one of the few people I trusted.

"Then let's get out of here."

THE SECOND CELESTE headed toward The Row, I knew I'd made a huge mistake.

"What the hell are you doing?" I snapped.

"I figured since it isn't probably a good idea for Nix to come to our side of town, we could go to his."

"Have you lost your goddamn mind?" I glared at her, but she kept her eyes on the road.

"You should call him, let him know we're on our way."

"Turn around. Turn around right now," I said, panic swelling like a riptide inside me.

"I can't turn around, Harleigh." Strained laughter escaped her lips. "It's a solid plan."

"Stupid. It's a stupid plan."

"You'll have to direct me to his trailer. I'm not—"

"His trailer?" I balked. "We can't turn up at his trailer, Celeste."

"What? Why?"

"Because… because we wouldn't be welcome."

"I don't understand." She shot me a confused look.

"Nix's dad isn't a nice guy."

"What? Does he beat on Nix or something?"

"Or something," I murmured, years of memories bubbling to the surface.

"God, I didn't know."

"Joe Wilder isn't a good man. But his stepmom Jessa is nice."

"I guess I didn't really think this through. I just thought—"

"It's okay," I said. "I'll text Nix and see what the guys are up to."

"Yeah?" There was a definite pep in her voice.

"Did you tell Miles where we were going?" My brow arched.

"I told him we needed some girly time." Her eyes slid to mine, swirling with shame. "I didn't want him to worry."

"Worry that you're headed to The Row, or worry that a certain brooding bad boy—"

"Don't say it," she rushed out. "Just… don't."

I lifted my hands in defeat. "You got it. But, so you know, I think this is a bad idea."

"Nothing is going to happen with me and Zane. I'm with Miles."

"Good. I'm pretty sure you're not Zane's type anyway."

Her brows furrowed. "What's that supposed to mean?"

I shook my head gently. "Nothing."

My cell vibrated and I opened Nix's reply.

Hot Tub Guy: Seriously? You're in The Row?

Me: Yeah. It's all part of Celeste's grand plan.

My cell phone started ringing.

"Hello?" I answered.

"Grand plan, huh? Do I even want to know?" Humor laced his words.

"It's probably better you don't. What are you up to?"

"We're at Kye's. Come over."

"I'm not sure it's a good idea for us to hang around. But we could go somewhere."

"I'll go anywhere with you, B. You know that, right?" My heart pounded in my chest. He had such a way with words. A way of making me feel like I was the only girl in the world.

It was astonishing, and a little intimidating at how easily we'd fallen back into this routine. Of me hanging on his every word. Eager for whatever he might say next.

But it had been innocent back then. An unrequited crush. At least, that's what I'd thought.

"Birdie?" His voice turned thick, low and gravelly. It rumbled through me.

"I'm here."

"Remember the old grain mill?" he said, as if I could ever forget.

"I remember." It had been one of the best and worst nights of my life.

"Meet us there." He inhaled a deep breath, and I could imagine him scrubbing a hand down his face, his brows drawn together in deep contemplation. "We'll bring supplies."

"Okay," I breathed.

"And B?"

"Yeah?"

"I missed you."

2

NIX

"You missed her?" Zane snorted. "Bro, it's barely been a few hours."

I flipped him off, not dignifying him with an answer. I didn't mean I'd missed her for the few hours since we had said goodbye outside Miller's house. I'd meant the last nine months.

All those wasted days, weeks, months. Thinking she'd chosen her father over me. A better life over the one I could give her.

Fuck.

I didn't know how the hell to deal with all the rage coursing through my veins. The bone-deep anger at the fact her father had kept her from me. Lied through his pearly white teeth to break us apart. As if he hadn't hurt her enough already.

I couldn't get my head around it. The vindictiveness

and malice. But most of all, I couldn't believe that I'd fallen for it. That I'd bought his lies so easily.

Growing up, Harleigh rarely talked about her father. As far as I knew, she'd known little about him. Known little about her mom's life in Old Darling Hill. There were no grandparents on the scene. No aunts or uncles. Nothing.

It was almost as if when Trina left, she hadn't looked back.

And it killed her.

Slowly and painfully, it drove her to the brink of madness. The wounds so deep that they festered, only made worse by all the liquor.

I'd known Harleigh for over ten years, and I'd never known a time when Trina Maguire wasn't drunk or sleeping off a hangover. Michael Rowe did that. He ruined her and then he ruined Harleigh.

I pressed a fist to my thigh, trying to rein in the tidal wave of emotion inside me. "She's in The Row," I said.

"What? Now? How—"

"The sister."

Zane's eyes narrowed. "You're shitting me?"

"You sound surprised."

"Didn't know she had it in her." He almost sounded impressed.

"Could be there's a lot about her you don't know?" I arched a brow.

"What the fuck is that supposed to mean?"

"Nothing… just thought that maybe a girl has finally gotten under your skin."

He made a choking sound. "Not fucking likely."

"So you don't want to come to the old grain mill with me to meet them then?"

"Where we going?" Kye appeared with fresh bottles of beer.

"Birdie is in The Row," Zane answered.

"No shit. She coming here?"

"That'd be okay with you?" I asked.

"Hell yeah, it's B. She's one of us."

Something loosened in my chest. It was that simple with Kye. Zane was different. More guarded and suspicious of the world. But with Kye everything was easy.

"Invite Chloe," I said. "And ask your mom if we can grab some supplies."

"Supplies?" Zane balked. "We're not taking a fucking picnic."

"I didn't say a picnic, asshole." But it was B. She was here, and I wanted to make it nice for her.

Fuck, Zane was right. I was turning into a pussy. But Harleigh was important to me—the most important thing in my whole wretched life. I wanted to be the kind of guy who surprised her, who made her feel special. If that meant grabbing a couple of blankets and some of Ms. Carter's home-baked cookies, then so be it.

An idea sprang into my head and I grinned at the guys.

"Oh no," Zane grumbled. "I know that look."

"What do you say to a little barbecue?"

"Barbecue? Where the fuck are we going to get supplies for a barbecue?"

"I've got an idea."

"This should be interesting." He rolled his eyes.

Interesting, maybe.

Reckless and guaranteed to end up with me and my old man going at it again, most definitely.

But Harleigh was worth it.

She was worth every damn thing.

"YOU LITTLE FUCKING SHIT," my old man bellowed after us as we hightailed it toward my car, arms full of supplies.

Once a month, my old man usually brought home a ton of meat to grill out. Burgers, steak, ribs… it was one of the few days I saw Jessa happy. She used to make me eat with them. Play happy family. She'd ask me about school, about football, and my friends, and I'd end up saying something to piss my old man off and it would be ruined. So over the years, I'd started making myself scarce.

"I left you and Jessa enough," I shouted through the window, laughter rumbling in my chest.

"You'll pay for this," Zane grumbled.

"Worth it though." I fired up the engine and watched the blood vessels in my old man's forehead fizzle and pop as I drove off, leaving nothing but dust in our wake.

Kye whooped, Chloe giggling beside him. "Seriously, who eats all of this?" she asked, eyeing the bag of bloody meat.

"Don't let my old man's physique fool you, Clo. The guy is an animal."

"Last night was fun." She caught my eye in the rearview mirror and smiled.

"Yeah." A lick of heat went through me.

It hadn't been fun, it had been… the best night of my fucking life. Feeling Harleigh naked and wanting beneath me. The way her body hugged mine, the way we fit together, so perfect, so right.

Part of me was pissed that I hadn't waited. That I'd tainted myself with all the girls before her. Because what I'd felt with Harleigh was like nothing I'd ever felt before.

"Are Miles and Nate coming?" she asked innocently enough, but it didn't stop Kye from pinning her with a sharp look. "What?" A knowing smirk played on her lips.

"I'm serious Clo, Miller is off-limits."

"You're being a dick."

"You think I didn't see you draped over him last night like a cheap fucking throw?"

"I was not." She huffed indignantly.

"Yeah, whatever. And no, Miles and Nate aren't coming. Right?" He looked to me for confirmation.

"Right."

I didn't really give a shit if they came, so long as I got some alone time with B.

I took the road toward the old grain mill. It was somewhere I came to clear my head, to get away from it all and just think. It was also where I'd brought Harleigh last Halloween. The place where I'd touched her for the first time.

Fuck. Maybe coming back here wasn't such a good idea. It held memories. Tainted memories. Bittersweet with the half-truths and lies that existed between us.

"You good?" Zane asked, and I glanced over at him, nodding.

But the truth was I was nervous. Restless energy zipping through me, making my leg jostle.

Last night had been urgent, driven by some base need to comfort and protect Harleigh. This morning had been… fuck, it had been perfect, waking up with her in my arms. But space, time, and distance weren't my friends. It allowed the seeds of doubt to take root and anchor themselves to my soul. Because there were some truths I couldn't deny.

Starting with the fact that Harleigh no longer lived in The Row. That she wasn't right across from my trailer, always there. A stone's throw away.

It shouldn't have mattered; I knew her heart. But her father was a problem.

A big fucking problem.

One I hadn't quite worked out how to fix yet.

"They're already here," Chloe said, just as I spotted Celeste's Range Rover parked over by some trees. My heart lurched into my throat, blood pounding in my ears.

She was here.

B was here.

This morning, when I'd left her, when I'd watched her walk away, doubt had quickly swept in, tamping down the lingering fire in my veins after my night with her. But she was here.

She came.

The car came to an abrupt stop and I shouldered the door open, climbing out, ignoring Zane's grumble of disapproval.

He didn't get it.

He would never get it.

I'd spent nine long months without her. My best friend. My anchor. The other half of my dirty, black fucking soul. I didn't plan on spending another second without her.

It was that simple.

Celeste spotted me first, a small smile lifting the corner of her mouth. But I only had eyes for Harleigh as she turned slowly, her breath catching as I strode toward her.

"Nix," she breathed, and I pulled her into my arms, pressing my head to hers.

"Hey, Birdie." The tension I'd felt since this morning seeped out of my shoulders.

She slid her hands up my chest, clutching my dark-gray t-shirt. "We have an audience." Her whispered words made my chest ache.

"Don't care," I murmured, inhaling her. Breathing her in. This, this is what I needed. Her. Me. The two of us facing the shitshow that was life. Together.

Soft laughter spilled out of her, and she tried to bury her face in the crook of my neck, but I gripped her chin gently, staring at her. Silently telling her everything I felt. "Gonna kiss you now, B."

Fixing my mouth to hers, I kissed her slowly. Deeply. My tongue snaked out, licking her lips, tasting her. A whimper escaped her as my tongue found hers.

Jesus. Kissing her was like a shock to my body. It wanted more. *More, more, more.* My hand slipped down her spine, clamping around her hip and dragging her closer. "Fuck, you drive me wild," I said, touching my head to hers again, forcing myself to calm the fuck down.

"The feeling is mutual." She gazed up at me all doe-eyed and lust drunk.

"We should go join the others before I do something reckless." Like drag her somewhere quiet and finish what I started with that kiss.

This was new for her. I didn't want to overwhelm her or scare her away. But the way I wanted her, the need I felt deep inside… it scared even me.

Harleigh had always been my weakness, but I didn't think she'd ever realized the power she wielded over me.

Neither of us went to move though, unwilling to end the moment.

"Keep looking at me like that, B, and I'm not sure you'll be prepared for what happens next."

"Why?" She swallowed. "What will happen?"

Sliding my hand against her neck, I pushed her hair away and ran my thumb over the skin along her jaw. "You know."

Her eyes flared with heat. No doubt with memories of last night. Of the moment she gave herself to me.

"I… you're right." She flushed. "We should go join them."

She was too damn cute for her own good.

"Come on." I grabbed her hand and tugged her into my side.

Zane's brow quirked up as we approached our friends. Kye already had the disposable grill fired up, and Chloe had spread out the blankets.

"What is all this?" Harleigh asked.

"We're having a barbecue. Isn't that great?" Celeste grinned.

"That's… where did you get all this from?" B glanced up at me.

"Don't worry about it." I dropped a kiss on the end of her nose and went to join the guys. But she grabbed my wrist and yanked me back to her.

"Nix, what did you do?"

Irritation flickered through me, but I stuffed it down. "I said don't worry about it. Help the girls unpack the rest of the food."

I shirked out of her grip and walked away, but I could feel her eyes burning into my back.

Tonight was supposed to be fun. It was supposed to be a chance to do something nice together. I didn't want her to worry.

I didn't want Harleigh to ever doubt this. Us.

But she knew me better than anyone.

She always had.

3

HARLEIGH

"I'm stuffed," Chloe let out a satisfied groan, patting her stomach. "You'll have to tell your dad the steak was—"

"Dad?" I sat up and twisted around to glare at Nix. "You stole the meat off your dad?"

"Thanks a bunch, Clo," he grumbled, hooking his arm around my neck and pulling me back down so that my back was against his chest.

"Nix," I sighed. I didn't want him doing anything that could cause trouble between him and his father, especially not for me.

"Relax, B," he whispered, pressing a kiss to my shoulder. "It's not a big deal."

Zane scoffed at that. "Tell us that after he's—"

Nix must have sent him a hard look because Zane swallowed whatever he'd been about to say.

A sinking feeling spread through me and it was on the

tip of my tongue to ask Zane what he he meant. But I knew. I'd always known, back from when we were kids growing up in The Row, just trying to survive. Me, my mother and her addiction to liquor; Nix, his father and his unpredictable temper. Over the years, I'd lost count how many times Nix had turned up on my porch with a black eye or split lip. He hadn't liked to talk about it back then, but I'd known.

I'd always known.

My stomach churned, but Nix's arms tightened around me. "Stop overthinking it," he said quietly. "I'll be fine."

"We're talking about this, Nix." I twisted to look at him. "Not here, not now, but soon."

Intense gray eyes stared back at me, full of vulnerability and pain.

There was so much we had yet to talk about. Things we'd been through, things we were still going through.

"I like it out here," Celeste said, cutting through the heavy tension around us.

"It's an abandoned mill. What's to like?" Zane muttered.

"I don't know." She shrugged, refusing to meet his eyes. "It's peaceful and it feels off the grid."

"Off the—"

"She's right, bro." Kye added around a teasing smile aimed right at Zane. "It is kinda cool."

"I bring my girl to all the best places," Nix said, letting his lips brush my shoulder again, making me shudder.

His girl.

His girl.

The words spun around in my head, giving me a warm fuzzy feeling like a hit of dopamine as Kye started telling Celeste the history of the mill, much to Zane's annoyance.

I was only half-listening, too busy soaking up Nix's solid presence behind and around me. One of his hands had slipped inside my t-shirt, stroking the skin there.

"First game of the season next weekend. You gonna come support your guy, B?"

"You all play football?" Celeste asked.

I rolled my eyes at her attempt at playing dumb, and Zane snorted, seeing straight through her.

"What?" She glowered at him.

"Does this little act usually work?"

"Act? What the hell is that supposed to mean?"

"Come on, Z, man," Nix said. "We're supposed to be chilling."

"Yeah, whatever," he conceded, digging in his pocket and pulling out a blunt.

"Not that kind of chilling," Nix grumbled.

"B doesn't mind, do you?" Zane gave me a wicked grin.

"Quit being a dick, Z." Kye threw something at him and Zane snarled.

"Boys." Chloe shook her head. "Are Miles and Nate like this?" she asked Celeste, who glanced at me with a confused expression.

I chuckled. "Someone has a crush."

"I do not," Chloe protested, narrowing her eyes at me.

"Nate is…"

"Someone I don't want to talk about." Nix nipped my collarbone.

"Nate Miller is complicated," Celeste added. "He doesn't really let people get close."

"Except Harleigh, right? You two seem tight."

"Clo," I chided, aware of Nix silent and still behind me.

"What?" She shrugged. "Nix knows you're his. You've always been his."

Her words hit me dead in the chest.

I had always been his, hadn't I?

He just hadn't realized it until it was too late.

"Whatever you're thinking." He leaned in, whispering against my cheek. "Stop, right now."

"How did you know?" I breathed.

"I know you, B. I know you better than anyone. Want to take a walk with me?"

"Nix, we can't just—"

"Sure we can. Come on." He got up and offered me his hand. "We'll be back."

Zane muttered something under his breath as he leaned back on his elbows, taking a deep hit on his blunt.

"Try not to kill each other, yeah?" Nix gave his best friend a knowing look before sliding his eyes to Celeste.

"Have fun." She waved.

It still surprised me how accepting Celeste was of all... this. Me. My past. Nix and the guys. She seemed totally unfazed by it. In fact, she seemed curious. Maybe a little too curious if the tension crackling between her and Zane was anything to go by.

Nix hooked his arm around my waist and tucked me into his side.

"Where are we going?" I asked.

"Somewhere a little more private." He guided us over to the abandoned mill.

"Is it safe?"

"Safe enough." He dropped a kiss on my head and there was something so intimate about it, so right, that I got a little choked up.

Silence followed us into the rickety old building. Nix was right; structurally, it seemed sound, but the rest of the place was a mess. The windows had long been blown out, destroyed by the elements and kids looking for a quick adrenaline rush no doubt. Dirt and debris littered the floor, crunching underneath my sneakers.

"How many times have you been out here?"

He shrugged. "A few. Usually, I just sit in my car, but when I first started coming out here, I used to explore the place. There's an office back here."

We left the main warehouse and slipped into a hall, the air thick with dust. Anticipation vibrated inside me, making my skin tingle, as my thoughts flickered to last night again.

A small puff of air left my lips as Nix pulled me into a small room and pushed me up against the wall. "Alone at last." His eyes glittered in the murky light, provided by a single small window high up on one of the walls. Hands pressed at either side of my head, he leaned in, rubbing his nose along my jaw.

"This is harder than I thought it would be."

"What is?" I raised a brow, though my voice quivered.

He chuckled softly. "I meant keeping my hands to myself. Behaving." Inhaling a thin breath, he whispered, "I can't stop thinking about last night."

"Me neither." My lashes fluttered as I gazed up at him.

The torrent of emotions bubbling inside of me were how I'd always imagined it would be, when I was just a girl with stars in her eyes and love in her heart. I'd worshiped Nix as a girl. A young, naïve girl who'd truly believed that she'd found her soul mate. The other half of her heart. All the girls, the drama, the endless disappointment of watching him kiss lips that weren't mine and hold hands that didn't belong to me had sucked, it had sucked so damn much. But deep down, it didn't matter because Phoenix Wilder was mine. Just as I was his. And nothing could come between that.

Nothing but my father.

The thought was like a lead balloon in my stomach.

"Harleigh?" Nix slid one of his hands into my hair, cupping the nape of my neck. "What is it?"

"I hate him, Nix. I hate him so much. What he did… what I did because I thought you…" Tears burned the backs of my eyes as I inhaled deeply.

"I know, Birdie. I know." He brushed his lips over mine. "But he didn't break us. He didn't break you."

Nix's conviction should have reassured me, but I still had doubts. Because something had broken in me that night. Something I wasn't sure I would ever get back. Being here with Nix helped. His touch, his heated gaze, and reverent touch all eased the gaping hole inside me. But some scars were simply too deep to heal.

"Hey," he whispered when I stood there, rooted to the

spot, my body quivering. "What is it? What's wrong?" His eyes searched mine, shining with nothing but unconditional love.

I'm broken, I swallowed the words. *Fractured and lost.*

I loved him, I knew that. Loved him with every fiber of my being. But sometimes love wasn't enough.

It hadn't been enough for my father. And it hadn't been enough for my mom. Just like it hadn't been enough for Nix's mom either.

We were surrounded by people who had proved that love didn't fix anything. So could we really believe love could fix this?

"B, talk to me," he pleaded.

"I'm okay." I lied, kissing him back. Letting the taste of him, the glide of his tongue against mine distract me from the dark thoughts pushing to the surface of my mind.

He tried to pull away, no doubt to finish the conversation. To push me for answers. But I laced my arms around his neck, anchoring us together.

"If I didn't know better," he rasped onto my lips. "I'd say you were trying to distract me."

"Is it working?" Soft laughter chased my words, so soft it was almost believable.

"The things I want to do to you, B." His hands skated down my waist, slipping around my hips and yanking me closer. Erasing every inch of space between our bodies as he pressed me against the wall, grinding into me.

"Nix." His name was a choked sigh.

"Tell me what you want, B. Anything, I'll give you anything."

"I-I..." Nothing came out, a heavy weight settling on my chest. I wanted him. I wanted his hands on my body and his mouth on my skin. But suddenly, I felt out of my league.

Nix was experienced. He knew what he liked, he knew how to make a girl feel good.

I didn't know any of those things.

"B?" His brows drew together.

"I've never..." My gaze darted away from his face. "I don't..."

"Hey, look at me." A playful smile traced his mouth, but he wasn't teasing me. He would never do that. "Do you have any idea how fucking good it makes me feel knowing I'm the only guy who's ever touched you here." One of his hands snaked around my thigh and cupped me *there*. My breath caught in my throat as he rubbed gently, applying the right amount of pressure to make me squirm.

"Are you wet for me, B?"

I pressed my lips together, nodding.

"Do you want me to make you feel good?"

Another nod as my head dropped back against the cool wall. It felt good, too good.

The self-doubt, the crippling anxiety I felt every time my thoughts flickered to dark, dark places edged away, replaced with something needier. Something hot and fiery.

Nix dipped his head, dragging his tongue up my throat and kissing my jaw, sucking and nibbling the skin there as his fingers moved in circles. It was too much... and not nearly enough.

"More," I breathed, falling into him. Into the sensations tumbling through me. "More…"

"Shit, yeah." His hand moved up, finding the waistband of my shorts. The elastic stretched with ease as he slipped inside. But he didn't stop there, sliding his fingers into my underwear.

"Fuck," he hissed, his eyes almost black as he watched me. Watched my reaction as he pressed two fingers inside me, curling them deep.

"Nix," I whispered, wriggling against him.

"You want me to stop?"

"No, no…" God no. I wanted more. I wanted to drown in him. In this.

I wanted to drown and never ever come up for air.

NIX

Harleigh's little sighs and moans of pleasure were going to be my fucking undoing. She looked beautiful, head dropped back against the wall, eyes heavy-lidded, and cheeks flushed as I worked her with my fingers.

Clutching my arm, she moaned. Panted my name over and over as she rode my hand, chasing the inevitable fall. "Nix, Nix… *Phoenix.*"

I wanted more.

I wanted to lift her up the wall and impale myself inside her, but this wasn't about me.

I'd seen how tense she'd gone when I'd asked her what she wanted. Before last night, Harleigh had been a virgin. She wasn't experienced, and from her response just now, I assumed she didn't know what she liked or how she wanted it.

But I was more than okay with that because we could

learn together. She could use me however she wanted to explore her body, all the ways she liked to get off.

"God, Nix... it's..." Harleigh's breath caught as I circled my thumb over her clit in small, precise circles. Her body was tense as she fought her oncoming release.

Touching my head to hers, I forced her to look at me, to see me. "Let go, B," I said. "Fly."

She clenched, panting my name.

"That's it, Birdie... give it to me." I kissed her, swallowing her little cries of pleasure. She tried to bury her face in my shoulder, to escape the intensity of the moment. But I didn't give her the chance, cupping her cheek and holding her there. "So fucking beautiful." I grinned.

"I... that was..." She flushed crimson. "Unexpected."

"Really?" My brow arched. "Because I've thought of nothing else since we got here."

"Nix..."

"Yeah, B?"

"Stop looking at me like that." She frowned, but I didn't miss the faint smile tracing her mouth.

I leaned in, brushing my lips over hers. Once. Twice. "Why?"

"Because it makes me feel... nervous."

"It should." Tucking a strand of her hair behind her ear, I chuckled. "I want to fucking devour you."

"You're so confident," she said quietly, a hint of sadness there.

"Because I know what I want, B and I'm not afraid to take it. You shouldn't be either."

A soft sigh left her. "You make it sound so easy. You know what you like, how you like it… I don't know—"

"I'm gonna stop you right there," I said, smoothing my thumb over her cheek. "You think I don't get nervous every time I touch you? I do. This, us, the way I feel about you…it's new for me too."

New and scary and intense.

But it was B.

Harleigh.

My Wren.

"If you need to go slow, we'll go slow." It would fucking kill me now that I knew how she felt, how perfectly our bodies fit together. But I could rein it in. I could go at her pace.

Anything for her.

"That's not—"

"Shh." I kissed her again, letting my hand glide along the side of her neck until I felt her pulse flutter beneath the tips of my fingers. Harleigh kissed me back, boldly plunging her tongue into my mouth and taking control.

Heat licked down my spine, stoking the flames inside me higher and higher until I thought I might explode.

"Stop," I breathed, hardly able to believe I'd said it. "We should stop."

"But I thought—"

"I want you, B. More than you'll ever understand. But not here, not like this."

"Oh, okay."

"You deserve more, Birdie." So much fucking more.

"I only want you," she said, peeking up at me through those thick, dark lashes.

Jesus, looking at her hurt sometimes. The vulnerability and honesty in her bewitching green eyes.

Harleigh had always had an expressive gaze. Everything she thought, everything she was feeling was usually right there, simmering in her eyes. You just had to look closely enough to see it.

"We have time." I put some space between us, trying to think of anything but my raging hard on.

Mrs. Feeley's ice cream.

Jessa's cookies.

My old man's dirty stained wifebeaters.

Yeah, that did the trick, the tension melting out of my body.

"Do you think Zane and Celeste have hurt each other yet?" Harleigh asked, and I was grateful for the change of subject.

"You noticed that, huh?"

"She's not exactly discreet."

"But she's with Mulligan."

"I guess." She shrugged. "It could get messy."

"Not likely. Z is… well, you know how Z is."

"Yeah. Would it bother you though if they did hook up?"

"They won't," I said, not entirely sure I believed my own words. Celeste got under Zane's skin. I'd seen it with my own eyes.

"But if they did…"

"That's their business." It was my turn to shrug. "Why?"

"Celeste isn't like us… I mean, you. The guys. She doesn't—"

"Know what it's like to grow up in The Row." I stiffened and Harleigh nodded.

"Michael would never approve of her being with someone like Zane."

Someone like me, the words flashed in my mind.

"What is it you're trying to say, Harleigh?" I snapped, feeling coils of shame snake through me.

"N-nothing, I didn't mean… I shouldn't have said that." Her expression fell. "I don't care what he thinks. But he could make things difficult for her. For them."

She wasn't talking about Celeste and Zane. She was talking about us.

Saying everything she couldn't, using words she could.

"Come on, let's go back to the others." She didn't look at me as she grabbed my hand and moved past me.

And I let her.

Because there were some things I still wasn't ready to hear.

"So where are you playing next weekend?" Celeste asked innocently enough.

It was getting late, the sun already sinking behind the tree line. But none of us were in any rush to leave.

Kye had used his Boy Scout skills to start a fire, the flames licking the dusky sky while he and Zane drank their beers.

They each looked to me and I let out a small sigh. "DA."

Harleigh went rigid beside me. "Your first game is at DA?" she said. "But that's—"

"Some real bad luck?" Zane quipped.

"Can't Coach Farringdon get it changed? Can't he—"

"The schedule was already changed. Our first game was supposed to be Dartford, but it got moved to DA."

"At our stadium?" Celeste asked, and I nodded, a ripple of frustration going through me.

Playing Denby at his place would have been irritating enough but playing him at his place now that Harleigh was back in my life... it made me want to punch something.

Preferably that smug fucker's face.

"Well, we can't exactly sit in the visiting fans section, but we'll be there."

"We will?" B blinked at her half-sister.

"Yeah, well. You want to support the guys, right?"

"I..."

"Come to the game, B." I nuzzled her neck. "I want you there."

She twisted around to look at me. "You know it's not that simple. If anyone—"

"We'll figure it out." Because I wouldn't be able to focus without her there, in the bleachers watching.

It was a little unnerving how possessive I felt toward her. But I'd lost her once. I had no fucking intention of it ever happening again.

"Nix, I'm not sure—"

"You should come, B," Z said, surprising me. "He'll be useless if you're not there, and we've got a lot riding on the game."

I pinned my best friend with a hard look, and he quirked a brow. "What? It's true. We all want to kick DA's ass, but it's more than that. Every game is one step closer to—"

"Z," I hissed.

"What?" Harleigh glanced up at me. "What's going on?"

"Albany U is interested," Kye said. "Coach thinks Nix has a real shot at getting a full ride but he's being... difficult about it."

"Is that true?" She sat up and turned fully around to me. "They want you?"

"Maybe," I said, barely meeting her eyes. "It's not a big deal."

"Nix," she breathed. "It's a huge deal. This is a good thing. A great thing." Her voice dropped to a whisper.

"I don't want to talk about it right now."

Confusion flickered in her eyes. "But—"

"Leave it, yeah?"

Harleigh turned back to the fire and guilt rolled through me. I was being a dick. But the truth was, I couldn't talk about it. Not here. Not surrounded by our friends.

I'd gotten her back. Harleigh was here. She was mine. And there was a ton of shit just waiting to try and separate us again. I didn't want to add a scholarship that may or may not happen to that list.

I didn't want to think beyond the here and now. Because this—her—it was all I needed.

For now, it was enough.

I slipped my arm around her waist and pulled her

back against my chest. "I'm sorry," I said quietly, breathing her in. "I didn't mean to snap."

Harleigh slid her hand over mine. "It's okay."

It wasn't, but I'd take it.

Zane caught my eye, silently asking me if I was okay. Lips pressed together in a thin line, I nodded.

Harleigh was here. She was here and she was okay. Everything else would figure itself out. Because no matter what happened, I would never leave her side again.

"You know, she's kind of cool." Kye flicked his head over to where Celeste, Chloe, and Harleigh were talking.

It was time to go, and I could already feel anger bubbling inside my veins. I didn't want to leave her, not again. And I sure as fuck didn't want her going back to *his* house. But this was our reality for now, and I had to find a way to live with that.

"Celeste is cool," I said, knowing that I owed her for bringing Harleigh here today.

"She's annoying," Zane grunted.

Kye chuckled. "You would say that."

"Fuck off."

Zane uncapped a bottle of water and doused the fire until it was nothing more than a pile of ash and embers. "Do we have a plan for the game?"

"A plan?" Kye's ears perked up.

"Harleigh's gonna be there, right? No way Denby won't try to use that to his advantage."

"Yeah." My eyes slid over to where she was standing, smiling at her sister and Chloe. Fuck, that smile. I wanted more of that. More of her smiles and laughter and her happiness. But I knew better. Because life was hard. It was messy and fucked up. And few kids from The Row ever made it out.

"Come on," I said, taking off toward the girls.

My girl.

My chest swelled. But an icy sensation washed over me as I heard Chloe say, "Oh shit, have you told Nix?"

They hadn't noticed me yet. But their heads soon whipped around when I said, "Told me what?"

"I..." Guilt flooded Harleigh's expression. "It's nothing."

"Just tell him, Harleigh. He'd want to know," Celeste said.

I was beginning to like her more and more.

"What's going on?" I asked coolly.

"Max knows."

"Your brother?" She nodded, and I asked, "What exactly does he know?"

"I'm not sure. But when I got back this morning, he said some things."

"What things?" My jaw clenched as Harleigh began to shut down. To shut *me* out.

"It doesn't matter. I can handle Max."

Grabbing her hand, I pulled her away from everyone else, not stopping until we were out of earshot. "When were you going to tell me?"

"Nix... it's not a big deal."

"Fuck that. He knows. He could tell your dad. I don't want him to cause trouble for you."

"But that's just it," she said, sadness bleeding into her words. "This, us… it is going to cause trouble and there's nothing we can do about it."

"What are you saying?" I gritted out.

"Nothing. I'm not saying anything." She let out a resigned sigh. "But we can't pretend that things aren't complicated."

Backing her up, I crowded her against a huge tree. "Nothing, *nothing* will come between us again, B. I won't let it. I promise."

"Nix… you can't—"

"I believe it." I had to believe it. "This, us, it's real. It's permanent. It's not something I'm prepared to walk away from again. But I need you to talk to me. I need you to be honest with me, okay? I can't do this without you, B."

I can't be the only one who fights for us.

5

HARLEIGH

Guilt was a thick, sticky thing inside me, making it a little hard to breathe as Nix stared at me. Begging me to meet him halfway. It wasn't that I didn't want to. I did.

Of course I did.

But everything was happening so fast. It was already time to leave him again. To go back to that world—*their* world—and pretend that my heart didn't belong to a boy who was born and raised in The Row.

"Say it, B. I need to hear you say it."

"I'm with you." My voice wavered. "I am. I just…"

"I know, I fucking know, okay." He pulled me into his arms and held me tight. "We'll figure it out. But I need you to promise me that you won't flake out on me."

Nix gazed down at me, the way I'd always dreamed of. Things had been simpler back then though, and I couldn't help but wonder how different things might have been if he'd only realized how he truly felt about me then… instead of now.

"Harleigh," Celeste called. "We should go." She was holding her cell phone, a frown etched into her face. "Dad texted."

"Did he—"

"It's okay. He just wants to know where we are and when we're coming back."

The heat that existed between me and Nix guttered out, and I inhaled a thin breath.

"I guess you need to go."

"Nix…"

But his walls were already up, reinforced by everything that existed between us now.

My father.

Max.

Where I lived.

Where I went to school.

I'd been plucked out of The Row and deposited in the one place he hated more than anything. How were we supposed to just forget that?

The answer was, we couldn't.

"It's okay," he said, grabbing the back of my neck and dropping a kiss on my head. "Go. I'll text you later."

"Thank you, for today. For everything."

He gave me a small nod, the invisible tether between us stretching taut. I wanted to go to him. But I didn't. Instead, I gave him one last lingering look before heading back over to Celeste.

"All set?" she asked me, noting that Nix didn't join us.

"Yeah, let's go."

"See you soon," Chloe called after us. I gave her a small wave as I climbed into Celeste's car.

"You good?" My sister eyed me carefully.

"Yeah, I'm fine."

"If you say so."

"I do." Pressing my head against the glass, I watched Nix watch me. He reminded me of a predator stalking its prey, biding its time. But he wouldn't catch me, not this time.

"Did you two get a chance to talk?"

"A little." But there was still so much we hadn't aired.

"I'm sorry if I pushed you to come here. I just thought—"

"It's okay, Celeste," I said quietly. "I don't want to hide or avoid everything, but sometimes it just feels easier, you know."

"Yeah. How can I help? Maybe I could speak to Da—"

"No, don't do that. I don't want you to do that."

"Okay, sorry." Her eyes flicked to mine, brimming with apology. "I won't say anything."

"I appreciate your support, Celeste, I do. But I need to do things at my own pace."

"Of course. I know I can be a little much sometimes. But it's only because I care about you, and I want you to be happy. And I know living at the house with us doesn't make you happy."

No, it didn't.

But it didn't matter.

The simple truth was, I had nowhere else to go. Sure, I turned eighteen in a few weeks, but if I left, the money I had access to would quickly deplete.

It wasn't enough.

Not if I wanted to truly escape Old Darling Hill and my father's clutches.

"It's not like I have much choice," I murmured.

"I know." She sighed. "But it won't be like this forever. You're eighteen soon and you graduate next spring."

As if I needed any reminder.

Nine months.

I just had to survive nine months.

It wasn't lost on me that's how long I'd survived *without* Nix.

We drove the rest of the way back to the house in silence. When we eventually drove through the automatic gold-tipped gates, Celeste broke the tension.

"What are you going to do about Max?" she asked, cutting the engine and twisting around to me.

"Honestly, nothing. It's obviously a game to him. I figure it's better not to provoke him."

"Are you sure that's the right approach? I mean, he's my brother, yeah. But he's also a sociopath."

A small chuckle left my lips. She wasn't wrong there.

"He's clearly baiting me for leverage." I shrugged. "I'm sure he'll let me know what he wants eventually."

"You're sure you want to do this? Go up against Max, I mean?" Concern flitted across her expression.

"What else would you suggest? Tell Michael about Nix? Because that's not an option."

Not yet at least.

"Yeah." She let out a resigned sigh. "You're right, he wouldn't like that at all. God, why do things have to be so complicated?"

"Because our father is a selfish ass who does what he wants with little regard for others?" My brow arched and Celeste spluttered over the breath caught in her throat.

"I wish I could argue but…"

"Yeah, I know." I stared up at the house, the invisible shackles around me already tightening.

"You know, he isn't all bad." I glanced over at Celeste and she gave me a weak smile. "It's true. Growing up, there would be these small moments. Rare little glimpses of a man who could laugh, have fun, and enjoy life."

"I find that hard to believe." I didn't think I'd ever seen the man crack a smile, let alone have fun.

Heavy silence settled over us and I lifted my gaze to hers. "Can I ask you something?"

"Of course."

"Why do you think he brought me here? I mean, he didn't want me… he didn't want my mom." Pain sliced through me.

He'd killed her.

Maybe not by his hand, but his abandonment, his cruel treatment, had broken something vital inside her and she'd never recovered.

I didn't know much about her life before The Row, before me. She'd rarely talked about it. But I knew enough to know that Michael Rowe had been her world. Trina Maguire hadn't been like the other kids growing up in Old Darling Hill. Her parents—my grandparents—had died in a tragic accident years before I was conceived. So she'd grown up with her ailing grandmother. They'd had money like everyone else here.

But I always got the impression my mom had been a lost soul.

Until she'd found my father.

"You're his daughter, Harleigh. His blood. I know he didn't do right by your mom… by you." Pity shone in her eyes, and I hated it. I hated that a man who meant so little to me could still make me feel such things. "But despite what you might think, he isn't a monster."

I wasn't so sure about that.

Before I could find the words to answer her, Celeste added, "I know he messed up, but I think in his own way, he thought he was protecting you."

"Protecting me? From what? My friends? My…" The words got stuck in my throat as my body shook with frustration. "He took away the one thing I needed most, Celeste. The one person who—"

I tamped down those dark, dangerous thoughts, anger rising inside me like a tidal wave.

"I know. Crap, I know." She reached over and grabbed my hand, tears pooling in her eyes. "And I'm sorry. I'm so sorry. I didn't know… I didn't—"

"I know." I inhaled a shaky breath, trying to smother the intense emotions threatening to consume me. I was okay. I was stronger. I wasn't the same girl I'd been back then when my world had fallen apart.

"I don't think he knew you would… hurt yourself. He couldn't have."

It wasn't easy for Celeste, being stuck in between me and Michael. He'd been there for her. Raised her. Given her everything she could ever want.

When I'd first arrived at their house, I hadn't wanted

anything to do with her. My half-sister—the daughter he'd wanted.

The daughter he'd kept.

But Celeste had wormed her way into my heart. She was never jealous of me or wary, she was patient and kind and consistent.

She was *there*.

She'd been there for the last nine months whether I wanted her to be or not, and I was grateful. I was. But I also knew we would never agree on some things.

Like the kind of man our father really was.

"We should go inside," I said, shouldering the door.

"Harleigh, wait, I didn't—"

But I'd already climbed out, needing to feel fresh air in my lungs. I loved Celeste, I did. But sometimes, it was too much. Sometimes it was too hard to forget that she'd had the life I should have had. That while I was living in The Row—barely surviving—she was here, playing princess in her pristine white castle.

It wasn't her fault, I knew that. But it didn't make it any easier to accept.

"Hey." She caught up to me as I slipped inside the house. "I didn't mean—"

"It's okay," I said a little hastily. "I just can't talk about it right now."

"Oh, okay." Her words were as tight as her smile. "Do you want to watch a movie or something? We could—"

"Girls?" Michael's voice clanged through me.

"It's us, Dad," Celeste called.

"Can you come in here please?"

She shot me an apologetic look before taking off down the hall.

I took a second to calm myself. I didn't want to see him. Didn't want to spend even a second longer than necessary in his presence. But I couldn't avoid him; not without raising suspicion. And I wasn't ready to call him out on everything, not yet. Because it would mean ripping open wounds that were barely healed, and I didn't know how that would affect the shaky progress I'd made.

"Harleigh?"

God, he couldn't just leave me alone. He didn't sound particularly pissed though, which was a saving grace. Obviously, Max was keeping the truth to himself for now.

I padded down the hall and entered the kitchen. "What's up?"

My father's brows pinched, that cleft in his chin more prominent as he frowned at me. "Did you have a nice evening?"

"It was fine." My lips pursed.

"We hung out with Miles."

"I see." His gaze swung to Celeste. "Things are getting serious between you and him?"

"Daddy." She flushed. "It's very… new. But it's Miles. He's a good guy."

"That he is. And Nate Miller, was *he* there?"

"Yeah, I'm not doing this," I said, distaste curling my lip.

"And what is it you think we're doing?" Michael

studied me, deep and probing as if he was trying to figure me out.

"This attempt at a father-daughter chat." Bitterness coated my tongue.

"We're just talking, Harleigh." He smiled. An honest-to-God smile that made my insides shrivel and die. "Is that such a bad thing? That I'm taking an interest in your life?"

"Whatever," I murmured. "I'm going to my room."

"Harleigh, wait—"

But I didn't wait.

I hightailed it out of there as if the hounds of hell were nipping at my heels. He was deluded if he thought I wanted to bond over boys. I didn't want anything to do with him. Never had. And that was before I'd found out just how deep his betrayal ran.

My entire life Michael Rowe had been nothing but the villain in my story.

That wasn't ever going to change.

6

NIX

"Wondered when you'd show your face, you little shit," my old man spat the words as he sat stretched out in his armchair, sipping on a beer.

"It wasn't like I took all of it."

"I should make you pack up your stuff and get the hell out of here before—"

"Nix, sweetheart, you're back." Jessa appeared, wearing a tentative smile. She glanced between us, her expression falling. "Joe, you promised."

"Relax, woman. I haven't laid a finger on him, have I, kid?"

Anger rolled up my spine and it took everything inside me not to respond. Jessa touched my arm, demanding my attention. "Did you have a nice time?" Her eyes twinkled.

She knew.

She knew exactly who I'd been with and why I'd stolen a bunch of stuff out of our refrigerator.

"Yeah. It was good, thanks."

"That's nice, sweetie. Real nice. Me and your dad had a nice evening too. In fact, he has some news, don't you, Joe?" He grumbled something inaudible, but Jessa added, "Go on, baby. Tell him."

"Gotta go out of town for a few days next weekend."

"And he's taking me with him. We're going to the city, Nix."

"Albany?" I asked.

"No, New York City. Isn't that exciting? I've always wanted to go to the Big Apple." Jessa's enthusiasm made my skin itch.

"New York? What business do you have in New York?" I asked.

"Watch it, kid." My old man glared at me, annoyance shining in his half-drunk eyes.

Something didn't add up. It wasn't unheard of for him to disappear on business now and again, but he never ventured as far south as NYC. At least, not to my knowledge.

Joe Wilder was small-town. He wasn't a city guy.

"Are you sure it's a good idea taking Jessa?"

"Oh, Phoenix," she cooed. "I'll be okay, sweetheart. Your dad said while he's taking care of business, I can go shopping. How about that? Little old me shopping in NYC." She clasped her hands together and let out a dreamy sigh.

"That's… great." I swallowed over the lump in my throat.

"You'll be okay? Home alone for a few nights?"

"I think I can handle it."

My old man snorted at that. "No parties."

"Would I ever?"

His brow quirked up. "I mean it, Nix. Keep your punk ass friends the fuck out of my home."

"Yeah, yeah, keep your hair on. I've got my first game of the season Friday, so we'll probably party down at the res."

"Ooh, first game of the season. How exciting. You don't mind if I give this one a miss, do you?" Jessa nudged my shoulder and I managed a weak half-smile.

"Mind? Why would I mind?"

It wasn't like it was unusual for me to not have anyone in the crowd. Sure, Chloe always came to our games, and Ms. Carter if she felt up to it, but I couldn't remember the last time my old man watched me play. Jessa had dragged him along once or twice in junior high, but we'd gotten into it afterwards.

He never came again, and I never asked.

But Jessa had been there sometimes. And when she wasn't, she'd still cheered me on, celebrating the wins and commiserating the losses with me.

"You think you'll get offered a scholarship?" my old man grunted, surprising me.

He'd never paid any interest before.

"Coach said it's a possibility."

"Oh, Joe, a scholarship. How wonderful."

"They pay for your board too?" He sneered.

My stomach sank. Of course it came back to whether

they'd give me a place to stay or not. Because come graduation, he wanted me gone.

A ripple of tension went through the air as Jessa looked at me and then to my old man.

"What's going on?"

So he hadn't told her then.

Fucking coward.

"Nothing you need to worry about, baby."

"Nix?" She turned to me.

"Ask him." I shrugged, moving past her. "I'm going to take a shower."

"Nix—"

But I was gone. Out of there. So he hadn't told her, though it wouldn't change anything. Joe Wilder didn't listen to anyone, least of all to Jessa. He didn't listen all the times she'd begged him to stop hitting me, hurting me. And he didn't listen over the years whenever she'd tried to stand up for me. Fights over school, on the field, around The Row. Growing up, Jessa constantly tried to stand in my corner. But my old man didn't care. He was never on my side.

Ever.

Sometimes, I thought it was a fucking miracle that we'd gotten here, to this point, without killing each other. But I guess he had some shred of conscience left because he hadn't turned me out on my ass yet. Then again, I probably had Jessa to thank for that.

I blew through the trailer to my room, slamming the door behind me. Thankfully, I had the benefit of a small private bathroom. Tearing my clothes off, I tramped inside and turned on the shower. Anger vibrated deep inside me and I wanted nothing more than to lash out. To hit something, hurt something. I needed to go to Buster's. To get in the ring and work off the restless energy zipping around my body like a live wire.

The tepid water sluiced down my body as I dropped my head against the tile. What I really needed was B. I needed to feel her close, her soft skin and mesmerizing green eyes. She grounded me, always had.

But she wasn't here. She was there. My fist slammed against the tile, the water drowning out the thud. She was there, playing happy family with Michael Rowe.

Thud.

She was one of them now, even if she didn't want to be.

Thud.

Thud.

Thud*.*

Pain exploded in my wrist as I roared into the jet stream, my body shuddering with frustration. Anger and helplessness.

This life… this fucking life. It was cruel. Unforgiving and brutal. And I was one of the lucky ones. I had a roof over my head, food on the table, and a stepmom who cared. A few bruises here and there, a black eye or two, was getting off lightly compared to what some kids in The Row went through.

Football was my shot at getting out. I knew that. But I couldn't commit. I couldn't let myself believe I was good enough. Because I didn't *feel* good enough.

Pressing my hands flat against the tile, I dropped my

head, letting the water wash away my sins. My dark, desperate thoughts.

I needed a plan.

I needed a fucking way out of this place.

For me.

For her.

For us.

"You need to snap out of it," Zane said as we piled out of my car Monday morning.

"He's lovesick." Kye chuckled and I flipped him off.

"Yeah, well, it was one day. One fucking day and he's acting like it's been weeks."

"Fuck you, Z. Fuck. You."

He had a point though. Harleigh hadn't been able to get out to meet me yesterday, and it wasn't for lack of me trying to persuade her.

It had only fueled the restlessness inside me.

"Look, I'm happy she's back, I am. But be realistic, Nix, how the fuck is this gonna work? You're here, she's there. You have school, the team, she has... her new family."

"Can we not do this?" I shoved my bag up my shoulder. "We have practice. I need to get my head in the game."

"Hell yes, you do." Kye nudged me. "Albany U is your ticket out of here. Harleigh could look into applying and the two of you could ride off into the sunset and never look—" I cut him off with a please-shut-the-fuck-up look, and he shrugged. "Just saying."

I dug my cell phone out of my pocket and checked for messages, a bolt of annoyance going through me at the blank screen.

"Pussy-whipped," Zane coughed into his hand.

"You could just text her, you know?" Kye said.

"He's trying to play it cool, asshole."

"Z's right. I don't want to smother her."

"Seriously?" Zane smirked. "Because I kind of got the impression—"

"Oh shit, crazy bitch alert two o'clock."

I looked up just in time to see Cherri making her way over toward us. "We need to talk," she said, hand fisted on her hip.

"I have practice." Moving around her, I fully intended on walking away, but she grabbed my arm. "Nix, come on. You owe me."

"I don't owe you shit, Cher, and you know—"

"Please." Her expression crumpled. It was strange seeing her like this, vulnerable. Maybe even a little sad.

"Fine, two minutes." I needed to make sure she understood that we were done, over. Because I couldn't be worrying about what Cherri might do when I had bigger things to worry about.

"I'll see you in the locker room," I said to the guys, motioning for Cherri to follow me. We walked in silence around the side of the main school building toward the football field.

"How have you been?" she asked me once we were alone.

I let out a weary sigh, scrubbing my jaw. "What do you want, Cherri?"

"I… I just wanted to say I get it, okay? She's your lobster."

"My what?" My brows pinched.

"You know, *Friends?*"

"You're quoting *Friends* at me?" What the fuck was happening right now?

"I'm just saying, I get it. I can't compete with her. I never could."

"Cher, I don't know what you think you know, but there's nothing going on with me and Harleigh." The lie was bitter on my tongue but I needed to throw her off Harleigh's scent for as long as possible.

Her soft smile morphed into something darker, something with more bite. "We'll see," she said. "See you around, Nix."

Sauntering off, Cherri took the air with her. It hadn't been a threat, but it sure felt like one. Or maybe the Queen Bitch of Darling Hill High had simply had a change of heart.

I didn't buy it, but whatever.

I dug my cell phone out of my pocket again and clenched my teeth at the blank screen.

Why hadn't she texted me?

I was trying to give Harleigh space, to let her come to me, but it was fucking with my head. What if her brother had outed us to her father? What if she was suddenly having doubts about me? About us? What if—

The vibration of my cell startled me and relief slammed into me as her name flashed up.

B: Monday mornings suck.

Me: Mine just got considerably better.

I DIDN'T EVEN BOTHER TRYING to fight the grin tugging at my mouth.

B: You are such a cheeseball. Good luck at practice.

Me: I wish you were going to be here to watch.

B: Nix...

Me: I know, I know. But you'll be at the game Friday, right?

B: I'll try. I have to go, morning bell just rang.

Me: Okay, have a good day. I'll text you later.

B: Bye, Nix xo

Me: Bye, B xo

"Let me guess, she finally texted?" Zane asked, strolling over to me.

"Yeah." I smiled, re-reading the message thread. It wasn't anything life-changing, but she'd texted me. It was enough, for now.

He shook his head, slinging his arm over my shoulder. "Jesus, you have it bad."

I bit down on my lip and smiled.

He had no fucking idea.

7

HARLEIGH

I POCKETED MY CELL PHONE, STILL SMILING FROM MY BRIEF text conversation with Nix, and headed for my locker.

"Oh look, if it isn't Wilder's pet," Marc stepped into my way, smirking down at me.

"Move." I went to move around him, but he followed my direction, cutting off my exit.

"Nuh-uh, say please."

"Move, *please*." I glowered at him, trembling with anger. He'd sent that text—or at least, one of his minions had. But I wouldn't rise to it, I wouldn't let him know how much he affected me.

"How was your weekend?" he asked, the perfect example of the-boy-next-door. But I knew better. I knew he was nothing more than the devil in sheep's clothing.

"I'm not doing this," I said, ducking around him. But he was too fast, too wily for me to slip past.

Damn him.

"And what is it you think we're doing?" His brow went up, that smug smirk still painted on his face.

God, I hated him so much.

It was a strong word, an even stronger emotion, but I felt it in every fiber of my being.

I hated Marc Denby. Plain and simple.

"A little birdie told me you hung out with Nate on the weekend."

"So what if I did?"

"You should be careful with the company you keep, Maguire. Nate is… messed up. Then again, I can see why you two would hit it off."

"Nice, asshole. Real nice," I mumbled before barging past him. This time, I didn't stop, sending him careening into the locker bank.

"Fucking bitch," he spluttered, righting himself.

"Oops," I drawled, smug satisfaction spreading through my chest. "My bad."

"Nate can't protect you forever, you know?" he called after me. But I kept walking.

Nate wasn't protecting me. He was… well, it was complicated. Even more complicated given that I didn't know if he was responsible for Max knowing about me and Nix.

I let out a weary sigh as I made my way toward class. Nate would be there and so would Angela. Just what I didn't need.

He'd texted me yesterday and I'd all but avoided him. I didn't want to accuse him of anything, but Max knew something, and it was highly unlikely Nix, Chloe, or the guys had been the ones to tell him. Which left Celeste,

Nate, and Miles. I trusted Celeste; she'd given me no reason not to. As for Miles, he seemed a little scared of Nix and the guys, so I couldn't imagine him saying anything to anyone. Plus, he wanted to stay in Celeste's good books.

Which left Nate.

Just as I reached the classroom, my cell phone vibrated. I quickly dug it out of my bag and smiled when I saw the photo message.

Clo: Thought you'd appreciate this.

IT WAS a photo of Nix mid-play, his hands up around the ball, and his white pants fitting very snugly over his ass.

Me: Does he know you took this?

Clo: What do you think?

I CHUCKLED, and before I could type out a reply, another text came through.

Clo: You owe me!

"HARLEIGH, WAIT UP."

I looked up to find Nate jogging toward me. "How are you?"

"I'm okay, thanks."

"Good, that's... good. Although I kind of got the impression you're ignoring me."

"I..." Pressing my lips together, I stared up at him. What was there to say? I had ignored him. Because I didn't know what to say, but not for the reasons I suspected he thought.

"You know, I get you're with Wilder," he whispered.

"That's not..." *Just ask him. Just rip the Band-Aid off and ask.* "Did you tell your brother that we were all over at your house the other night?"

"What? No." He blanched. "No way. I swear, I didn't. Why, what happened?"

"Max said some things."

Concern flitted across his expression. "What kinds of things are we talking about?"

"Not here." I glanced at a couple of kids walking past us.

"Yeah, shit, okay." He ran a hand through his hair. "I swear though, Harleigh, it wasn't me. I would never—"

"Yeah, I know." And part of me did.

But if it wasn't Nate, and it wasn't Celeste or Miles, who was it?

My head hurt. The last thing I needed was Max holding me to ransom. I'd managed to avoid him all day yesterday: feigning a headache, and binge-watching TV in my room. But I couldn't avoid him forever.

"Mr. Miller, Miss Rowe," the teacher said. "Will you be joining us this morning?"

"Be right there, sir." Nate nodded, flicking me a concerned gaze.

"Come on, Maguire. Class awaits." He went to sling his arm around my shoulder but hesitated, something flashing in his eyes. "My bad," he murmured, moving ahead of me, and slipping into class.

I inhaled a shaky breath, wondering when life had gotten so complicated.

AFTER THIRD PERIOD, I went in search of Celeste. She hadn't texted me to arrange to meet for lunch which was strange. But I quickly realized why when I spotted her and Miles arguing over by the stairs.

"Hey, guys." I approached with caution. "What's going on?"

"Oh, Harleigh, hey." She swiped at her eyes, smiling. But it was a little too bright, too forced. "Nothing. We were just talking."

"Talking, yeah." Miles barely looked at me.

"What's the matter?" I looked between them, the air thick around us.

"Honestly, it's nothing." Celeste glared at Miles and he recoiled, backing away slowly.

"I have an appointment with Miss Hanley, so I'll see

you guys later." He took off down the hall, not sparing us a second glance.

"Okay, what happened?" I pinned Celeste with a knowing look.

"He… he's pissed about Saturday."

"Sat— you mean he's pissed we hung out with Nix and the guys?"

She nodded. "I told him it was nothing, but he's a guy. They get jealous."

"That isn't a guy thing, Celeste. It's a people thing," I said, thinking of how jealousy had been my best friend for pretty much my entire life growing up with Nix and his harem of girls.

"He'll get over it." Hitching her bag up her shoulder, she shrugged. "You want to get lunch?"

"Yeah," I said, not really caring if I ate or not thanks to the permanent knot in my stomach.

Celeste moved ahead of me a little as we fought our way through the lunchtime rush. The cafeteria was a hive of activity, loud and crowded. Marc, Ange and their friends immediately spotted me, glaring in our direction. I stared right back.

"Harleigh," Celeste warned. "Don't poke the beast." She grabbed my hand, tugging me toward the lunch line.

My cell vibrated and I dug it out.

Hot Tub Guy: How's it going?

"Hᴏᴛ ᴛᴜʙ ɢᴜʏ?" Celeste peered over my hands and chuckled. "Original. Has he said anything about the game yet?"

"Like what?" My thumb hovered over the reply button.

"Well, we're going to watch, right? Afterward, we could all hang out again. Maybe ask Nate—"

"No," I rushed out. "I don't think that's a good idea."

"Because he likes you?"

"I… I don't know. It's just weird."

"Nate knows you're with *Hot Tub Guy*, Harleigh." Amusement danced in her eyes, but I didn't find it funny.

"Do the Hawks usually party after a game?"

"No. No way."

"What?" She was the picture of innocence.

"Whatever you're thinking, unthink it." I leaned closer, lowering my voice. "We cannot go to a Darling Hill High party."

"Why not? It could be fun."

"*Celeste*! Too many people know me." Too many girls who all wanted a piece of Nix and wouldn't hesitate to cut me out of the equation.

"Yeah, that could be a problem." She tapped her cheek. "Maybe we could hang out with the guys and Chloe again?"

"What about Miles?" My brow arched.

"He can come, or not. Whatever."

"Celeste, don't be that girl. Don't risk what you have with Miles for a guy like Zane."

She made a derisive noise in her throat. "I told you I don't—"

"Like Zane, yeah." My eyes rolled. "Keep telling yourself that."

Grabbing my hand, she looked me dead in the eye. "I promise I will not make any mistakes where Zane Washington is concerned."

We moved down the line, and I grabbed a salad.

"Did Dr. Katy call you back yet?"

"No. She'll probably pick up my message today."

"And how are you feeling… about everything?"

"Okay, I guess." Smoothing things over with Nix had helped. But it had also brought to light a bunch of other issues. My father's betrayal mainly.

She narrowed her eyes at me and I went on the defensive. "What?" I groaned.

"Nothing. Nothing at all."

"Celeste, I'm okay. Things got a little intense, but I feel more grounded now."

"Because of Nix?"

"It isn't like that."

"Listen, I get it. He's your person. But don't let your feelings for him mask—"

"I know, I know." I glanced away, pressing my lips together, uncomfortable with the way she saw through me so easily.

I'd called Dr. Katy, and that was huge for me. But despite the pressure in my chest, I did feel calmer, and I knew it had to do with Nix being back in my life.

And mine.

He's mine.

It still felt like a dream, a wild fantasy where I was the shining star. Except, I wasn't a star. I was the moon.

Radiant during the night, but only a wispy reflection in the day.

I sent Nix a quick text back, and paid for my lunch, following Celeste to an empty table. The second I sat down, a reply came through.

Hot Tub Guy: So my old man and Jessa are going out of town on the weekend...

"What?" Celeste asked. "You just went as red as a beet."

"I... his stepmom and dad are out of town on the weekend." Heat trickled through me.

"Ooh, you can have a romantic night at his place."

"I'm not sure that's a good idea."

"It's a great idea. You can sneak in under the cover of darkness and play house." Her brows waggled suggestively.

"I'm sorry, are you pro-Nix or anti-Nix? I can't keep up".

"Ha ha." She poked her tongue out at me. "I'm pro-whatever-makes-you-happy."

"And where would I tell Michael and Sabrina I'm staying?" Because I couldn't deny the idea of a night alone with Nix was appealing.

"Maybe I can stay at Miles's and we can cover for you? We'll figure something out."

Another lie to add to the web of lies I was already

caught in. But why should I care? Michael had lied—lies that had changed everything.

That had changed me.

"What are you two talking about?" Max slid in beside Celeste and we both gawked at him.

"What the hell are you doing?" she hissed.

"Saying hello to my two favorite sisters. Problem with that?"

"I don't know how else to say this, Brother. Get. Lost."

"Is that anyway to talk to your favorite—"

"What do you want, Max?" I sighed, trying to play it cool, when really I felt like the ground was falling away beneath me.

"I need you to hook me up."

"Hook you up?" My brows furrowed.

"Yeah. There's a guy across the res. I want an introduction."

"No," Celeste said. "No freaking way."

"I think Harleigh wants to help me. Isn't that right, Harleigh?" A smug grin spread over his face.

"Max, come on… this isn't fair—"

"What do you say, Harleigh? Want to help me out? I'll make it worth your while."

"I don't trust you." I folded my arms on the table.

"You don't exactly have much of a choice. Not unless you want me to reveal all your dirty little secrets to Dad."

"Max!"

"Butt out, Sis." He cut Celeste with a scathing look. "This is between me and Harleigh. So what do you say?"

"Harleigh, you don't have to do this."

But what choice did I have?

I'd just got Nix back. I didn't want to jeopardize that, not yet. Not until we'd figured out things.

"Fine," I said. "I'll help you."

Max slammed his palm down on the table, a wicked glint in his eye. "Right answer, Sis. Right fucking answer."

8

NIX

"You wanted to see me, Coach?"

"Come in, son. Take a seat." He motioned to the empty chair.

"Should I be worried?" Strained laughter rumbled in my chest.

"You had a good practice this morning."

"Thanks, Coach. I felt good."

It was the truth. I'd nailed every pass, every play. Our defense had barely been able to touch me. I was on fire. And I was pretty sure I knew the reason.

"Something you want to tell me, Nix?"

I rubbed a hand over my jaw. "Nothing I can think of."

"No? No reason for the extra spring in your step today?" His brow lifted with mild amusement.

"Something you want to ask me, Coach?"

"You saw her, didn't you? Harleigh Wren?"

"I… yeah." I couldn't lie to him. Not Coach, the one man who had always believed in me. "Yeah, I did."

"And the two of you figured things out?"

"It's complicated."

"I'm sure it is, son." He sat back in his chair. "I'm sure it is."

It was on the tip of my tongue to tell him the truth: about the text messages, Michael, all of it. But the last thing I needed was him getting involved.

"Look, Coach, I appreciate your concern, but you don't need to worry."

"Famous last words." He chuckled but it didn't reach his eyes. "We have a big opening game Friday. I need you to keep a cool head. No matter what shit they try, no matter how much they try to provoke you, you need to rein it in."

"I can handle it, I promise."

His eyes narrowed. "And will Miss Maguire be in the crowd?"

"I'm not sure."

"Hmm." He stroked his jaw. "Have you given any more thought to Albany U? I spoke to their recruiter earlier and they want to come out and see you."

"I…" Fuck. What was I supposed to say? That I wanted it, but I was scared as hell that I wasn't good enough? That I'd get to college and realize I didn't have what it took to play with the Falcons?

I was just a boy from The Row. What did I know about college football, and dreams of going pro?

"Nix, I don't know how many times I need to say this,

but you've got it, son. The spark. The talent. The charisma. But none of that means a thing if *you* don't believe it.

"I know things at home aren't easy." Understatement of the fucking century. "But football could be your ticket out of here. I know you're worried about Jessa, about leaving her. But this is your life, Nix. She made her choice, son." His expression softened, full of pity and helplessness. "Maybe it's time for you to make yours."

"I'll think about it."

"Good, that's good. Let's get Friday out of the way and see where we're at."

He knew as well as I did, Friday's game was not the place to invite scouts to attend. It would be a dogfight, the rivalry between the Devils and the Hawks too entrenched in years' worth of bitterness and resentment.

"Yeah, okay."

Part of me couldn't believe I'd agreed, but there wasn't only me to think about now. There was Harleigh too. I wanted to be the kind of guy she could be proud of. The kind of guy she could depend on. How the fuck was I going to do that if I was homeless with no prospects after graduation?

"I'm real glad to hear that," Coach said. "Now get out of here, and Nix?"

"Yeah?" I stood.

"Try to stay out of trouble."

I gave him an imperceptible nod because I didn't want to make a promise I couldn't keep.

Me: What are you up to?

B: Studying.

Me: Boring.

B: But necessary. What are you doing?

THE CORNER of my mouth tipped as I texted Harleigh back. I was heading to Buster's to meet the guys. I had a ton of restless energy to burn, and since Harleigh had blown me off when I'd asked her to meet me later, a few rounds with the punch bag and a cold shower would have to suffice.

My thumb hovered over the call button, and I hesitated. I didn't want to get her into trouble, to make things difficult, but I also really wanted to hear her voice.

I hit call and waited as I headed for the gym.

"Hello?"

"Can you talk?" I asked.

"Yeah, I'm in my room, studying."

"How very studious of you."

"We can't all be hotshot football players like you." I heard the smile in her voice.

"I can't believe you blew me off for homework."

"I've got a lot of work to do if I want to catch up."

"Because of last year?"

"Something like that," she whispered. "Where are you?"

"Just heading to the gym."

"Buster's, you still go there?"

"Why wouldn't I?"

There was a beat of silence and then Harleigh said, "Do you still fight?"

"Not as much as I used to."

"Nix…"

"It's not something I do regularly. There was an incident last year, right after… Anyway, Coach made me promise I wouldn't fight anymore."

"Good," she huffed.

"Come on, B. You more than anyone should get it."

"It's dangerous."

"So is a ton of other stuff. But sometimes, I need it." I needed the release. The pain and distraction.

She was quiet for a long time. "Is that where the bruises came from? Or was that…"

"My old man?"

"Yeah," she breathed.

"I got my ass handed to me by some meathead the other week. I'm only going to train tonight."

"Good."

"Worried about me, Birdie?"

"Always."

My heart thumped against my rib cage. "Why can't you sneak out to meet me again?"

"Studying. My father… Max."

"Yeah, okay." My jaw clenched. "But I need my Birdie fix before the game Friday."

"Celeste is working on it. She's also working on my

cover story for after the game…" I swear I heard a hitch in her breath. "There's something else," she said.

Why didn't I like the sound of that?

"Go on."

"Max, he uh, he wants an introduction with Bryson."

"*What?*"

"Yeah, I don't understand it either, but that's his price. If I… well, you introduce him to Bryson, he'll keep our secret."

"You trust him?"

"Not even a little bit. But I didn't know what else to do. I don't want Michael to know about us yet. Not until we…" She trailed off and my insides twisted.

"We have a lot of shit to figure out," I said, pausing outside Buster's.

"Yeah. The less people who know right now, the better."

I ignored the flash of hurt at her words, and said, "Bryson is a friend, but he's not a good guy, B. You know that."

The illegal fight ring wasn't the only thing he was into.

"I know. I don't like it either, but maybe whatever Max wants will work in our favor."

"It'll give you leverage over him too." I realized. "How old is he again?"

"Sixteen."

"Fuck." No way Bryson would want a sixteen-year-old rich kid from across the res sniffing around. But Harleigh was right, it was better than her father.

"Tomorrow night. Bring him by and I'll make the introduction. But, Birdie, if he screws us over…"

"He seemed dead set on the meet, so I think we can trust him. With this at least."

"Okay." I blew out an exasperated breath. What the hell could this kid want with a guy like Bryson?

I guess we were going to find out.

"I'm outside the gym so I'll let you get back to your studies."

"Okay, don't work out too hard."

"Don't you study too hard," I teased. "I'll text you later."

"Okay."

"Bye, B."

"Bye, Nix."

Neither of us hung up.

"Nix…"

"Yeah, I'm going. Talk later." I forced myself to end the call, stuffing my cell in my pocket.

Taking a deep breath, I shouldered the door to the gym and slipped inside. The smell of blood, sweat, and testosterone hit me, but it gave me a strange kind of comfort. There was something about the sound of fists hitting bags, the grunts and groans of guys going at it that soothed something inside me.

What that said about me, I didn't know. But it was hardly a surprise that a place like this settled me when I'd grown up with Joe Wilder's temper. Because it was the one place I got to unleash myself.

Although I hadn't been back since I'd got my ass

handed to me by that asshole Sy. A couple of the guys dipped their chins in greeting. Zane and Kye were already working with the free weights, so I dumped my bag on the bench in the corner of the room and yanked off my sleeveless hoodie.

"You made it," Zane said as I reached them.

"Yeah. But something weird happened."

"We're listening."

"I spoke to B. Her brother Max wants an introduction with Bryson."

"The fuck?"

"Exactly what I said."

"Isn't he like fifteen or something?" Kye asked and I corrected him.

"Sixteen."

"What the fuck does he want with Bryson?"

"Fuck if I know, but Birdie said he was pretty insistent. He's threatening to tell his old man about us if she doesn't come through."

"He can't know for sure that you two are... whatever the fuck you two are doing."

"Seemed confident enough to blackmail her."

"What are you going to do?"

"Ask Bryson for an introduction, I guess." I shrugged.

"Come on, Nix." Zane scoffed. "He'll never go for it."

"Guess I'll have to find a way to convince him then."

"Shit," Kye murmured.

"No way, no fucking way." Zane pinned me with a hard look. "You can't be fucking serious."

"I make him a lot of money."

"Yeah, and risk getting thrown off the team... or worse."

"Let me worry about Bryson," I said as I searched him out. He was busy in the ring, refereeing two guys sparring. Although from the state of them and the bloodstained wraps on their hands, they'd obviously been going at it hard.

"You could always just ask him," Kye suggested. "What's the worst that could happen?"

Asking wouldn't get me anywhere. Guys like Bryson worked in favors. And the only favor he'd want from me would be me stepping into the ring on fight night pummeling some guy's face.

But I'd do it.

For B I'd do anything.

"I'm going to put it out there and say this is a bad fucking idea." Zane's expression hardened. Trust him to say what we were all thinking but what I didn't need to hear.

"Yeah, well, I don't have a choice."

"There's always a choice, Nix." His lips thinned.

If only it was that easy.

But this was The Row. I couldn't run back to mommy and daddy and ask them to fix my problems, throw money at them and make them disappear. And I sure as shit couldn't go to the authorities.

I clenched my fist, dropping my head and inhaling a shallow breath. Everything was out of my control. But there were some things I could do to retain a tiny sliver of it.

"I need to hit the bag," I said to no one in particular.

Flexing my hand, a zip of anticipation went through me. The punch bag wouldn't hit me back, so I'd have to go at it hard.

And make it hurt.

9

HARLEIGH

"This is a bad idea," Celeste hissed.

It was Tuesday evening and it had been the longest day of my life.

Nix had gotten Max the introduction with Bryson. He didn't say how he'd done it, but he had.

"What would you have me do?" I snapped back, feeling a lick of irritation up my spine.

Max knew. Even if he didn't know everything, I couldn't take that risk. Not when everything between me and Nix was so new and precarious.

"I don't know, but this doesn't feel right, Harleigh. You said it yourself, Bryson is bad news."

"I'm not ready to confront him, Celeste." I sighed.

"I know, I know. Dad messed up. But don't you think by bartering with Max you're only going to make things worse?"

"You don't have to come." I would have preferred it if

she didn't. I didn't want to drag her into this anymore than necessary.

"Yeah, okay. I'll just let you and Max—"

"Max, what?" He appeared dressed in navy sweats and a matching hoodie.

"What are you wearing?" Celeste balked.

"I wear workout clothes sometimes."

"Yeah, okay, *Rocky Balboa*." She snickered.

"Are we doing this or not?" He cut me a look.

"What exactly do you want to meet Bryson for?"

"That's for me to know and you to never find out." He smirked, barging past us. He grabbed Celeste's keys from the bowl on the sideboard and called out, "I'll drive."

"Like hell you will." She charged after him, the two of them spilling out of the house.

Rolling my eyes, I trudged after them. I didn't want to go to The Row, not tonight. Not under these circumstances. Introducing Max to Bryson felt like a huge mistake, but I didn't have a choice. Well, not one I was prepared to make.

It was either placate Max or go up against my father, and I wasn't sure I would survive that showdown.

By the time I reached Celeste's car, she was in the driver's seat and Max was sitting shotgun. I climbed into the back and gave her directions.

"Will your boyfriend be there tonight?" Max glanced back at me, his smirk still fixed in place.

"Have you always been such an asshole?" My brow lifted, but my icy response melted a little when I noticed Max's expression falter.

"Max?"

"Whatever, Maguire. I might be an asshole, but you're still trailer trash."

His words didn't matter.

They didn't.

So why did they hurt so much? Why did it feel like he'd sliced me open with tiny shards of glass?

"Max, that's not fair."

"A lot of things aren't fair, Sister," he snarled at Celeste. "But shit happens and then you die."

God, he was so angry. Bitter and twisted. I'd spent very little time with Max since moving into their house, but it was apparent he wasn't a nice kid. The total opposite to Celeste who was warm and kind and forgiving. Celeste saw the good in people while Max brought out the worst in them.

"What happened to you, Max?" Celeste whispered under her breath.

"Just drive," he bit out.

And she did.

Straight into the heart of Darling Row.

I'D NEVER BEEN inside Buster's before, and I wasn't about to start now.

Celeste had parked down the street in a small parking lot that belonged to a gas station. I knew every store, every road, and every alley of this place, but it no longer felt like home.

Hoodie up and hands in his pockets, Nix jogged

across the street and glanced around the lot before climbing in beside me.

"Hey," he said, his eyes dropping straight to my mouth.

"Hi."

"This is all very cloak and dagger," Celeste said dryly.

"You must be Wilder." Max twisted around and fixed his eyes on Nix.

"And you must be the brother, Maximilian."

He flushed, part embarrassment, part anger. "It's just Max."

"Well, *just Max*. You ready to do this?"

He nodded.

"I hope you know what you're doing. Bryson Shaw isn't the kind of guy you mess around with."

"Says you."

"What the fuck is that supposed to mean?" Nix went rigid.

"I've heard the stories."

"I don't know what you're talking about."

"Yeah, okay." Max's smile turned smug. "Are we doing this or not?"

"After we're done here." Nix leaned in, his mouth hovering over the corner of mine. "Can we go somewhere?"

"I... what about Max?"

"Don't worry, I'll handle it."

"Nix." I fisted his hoodie. "Promise me he'll walk out of there in one piece."

"Relax, I'll behave." His lips moved to right beneath

my ear. "The same can't be said for when I get you alone though."

A shiver ran through me at his dark promise.

"See you soon." He kissed me, uncaring that Max was sitting right there. It shouldn't have thrilled me half as much as it did.

Nix wasn't afraid. Something told me he'd shout our relationship from the rooftops if I let him. But he had to know it wasn't that simple.

"Let's go, Maxy." Humor laced his words as he climbed out of the car, waiting for Max to do the same.

Nix poked his head back inside and grinned. "Go to Strike One, we'll meet you there later."

"Nix, I'm not sure—"

"Please, B. For me." He pouted, and it was so freaking adorable I melted.

"Fine."

"Good, Chloe is going to meet you there." He winked and slammed the door.

"That wasn't weird at all," Celeste grumbled, reversing out of the parking spot.

I glanced back, watching Nix and Max disappear down the street. "Did he seem okay to you?" I asked.

"Who Max? Just his usual douchebag self."

"Yeah, I guess."

I was sure I'd seen something in his eyes though, a moment of hesitation. Of pain. Or maybe it was simply wishful thinking. That my own trauma made me look beyond someone's cold, cruel persona and search for a reason. As far as I knew—and I didn't know all that much about the youngest Rowe-Delacorte sibling—Max had experienced a pretty typical childhood for a kid growing up wanting for nothing.

Celeste's cell phone vibrated and she let out a little huff of irritation.

"Miles?" I asked.

"Yeah, we had another fight earlier."

"Why didn't you say anything?"

"Because it's stupid."

"It's not stupid, Celeste, and you can always talk to me about this stuff."

She met my gaze in the rearview mirror. "Thanks." She pressed her lips together, trapping a sigh. "Maybe we were better off as friends."

"But I thought you liked him?"

"I do. At least, I did."

"Do you know what I think? I think you need to push all thoughts of a certain brooding bad boy from The Row out of your mind."

"I'm not... fine, maybe Zane is a tiny part of the problem. I can't stop thinking about him."

"Celeste..."

"I know, I know. I'm such a cliché," she murmured.

"No, you're not." There was something about a misunderstood bad boy that called to girls like me and Celeste. Maybe it was the idea of breaking the rules, of taming the untamable. Whatever it was, I'd been there once, swept away in the fantasy. Except, my attraction to Nix was so much more than that.

It always had been.

It was something innocent that had slowly, deeply flourished into something more.

Silence filled the car, both of us lost to our own thoughts. The last time I'd been at Strike One, I'd seen Nix. It seemed like so long ago when in reality it was only a few weeks. But time was often an unquantifiable thing for me. Days sometimes blurred into each other or ran on and on and on. Sometimes, it was like time stopped and no amount of clock watching would speed it up.

Sometimes nine months apart from Nix felt like an eternity, yet at other times it felt like no time had passed at all.

"Harleigh?"

"Huh." My brows pinched as I realized we had arrived at Strike One.

"You were doing it again," she said with a hint of pity.

"Sorry, I was just thinking."

The second Celeste parked the car, Chloe appeared at the window grinning. Shouldering the door, I climbed out. "Hey."

"Took you long enough." She laced her arm through mine. "Come on, I already got us a lane."

"We're actually playing?"

"Well, yeah. I figured we might as well."

"Sounds good to me." Celeste joined us as we entered the building.

"So what's up with your brother wanting to meet Bryson?" Chloe whispered.

"We're as in the dark as you," I replied.

"Hmm, it can't be anything good."

"Clo." I shot her a harsh look.

"Crap, sorry. I'm sure he'll be fine."

We reached the booth and I slid into the soft leather seat.

"You're not bowling?" Celeste asked, and I shook my head.

"I'll watch."

"Fine, suit yourself."

I pulled out my cell phone and placed it on the table, waiting for it to light up with a text from Nix.

"He won't let anything happen to your brother," Chloe said.

"I know."

And I did. But it didn't make the waiting any easier.

Celeste threw her first ball, knocking down six pins. "Dammit," she hissed. "I miscalculated."

"Miscalculated?" Chloe asked. "I just roll it and hope for the best."

"I worked out the mass-to-force ratio and accounted for the angle, I should have knocked down at least eight pins."

"You know all that?" Chloe gawked at her.

"She's basically a genius," I mumbled.

"I wouldn't go that far." Celeste's cheeks turned a deep shade of pink. "But I have a thing for numbers."

"Genius," I coughed into my hand, fighting a smile.

"Wow, I don't think I've ever met a genius before. Can you show me how to throw the perfect ball? I almost beat Kye last time, so any help I can get would be appreciated."

The two of them launched into a discussion about the benefits of using mathematical equations to throw the perfect ball while I fixated on my cell phone.

Maybe I should have gone with them. Max wasn't my

friend, and I certainly didn't consider him family, but he was my blood. And the last thing I wanted was for him to be tangled up with the likes of Bryson Shaw. Even if he had brought this on himself.

But Nix didn't text.

Not after a couple of minutes.

Not after ten minutes.

Not after thirty.

And by the time Celeste and Chloe had started their second game of bowling, the knot in my stomach was telling me something was very, very wrong.

10

NIX

"What's the holdup?" Max grumbled as we stood in Bryson's back room. It doubled as his office and apartment, depending on what day of the week it was.

There was an old threadbare couch pushed up against the wall, littered with cushions and a ratty throw. Framed posters of some of boxing's greats hung around the room. The place smelled of old sweat, but it was familiar in all the ways that mattered. Bryson wasn't exactly what I'd call a father figure, but he'd been there for me when no one else had. And yeah, maybe he exploited that a little, but he'd never made me do anything I hadn't wanted to.

He just didn't believe in doing things out of the kindness of your heart.

In a place like The Row, everything had a price, and Bryson's favors were no different.

"Aw that's right, rich boy isn't used to waiting," Zane drawled.

"Fuck you, man. You don't know anything about me."

"I know enough. Walking in here like you're somebody when really you're—"

"Z, knock it off," I said.

"Seriously, you're taking his side?"

"I'm not taking anyone's side. But Bryson will be here soon, and I don't want—"

The door flung open and the man in question appeared. "You've got five minutes," he grunted, throwing his keys down on the table.

"I want to fight."

"Come again, kid?"

"You heard me," Max pulled to his full height, "I want to fight."

Deep, teasing laughter rumbled in Bryson's chest as I stood there dumbfounded. It was the last thing I'd expected Max to say. I'd assumed he'd come here to score drugs or some under the table work.

But to fight?

The kid had balls of steel, I'd give him that.

"How old are you, kid? Fifteen?"

"Sixteen."

"Give it a couple of years, beef up a little, come back and see me and we'll talk then."

"I can't wait that long. I need to fight now."

"Now? *Now?*" Bryson leaned back on the edge of his desk, crossing his ankles. "That's not how shit around here works. You think you get to waltz in here and start throwing demands around like a spoiled brat? I don't know what Nix told you—"

"Whoa, I didn't tell him shit," I said, holding up my hands. "I only set up the introduction."

"I can pay you."

A ripple went through the room. Zane and Kye both looked at me as if to say, 'What the fuck?'

"Let me get this straight. You want to pay *me* to let *you* fight? What's your game, kid?"

"No game, I swear. I'm just here to fight." For the first time since walking through the door to Buster's, Max looked visibly uncomfortable. The kid had swagger, that was for sure, and shit ton of arrogance. But there was something lurking beneath the surface that I couldn't quite put my finger on.

Bryson stroked his cheek, studying Max.

"You're not actually considering it?" Zane broke the tense silence. "He's barely out of kindergarten."

"I'd put you on your ass quick enough," Max shot back, and Bryson let out a low whistle.

"You've got balls, kid. Can't deny that. But Zane is right. You're younger than—"

"Just give me a shot. I'll fight anyone here you want."

"Easy now, don't be making promises you can't keep."

"I swear on my life, you let me get in the ring, and I'll step up to any opponent."

"Famous last words," Bryson murmured

"What's wrong with you?" I spat. "Do you really think you can take on Zane? Me?"

I'd fucking annihilate the cocky little shit.

"I think I could try." He puffed out his chest and I

couldn't figure out if he was plain stupid or believed his own bullshit. But if he was adamant about getting in the ring, I couldn't let him spar with anyone. Harleigh would never forgive me, even if he deserved a beating.

"I'll do it," I said much to Zane and Kye's grumbles of disapproval.

"This is a bad idea," Zane said. "A really fucking bad idea."

"Something tells me he's not going to quit until Bryson gives him a shot. You really want to do this?" I asked him, flicking my hard gaze to Bryson. He smirked back as if I'd played right into his hands.

Whatever.

I wasn't doing this for him or even Max. I was doing it for Harleigh.

"One hundred percent" he said, jabbing the air, relief flitting across his expression.

"Okay, then let's do it." I looked at Bryson for permission and he nodded.

"Have at it. You can consider this your audition, kid. Now get out of here and get ready."

"Yes, thank fuck." He punched the air. "I mean yes, thanks."

"You need to find some gloves from the bin and a helmet."

"What? I thought you sparred without all that?"

"We do, but we know what we're doing." I smirked.

"If you're not wearing it, I'm not wearing it."

"You don't get to make the rules, kid. Harleigh will—"

"I didn't realize you were pussy-whipped. You know, I've heard the stories about you."

"This isn't some weird fan worship, is it?" I frowned. "Because you're going to be sorely disappointed." His eyes narrowed, nostrils flaring with anger. "How badly do you want to hit me right now?"

His fists clenched by his sides. I knew that look. The look of someone trying to fight their inner monster.

What the fuck had happened to this kid to make him so angry?

Max stalked off into the gym, making a beeline for the equipment bins. I went to follow, but Zane grabbed my arm. "What the fuck are you doing?"

"Better it's me in the ring with him than any of these guys." I flicked my head to the group of guys over by the punch bags.

"She'll kill you if you hurt him."

"I'm not going to hurt him. I'll let him burn off some steam and hopefully get this stupid-as-fuck idea out of his head."

"What's with that? Surely he knows Bryson isn't going to let him fight? He's barely out of diapers."

Kye snickered at that, but I rolled my eyes. "He's sixteen, Z. Remember us at that age?"

"Nix is right. We were cocky little punks, thinking we always knew best. And Nix was already fighting by then."

"That's different. It's Nix. This is..." Zane glanced over at Max and ground his teeth together. "He's one of *them*."

"Yeah, it's weird as fuck, but he isn't going to quit until he gets his five minutes in the ring, so why not let him have it?" I shrugged, retrieving some wrap off the sideboard running one length of the wall.

"I thought we had to wear gloves?" Max said over my shoulder.

"No, I said *you* had to wear gloves. Ever had a bare fist come at you before?" He rolled his lips together in a half-snarl, and I added, "Where's your helmet?"

"Come on, Wilder. I'm not a total pussy. I'll go easy on you."

A couple of guys nearby heard Max's taunt and snickered. I shot them a hard look that soon had them quieting down.

"Last chance to back out?" I said.

"No fucking way."

"Just tell me one thing," I said, lowering my voice. "Why? Why come here at all? Surely, your side of town has somewhere you can work out?"

Hell, I bet he had his own personal gym at home.

He dropped his head a little and I was sure he said, "Because I need it to hurt."

But when he looked back at me, it was like the words were never there.

***

"You're hesitating," I baited Max as we danced around one another in circles. We'd drawn a crowd, but then, I usually did when I stepped into Bryson's sparring ring.

"Just getting a feel for you, Wilder. Don't worry, I'll ruin that pretty face of yours soon enough." His lips twisted with amusement.

"You talk a good talk, Maxy boy," I teased, darting

forward and jabbing his face. He ducked, rolling away from my punch. The little fucker was quick.

Really damn quick.

"Get him, Nix," someone yelled. "Teach the little punk a lesson."

I glanced over at Zane and Kye. Wrong fucking move. Max came at me with lightning speed, his knuckles grazing my cheekbone as they smashed into my face.

"Fuck," I grunted, leaping backward. "That was a sly move."

"Boo hoo." He chuckled.

Oh, it was on now.

We circled each other again, trying to learn the other's weaknesses. I hadn't actually expected him to know what the fuck he was doing, but it was all there in his posture: the way he bounced lightly on his feet, and held his hands up to protect his face.

Max Rowe knew how to fight, and it had me all kinds of curious.

He lunged again, his fist crunching against my shoulder as I dodged his uppercut. "I won't fall for that again, asshole," I drawled, baiting him.

It worked and he came at me harder, faster, growing sloppy. I deflected most of his shots, only a couple making contact. But my body was used to the flash and spark of pain, it reveled in it.

"You have skill, kid. But you're overconfident."

"You sure about that?" He swung again, catching my jaw. My head snapped back, the coppery taste of blood filling my mouth where my teeth snagged on the inside of my lip.

I wiped it away with the back of my hand and gave him a feral grin. "You're gonna pay for that."

Cracking my neck from side to side, I centered myself before attacking, landing a series of jabs and right hooks on him. Max grunted, staggering back against the ropes. "Ready to bow out?" I taunted.

I wanted to teach the kid a lesson. I didn't want to inflict any real damage.

"Fuck you," he spat, swinging for me again. But I preempted his move, ramming my shoulder into him and sending him flying backward.

"Ooof," someone hissed, as Max lost his footing and went down, the *thud* of his body hitting the mat echoing through the place.

I loomed over him, feeling a tiny stab of guilt at the bruise blossoming along his jaw. He pushed up to a seated position, rubbing the back of his head. "Let's go again," he said. "I almost had you."

"A good fighter knows when to quit."

"Bullshit." He glowered at me. "I've heard the stories. You don't back down."

"I know what the fuck I'm doing."

He leapt up, getting right in my face.

"You really want to do this?" I stood my ground, tension crackling around us. "I already put you on your ass, don't make me do it again."

"Come on, man," he goaded. "Don't be such a pussy."

"That mouth is going to land you in trouble if you don't watch it."

"Fuck you, Wilder. If you won't fight me, I'll find

someone who will." He went to shove past me, but I grabbed his arm.

"Not gonna happen, kid. I brought you here. I got you the introduction. I let you spar a little. You're done here."

"I…" His expression crumpled. "Fine." He shirked me off and stormed out of the ring.

I spotted Bryson leaning against the door jamb, watching us. Ducking under the ropes, I jumped down off the platform and walked over to him.

"That could have gone worse," he said.

"The kid's a liability. I won't bring him around again."

"Actually, tell him he can train here, if he wants to."

"What the fuck? You saw how hotheaded he was. He'll never—"

"Know what I saw, Nix?" The corner of his mouth kicked up. "I saw a young guy angry and pissed at the world. A young guy looking for some kind of release. I saw you, Nix."

"You're kidding, right? I'm nothing like him. He's…" I glanced over to where Max was sitting on one of the benches, chugging a bottle of water. Shoulders tense and hunched over, expression dark and moody, he reminded me of a thunderstorm about to break.

"The offer is there. But if he comes around, I want you to keep an eye on him."

"Brys, man, come on. I don't have time to babysit him."

"He's lost, Nix. Trust me when I say I know what I'm talking about." He gave me a knowing look. I didn't like it, the assumptions he was making about me and Max being the same.

We were nothing alike.

Max had the world at his feet. He'd probably never wanted for anything in his life. Whereas I'd had to claw for every scrap and moment of hope.

He was wrong.

He had to be.

Didn't he?

11

HARLEIGH

A SHADOW LOOMED OVER ME AS I SCROLLED AIMLESSLY through my social media app.

"Hey." Nix dropped down beside me.

"Oh my gosh, your lip, what happened?" I moved closer, reaching out to ghost my thumb over the swollen, puffy skin.

"Your brother has a mean left hook."

"You were fighting?" The air whooshed from my lungs.

"It's a long story. But he's fine, so don't worry. We gave him a ride back to Old Darling Hill."

"You did?"

"Yeah, told him I wanted some alone time with my girl." Nix's hand slid over my lap, tugging me closer. "You are, aren't you, B? Mine?" His warm breath fanned my face and my head swam with all things Nix. "How was your night?" he asked, his mouth precariously close to mine.

"Okay," I choked out.

"She sat sulking the entire time," Celeste said out of nowhere, and I glanced over to scowl at her.

"Miss me that much, huh?" Nix teased, lifting my legs so that they draped over his. It was intimate, too intimate given we were in public, but he didn't seem to care.

"We're going to play against the guys if you two can keep your hands off each other long enough to join us?" Chloe grinned.

"Play without us. I need to talk to B."

"Suit yourself." She shrugged. "Prepare to lose, Brother."

Kye flipped her off, the four of them crowding around the ball caddy.

"What did Max want?" I asked.

"It was weird. He asked Bryson to let him fight."

"What?"

"Right? Obviously, Bryson said no, but he was pretty insistent."

"I-I don't understand. Does Max even know how to fight? He's just a spoiled kid."

"This would suggest otherwise." He pointed to his mouth.

"I can't believe you fought him."

"It wasn't like I had much choice, B. He was determined to spar with someone. I figured it might as well be me. Your brother is kind of an asshole."

"He's not my brother, Nix." He was by blood, but family was so much more than that.

"Bryson said he can train at the gym. I told him it was a bad idea, but he seems to have taken a shine to him."

"What does that mean?" Dread snaked through me.

"Bryson collects broken things, B. And he has a talent for sniffing out talent. He saw something in Max tonight."

"This is a disaster," I groaned, staring out at the bowling lane. Celeste was laughing as she watched Zane take his turn. She looked so happy, so at peace. Max wasn't like that. Even when he was with his friends, hanging out by the pool or at school, he had a dark shadow hanging over him.

Nix nudged his nose against my cheek. "I didn't want him to get hurt any more than necessary. Not that I don't think the little shit deserves it."

Sliding my eyes to his, I sucked in a sharp breath. Our heads touched as we breathed each other's air. "You sound like you think we should give him a chance."

"I don't. That's not what this is… but Bryson said some things. Things that got me thinking. What do you know about Max, B? About his past? The skeletons in his closet?"

"Nothing, I don't know anything. We aren't exactly close, and he's made his hatred for me pretty clear."

Nix went still, his breathing turning ragged. "He say something to you?"

"It doesn't matter." I sighed. "I can handle Max, Nix."

He tucked a stray hair behind my ear. "Want to sneak off to my car and make out?"

"Nix…" Heat crept up my neck and into my cheeks.

"Is it such a bad thing that I can't keep my hands off

you?" The intensity in his gaze seared me, burning me inside out.

"No, but we're in public and I'm not..." *I'm not used to this.*

"So, no one here cares about us, B."

"Zane looks like he cares." My gaze flicked to where he watched us.

"Zane's just pissed that I got into the ring with Max."

"Something we can agree on."

"We can't control everything, B. Some things will always be outside of our reach."

"I know, I... I just wish things weren't so complicated."

Nix curved his hand along the side of my neck and fitted his mouth to mine, shaping my lips with his. His kiss was like a match to a flame, igniting a fire inside me. Our tongues tangled in soft lazy licks as my fingers twisted into his hoodie.

"Nix," I whispered, trying to catch my breath.

"Yeah, I know." His pupils were blown with lust.

"Is it always like this?"

Intense. Consuming. Overwhelming.

"It's never been like this." He kissed me again, hard enough that it had to hurt his swollen lip. But if it did, it didn't stop him.

Someone cleared their throat and I peeked up to find Zane watching us.

"What, Z?" Nix sighed.

"You think it's wise being here?"

"It's safe. Nobody from school comes here."

"I'm not talking about us, asshole." His hard gaze found me. "If someone sees the two of you…"

"We can go back to Chloe and Kye's house, hang out in their—"

"We should probably go," I said, unsure how I felt about going to the Carters' house. Their mom would have questions. Questions I didn't know how to answer.

"Go?" Nix frowned, that adorable pout of his making an appearance. "It's still early."

"It's a school night," Celeste said, joining us.

"A school night?" Zane snorted. "What are you, twelve?"

"Sore loser, Washington?" She quipped. "Although I can understand why you might find bowling a little difficult since it's a game of skill and well, you know, you have none."

"Ouch, burn," Nix howled with laughter. "She got you good there, Z."

"Fuck you, asshole." He folded his arms across his chest, drawing Celeste's eye to the muscles peeking out from under his t-shirt.

"You know, Celeste's practically a genius."

"Harleigh!"

"Is that true, Einstein?"

"Do not call me that." She glowered after Zane.

"What would you prefer? Voltaire? Aristotle? Galileo?"

"You know who Voltaire and Aristotle are?"

I don't think I'd ever seen Celeste speechless before, but her mouth hung open as she gaped at him like a fish.

"What? You think just because I'm from The Row I'm dumb or something?"

"No, Zane, that's not—"

"Yeah, whatever. I'm going for a smoke." He took off.

"Dammit," Celeste murmured, shame burning her cheeks. "I didn't mean—"

"We know. Z is a complicated guy," Nix said, hooking his arm around my neck.

"He just makes me so—"

"Horny?" Kye appeared, grinning.

"Oh my God," she breathed, blushing even harder.

"What are we doing then?" Chloe said.

"We're going to head back," I replied before Celeste could reply.

"Oh, that's a shame. I was hoping to show Celeste my book collection."

"Maybe another time?" she asked, hopeful.

Of course they'd bonded over books. I'd never met a girl who loved to read as much as Celeste. She was like a sponge, absorbing facts and information from everything she touched.

"Yeah, anytime. My mom would love to meet you, and you know she's asking when you're coming around to see her, Harleigh."

I curled my fingers over the leather seat, focusing on the soft, smooth feel of it.

"Come on." Nix said, nudging me. "We'll walk you out."

The five of us left together, finding Zane waiting by Nix's car. He gave us a small wave before ducking inside.

"Goodbye to you too," I heard Celeste mutter to

herself as she hugged Chloe and headed for her Range Rover.

"We'll see you soon, B." Kye slung his arm around Chloe's neck and led her toward Nix's car.

"Come here you." Nix pulled me into his chest. "I really don't want to say goodbye to you yet."

"And you think I do?" I gazed up at him, anticipation bubbling inside me.

"I don't know, B. Sometimes I look at you and know exactly where your head's at. But other times, I don't have a clue what you're thinking."

"I'm sorry."

"Don't be. It keeps me on my toes." He kissed the end of my nose. "I know shit is complicated, but it won't always be like this, you'll see. I spoke to Coach Farringdon today."

"You didn't say anything."

"Because I still don't know if I can do it."

"Do what?"

"Go after it. A scholarship, I mean."

"You can, Nix." I laid my hand against his cheek. "I believe in you."

I always had. But he'd never believed in himself.

"I told him I'd think about it."

"That's a good thing, isn't it?"

"I don't know. We haven't exactly talked about the future."

The word made my heart stutter in my chest.

Future.

Did he mean *our* future?

I think he did.

But he was right, we hadn't talked about it, not when there were so many other things to talk about first.

"I want you to chase your dreams, Nix. Always."

"And what about your dreams, B? They're worth chasing too."

"I…" I didn't have dreams. Not anymore. Not when just getting through the day sometimes felt like wading through mud or clawing my way out of an endless pit.

"Yo, Nix," Zane called out of the window. "Let's go."

Nix dropped his head to mine, a low groan reverberating through his chest. "Friday. Only three more days until Friday night." He hugged me tight, dropping a kiss on the end of my nose. I tilted my face toward him, and our lips grazed.

It would have been so easy for him to lose control, to pin me up against Celeste's car and kiss me hard and without restraint. But he didn't.

"Go, before I change my mind about letting you leave." He brushed my lips again. "Text me when you get back."

"I will." I inhaled deeply. Inhaled him. It hurt my already weary heart to leave him and return to Old Darling Hill, but I had to.

"Friday, Birdie," he said. "I want to feel your eyes on me when we crush DA, and then I want to feel your lips on me when we celebrate."

His heated words licked my skin.

"Friday," I whispered, slowly pulling out of his arms.

"Until then." He winked, inching away from me, his eyes refusing to break their hold on me.

"Until then."

My heart was a runaway train in my chest. I'd always known being with Nix would be intense, but I hadn't realized just how much of a roller coaster it would be.

He lingered, waiting until I got into Celeste's car. Waited until she pulled out of the parking lot and we disappeared down the street.

We hadn't even gotten around the corner when my cell phone vibrated.

Hot Tub Guy: In case you hadn't already noticed, I'm gone for you, B.

"GOD, I WANT THAT," Celeste was peering over.

"Watch the road," I snapped, pulling my cell phone closer to my body.

"Aren't you going to reply?"

"Later. When we get back." When I figured out what to say.

He was so good at telling me how he felt, what he wanted. But I'd been so used to suppressing my emotions, keeping them hidden, that I was out of my depth.

"I still can't believe Max fought Nix."

"Sparred, they sparred."

"Same thing." She shrugged. "And you saw the state of Nix's face. I dread to think what Max looks like."

"Do you know why he'd want to fight for Bryson?"

"You have met Max, right? He's not exactly an open book. Why?"

"I don't know, it just feels like we're missing something."

"He probably wants to brag to his friends," she said dismissively.

And I got it. Max wasn't a good person, and he definitely wasn't a good brother. But something didn't add up.

And I couldn't shake the feeling there was more to Maximilian Rowe than either of us knew.

12

NIX

"Morn— Nix, sweetheart, what on earth happened to your lip?"

"You wouldn't believe me if I told you," I murmured, sliding onto one of the stools.

Jessa made me a mug of coffee and pushed it in my direction. "You want some ice for that?"

"Nah, I'll live." The swelling had already gone down a little. Besides, I'd had worse.

"You want pancakes?"

"I never say no to pancakes." I smiled, wincing as the skin around my mouth tightened and stretched. "Where is he?"

"He left early. Had some stuff to take care of before we leave tomorrow."

"You're leaving tomorrow?" That was news to me.

"Yeah. Tomorrow afternoon. We'll be back Monday.

Are you sure you're going to be okay? I know it's your first game of the season—"

"Don't worry about it."

Harleigh would be there. It wasn't ideal, asking her to come to watch the game. Especially not since Denby had stuck a target on her back. But I had a plan.

"But I do worry." Jessa leaned over and cupped my cheek. "You're a good boy, Nix. I know life hasn't always been easy for you…"

"Can we not do this?" I said, sipping my coffee.

She turned back to the pan on the stove, using the spatula to flip the pancakes. "Anything else you want?"

There were a lot of things I wanted but would never get. That was life.

"Bacon? Eggs?"

"Pancakes is fine, thanks. Listen, Jessa, are you sure about this weekend? I know you're excited, but I don't want you to—"

She swung around and pinned me with a knowing look, letting out a soft sigh. "He's trying, Nix. He's really trying. I know he has his moments…" she trailed off.

Is that what we are calling them now?

"…but I can't remember the last time your dad took me anywhere. I think it'll be good for us. Practice for when you move out and go off to college."

My spine straightened. He still hadn't told her. Such a fucking coward. But he knew, he knew I'd keep his little secret. Because I didn't want to hurt Jessa any more than necessary. And finding out my old man wanted me gone at the end of senior year was going to be a huge fucking fight.

"Yeah, college," I mumbled.

"Here you go, sweetie. Just how you like 'em." She shoved a plate full of pancakes toward me and I grabbed the syrup. "How are things with Harleigh? You know, it would be nice to see her."

"Yeah, never going to happen." Because bringing her here meant risking her running into my old man. Which is why this weekend was perfect. We could finally spend some time alone without her worrying about who might see us.

A sinking feeling went through me. First, we had to survive the game against DA.

"Nix, what is it?"

"These are good." I shoved another mouthful of syrup-drenched pancake into my mouth and smiled.

"You're keeping something from me," she said.

"Who, me?" I mumbled. "Would I ever?"

Her expression fell. "I know you worry about me, Nix, about this life… but I'm okay, sweetheart. I need you to know that. I choose this, I choose your father. Even when things get tough."

Jessa didn't have family; she didn't have parents, or brothers and sisters, or aunts and uncles. We were it. Me and my old man. So it didn't surprise me that she clung onto the hope of her happily ever after with him. But guys like Joe Wilder didn't mellow with age. They didn't have a sudden epiphany where they realized all their flaws and strived to do better. To *be* better. They grew old and even more bitter and twisted.

I didn't want that for her, not when she had such a good soul. But she was a grown woman who could make her own choices, and as hard as it was, I had to accept that.

I wouldn't have much choice anyhow come graduation when my old man kicked me out.

If we even lasted that long.

Because now I had Birdie to think about.

My cell phone vibrated and I dug it out of my pocket.

B: Good morning, Nix.

I SMILED, all the weight evaporating from my chest. Fuck, how did she do that? How did she make everything seem better with a single text message?

"Harleigh, I take it?" Jessa fought a grin. "Tell her I said hi."

I quickly typed a reply.

Me: Morning you. I missed you.

B: You can't miss me when you're asleep.

Me: Wanna bet?

I TYPED out another message before she could reply.

Me: Three more days at school until I get you all to myself.

My dick twitched behind my sweats, so on board with my Friday night plans.

B: I have to get ready for school.

Me: Do I make you nervous, B?

She'd told me before I did. When I'd asked her what she wanted. Her innocence was cute. It was one of the things I'd always loved about her.

But I had no problem corrupting her either, making her want me the way I wanted her.

B: You know you do, you always have...

Me: I can't wait to get between your pretty little thighs again, B.

B: I'm going now. Have a good day, Nix.

Quiet laughter rumbled in my chest as I texted her back.

Me: Yeah, you too. xo

"You know, it's nice to see you like this, Nix." Jessa's voice pulled me back into the kitchen.

"Like what?"

"Smiling. Happy. She always did bring out the best in you."

But that was the thing. If something made you happy, it also had the power to make you sad. If something lifted you up and made you soar, it also had the power to drag you down and ruin you.

Birdie was my salvation...

As much as she was my weakness.

"Yo, Wilder, wait up." Darius Hench jogged up beside me as I made my way to the locker room. "Can I talk to you for a second?"

"Sure, what's up?"

"I was thinking of asking Cherri out, but I know you two are—"

"Firstly." I held up my hand. "Me and Cherri aren't anything, and secondly, you sure you want to go there?"

"Have you seen her? She's… fuck, I get hard just thinking about her tight little body."

"Too much information, dude." I scowled at him.

"Shit, sorry. I guess it's kind of weird, huh. You've banged her and now I want to bang her."

"Have at it." I shrugged. I honestly didn't give a shit if he asked her out. It would hopefully keep her off my back. "Just don't come crying to me when she breaks your heart in tiny little pieces."

Darius grinned. "I know something she can break." He cupped his junk and I shook my head with laughter.

"She's all yours."

I'd never wanted Cherri. She was a means to an end, and maybe that made me a cold bastard. But no girl—not Cherri or anyone else—would ever thaw the ice around my heart because no one would ever come close to Harleigh and the way she made me feel.

The way she'd always made me feel.

"Well, so long as you're cool with it." He nudged my shoulder. "You ready for Friday? I'm eager to kick some DA ass."

"You know it." I held out my fist and he bumped it.

We entered the locker room together and I joined Zane and Kye in our usual spot.

"Everything good there?" Zane asked, flicking his eyes to Darius.

"Yeah, Hench wanted to know if I minded him making a play for Cherri."

Kye snickered. "Seriously?"

"Yup." I pulled off my hoodie and t-shirt and started changing into my pants and jersey.

"What did you tell him?"

"To go for it. I don't care who she does or doesn't hook up with."

"She won't like it."

"Not my problem."

Zane scoffed. "You know her attempt at calling a truce was bullshit. If I were you, I'd watch your back."

"Yeah." I rubbed my jaw. "But she's the least of my concerns right now."

"Friday," Zane said because he knew exactly where my head was at.

"I want Harleigh at the game but I need to know she's protected."

"I take it you have an idea about how to make that happen?"

"Yeah, I have a couple. You think Chloe will be good with sitting with her and Celeste?"

"Is Miller going to be there?" Kye's brow lifted.

"I was going to ask him to go with them, yeah."

"You really trust him?" Zane asked, and I shrugged.

"Harleigh trusts him, and he did us a solid last weekend."

"I don't want my sister getting mixed up with him."

"Not sure you have much of a choice," I said to Kye. "You know what Chloe is like when she sets her mind on something. Could be worse, she could want someone like Denby."

"Jesus, Nix, did you have to put that visual in my head?"

"You've got visuals of your sister and some guy in

your head?" Zane teased. "What the fuck is wrong with you?"

"You know what I mean, asshole."

"We should head out," I said, grabbing my helmet.

"Two more days until we get to kick some DA ass." Kye leaped on my back to the sound of our teammates' laughter.

Denby had it coming to him.

I just had to figure out a way to hit him where it hurt all while protecting Harleigh.

"WONDERED IF YOU'D SHOW," I said to Max later that night as he appeared around the corner from Buster's.

"Yeah, well, I need to train and I want to do it with the best."

"Why?" Pushing off the wall, I approached him.

"Like I said before, I have my reasons."

"I'll figure out what you're hiding, you know."

"You can try." His lips thinned. "We doing this or what?" Max went to move around me to the door, but I slammed my palm against his shoulder.

"Your old man know you're here?"

"What do you think?"

"And what about Harleigh? This better not be some attempt at—"

"Don't worry, this has nothing to do with your precious girlfriend," he spat the words with so much venom, I jerked back.

"If you so much as hurt a hair on her head, I'll—"

"Relax," he murmured, the fire in his eyes guttering. "This isn't about Harleigh, I swear. I just... I want to fight, and I can't do that back home."

"Yeah, I guess it isn't very becoming of Michael Rowe's son to be brawling in an illegal fight circuit."

A ripple went through the air. "I'm risking a lot being here. If my dad finds out..."

"Say no more. And for what it's worth, your secret is safe with me."

Relief washed over him.

"But there is one thing," I added. "I need a favor."

His brows crinkled. "Why do I not like the sound of that?"

"You want to train at the gym, train with me? This is what it'll cost you."

"Bryson said—"

"I don't give a fuck what Bryson said. The guys respect me. If I want to freeze you out, I can."

Max narrowed his eyes. "You're a real piece of work, Wilder."

"Likewise. So what do you say, a favor for a favor?"

He glowered at me, exhaling a shaky breath. "Fine, what do you need?"

13

HARLEIGH

I'D FORGOTTEN HOW WILD GAME NIGHT COULD BE, LET alone the opening game of the season. Just like Darling Hill High had done all the years previous, DA went all out. The bunting and flags, a whole student population dressed in red and white, the constant hoots and hollers in the hall at school. The entire day had been a frenzy.

So much so, I wasn't sure I would make it through the actual game.

My muscles had grown tenser as the day went on, my skin tight and itchy. And if my body felt tense, my stomach felt hollow. A vast pit of nothingness that was slowly swallowing me whole.

But of course, I pasted on my best fake smile and armed myself with enough 'I'm fine' and 'I'm okays' to make it through the day.

Now I was here, at DA's impressive stadium, following Celeste as we weaved through the sea of rowdy spectators. Guys wearing foam Devil's horns, and girls with painted faces brushed up against me as I pressed closer to Celeste.

"Guys, over here," she yelled over the ruckus, and Nate and Miles burst through the crowd.

"Whoa, this is some turn out," Nate said, offering me a polite smile. Things had been a little weird between us all week. Friendly but strained.

"You've never been to a football game before?" I asked him.

"I have, but not like this."

"The Devils-Hawks rivalry is intense," Miles said. "Things always get kind of crazy."

I winced at his choice of words, but he didn't notice. And why would he? It was a colloquialism generally accepted by society and yet it held such painful connotations for me, and so many people like me.

In the early days of living with Michael and his family, Max had called me crazy so many times, I'd actually begun to question whether he was right. Whether I really was losing my mind. But grief was a strong emotion, and in many ways, it did change you. Even when the holes left behind by the people you lost began to heal, the scars were still there. Forever ingrained on your soul.

"Harleigh?" Celeste squeezed my hand and I blinked at her.

"Yeah?"

"Are you sure you're okay? I know it's kind of intense."

"I can handle it."

For Nix, I'd do it. I'd step out of the shadows and into the light.

"You girls want something to eat? A hot dog or some cotton candy?"

"Ooh, I wouldn't say no to some cotton candy." Celeste grinned at Nate.

"I'll get it," Miles said. "Want to come with me?" His uncertain smile was so freaking cute.

"Sure." Celeste accepted his hand and the two of them joined the line.

"Hey," Nate said, stepping closer. "You holding up okay?"

"It's… a lot."

"It's high school. Football is religion."

"Yet you don't seem all that interested," I said, noting his lack of team colors or Devils jersey.

"Yeah, team sports aren't really my thing."

"They're not mine either."

"Then we can begrudgingly watch the game together." He winked and some of the tension inside me loosened. "What's happening there?" he said, inclining his head to where Celeste and Miles were standing.

"Why, has he said something to you?"

"That would infer we're friends, and I'm not sure we are. But he's been walking around school like someone stole his favorite toy."

"It's complicated."

"Let me guess, Celeste is a fan of The Row and their special brand of bad boys?"

"That's not fair," I said, my hand drifting to my throat.

"No, you're right, it's not. I'm sorry. I didn't—"

"It's okay."

"You keep saying that but it feels like a lie."

I stared up at him and whispered, "Sometimes if you lie for long enough it starts to feel like the truth."

"Touché, Maguire. Tou-fuckng-ché."

"Hey, you guys." Chloe appeared. "I thought I'd never find you. Doesn't anyone check their cell phones around here?"

"My bad, I was too busy trying to stick close to Celeste."

"Where is— Oh, Miles is here. Cool."

"Yeah, really cool," Nate murmured under his breath. "Looking good, Clo."

"Why thank you. Thought I'd better try and at least fit in with the DA crowd. How'd I do?" She spun slowly on the spot, letting me get a full look at her skinny jeans and white cropped tee combo.

"You look cute."

Her eyes twinkled with delight. "Exactly what I was going for."

"You don't go here," a saccharine voice said from behind us.

Slowly, I turned to meet Angela's narrowed gaze. She was dressed in her cheer costume: a tight little red and white dress and blonde hair pulled high in a slick curled ponytail.

"Angela, always a pleasure," Nate drawled, flanking Chloe's other side.

"Who's your new friend?"

"I'm Chloe. Chloe Ca—"

"This is Chloe, my friend," I said.

"You have friends?" She smiled but it was full of bite. "Who knew?"

"Shouldn't you be warming up or something?" Nate asked.

"You know, Nate, you really should think about the company you keep these days. Marc offered you an in and you threw it back in his face."

"Excuse me while I go cry into my hot dog."

"Asshole," she murmured.

"Bitch," he shot back, and she snarled.

"Enjoy the game, Harleigh. Although it probably won't be any fun watching your old team get annihilated by the Devils."

Chloe went to speak, but I elbowed her in the ribs. "Break a leg," I called as she walked away.

"Okay, we hate her, right? Tell me we hate her."

"Oh, we hate her," Nate said.

"What a bitch. Are you okay?" Chloe asked me.

"Yeah. She's Marc Denby's girlfriend."

"More like his latest piece of ass." I glanced at Nate and he shrugged. "What?" he said. "It's true. Marc doesn't like to be tied down."

"Said every guy ever." Chloe's expression dropped, and Nate frowned.

"Bad break up?"

She twirled a strand of her hair around her finger but didn't meet his eyes. "Something like that."

"We got extra." Celeste and Miles reappeared, thrusting a bag of cotton candy at me. "Hold up, what happened?"

"Chloe met Angela."

"Ugh, unlucky for you."

"Is she always such a bitch?"

"Every second of every day. You know, it was probably her that sent the text message to Har—"

"Celeste," I hissed. I didn't need to be thinking about *that* particular thing right now.

"What? It's true."

"Well now I want to wipe that fake smile right off her stupid pretty face."

"No fighting," I said.

"Fine. I'll behave." Chloe laced her arm through mine. "We should probably find our seats."

Chloe stuck to my side as Nate guided us through the crowd, Miles and Celeste trailing behind. If people's curious stares bothered Chloe, she didn't let it be known as she talked about everything and nothing.

We filed into the bleachers and found our seats, but the second I spotted Max and Nate's brother Toby, my stomach sank.

"Seriously, you couldn't have sat somewhere else?" I snapped at Max.

He smirked, shrugging his shoulders. "Free country, weirdo."

"Ignore him." Celeste leaned around Chloe. "I do."

Nate snickered and I pinned him with an incredulous look. "Tell me you didn't arrange this?"

"Not my doing." He held up his hands. "But you might want to ask your boyfriend."

"Nix… but I don't understand." I glanced back at Max who was paying me no attention, the shadow of a bruise along his cheekbone. I'd heard him tell Michael he had a fight with a door, but I knew exactly whose knuckles had left that mark.

And it bothered me more than it should have.

Music exploded out of the PA system making me flinch. Nate touched my arm and mouthed, "Okay?"

I nodded, focusing on my breathing, the feel of the cool plastic seat under my thighs. But the blood pounding in my ears was overwhelming, like a second heartbeat reverberating in my skull.

Chloe's fingers slid through mine, offering me an anchor. I could do this. I could sit and watch a football game with my friends. With people who had been here for me regardless of what had happened last year. In *spite* of what happened.

Chloe had accepted me back into the fold as if I'd never left: no questions asked, no apologies required. It was the same with Celeste. I was her half-sister and that's all she needed to know to welcome me into her life unconditionally.

The music crescendoed as the team burst onto the field, tearing open the hand-painted banner. Our side of the bleachers were on their feet, clapping and cheering, but the red and white players weren't the ones I was waiting to see.

"Remember not to cheer when they come out." Chloe chuckled.

A quieter rumble filled the air as the Hawks walked onto the field. They were calm, collected; a solid wall of magenta and black moving as one.

My heart stalled at the sight of Nix, leading his team, moving ahead of them like a general leading his army into battle. His helmet hung loosely at his side as his long, powerful legs ate up the field. His eyes immediately scanned the crowd, finding me as if he couldn't resist the sharp tug I also felt in my stomach.

He smiled, his whole face lighting up as if we were the only two people in the stadium. And maybe it had always been that way for me to some degree. My world had always revolved around Nix. His was the sun, the center of my universe.

Only now, I was his too.

The reality of it flowed through me, wrapping around my heart and making it flutter. Slow, steady beats that bathed me in reassurance and comfort.

"He looks good, huh?" Chloe squeezed my hand.

"Yeah," I breathed, unable to drag my eyes off him.

He jogged over to Coach Farringdon, letting the older man pull him close and give him instructions and a pre-game pep talk. Playing DA was always a big deal, but for Nix it was even more important since it was senior year. The Hawks wouldn't go down without a fight. But neither would the Devils.

The referee called both quarterbacks onto centerfield for the coin toss, and an eerie silence fell over the stadium until the Devils won the toss and chose to kick off first, and the place erupted again.

"Marc looks like he's up to something," Nate whispered.

I glanced up at him and frowned. "What do you mean?"

"Look." He pointed to where Marc stood with some of his defensive players. To anyone else it might have looked like a captain commanding his team but I saw what Nate saw. How they watched Nix's every move. Like a predator stalking its prey.

"What do you think they'll do?"

"Knowing Marc, he'll go for blood."

"What?" I shrieked over the deafening noise. I wanted to run down there and warn Nix, but both teams were already on the field, moving into position.

"Don't worry," he added. "I'm sure Wilder will give as good as he gets."

A violent shudder ran through me. I didn't want Nix to get hurt, but I also didn't want him to do something that would jeopardize his place on the team.

Or his chance at a way out of The Row.

14

NIX

THWACK.

The air whooshed from my lungs as I went down hard. Everything ached. My shoulders, my thighs, and calves. The muscles in my arms were heavy and sore.

The Devils defensive line were all over me. It was a shitshow and it was starting to piss me the hell off.

"Jesus, Nix, you good?" Kye offered me his hand and pulled me up. I shook off the tension radiating through me and nodded. "What I need is for our guys to give me some fucking space."

"They're all over us, bro."

I glanced at the scoreboard. Despite having me pinned down, Denby was also struggling to get past our defense so they were only leading by one touchdown. Everything was still to play for, but I had a bad feeling. Like a storm rolling in on the distance, the air felt charged, full of anticipation.

I'd barely had time to breathe in the first two quarters and it was starting to show.

"We need to put some points on the board," I said to my guys as they joined the huddle.

"What you thinking, Nix?"

"We go with the play we've been practicing."

"You sure? It's a risky move. Puts you out in the open..."

"They won't be expecting it. If I can rush enough yards, we can tip things in our favor."

"Okay," Kye said, clapping his hands together. "You heard the man. Let's give these punks something to moan about."

We moved back into position. My center, a guy named Gunner, cradled the ball as the Devils defense moved along the scrimmage line. Adrenaline pulsed through me, my muscles pinging with exertion. We needed this win. It wasn't so much about the season as it was about proving to these rich boy assholes that just because we were from The Row—that our lives were hard and we didn't come from much—didn't mean we lacked skill. We had what it took to be here, on their field, playing at their fancy school.

"Ready to quit yet, Wilder?" one of their players snickered. "There's only one way this ends, and that's with you broken and bleeding."

"Fuck you, asshole," I muttered, rocking from side to side as I waited for the whistle. "Red seventeen," I called the play. "Red seventeen."

My players began shifting into position, laying the

diversion with precision just as we'd practiced again and again over the last couple of weeks.

"Hut," Gunner called, snapping the ball to me. I caught it and dropped back, keeping an eye on the defense as they barreled through our guys to get to me.

One of my running backs slipped past me, faking the pass, and took off down the left side, drawing the attention of the Devils defense.

And I ran.

Pumping my legs hard, I went wide around the scrimmage and shot down the right side of the field. It only took a second for them to realize but I was already flying like a rocket, blood pounding in my ears with every thud of my cleats against the ground. *Fifty... forty... thirty...* I ate up the yard markers as a swarm of red and white jerseys hurtled toward me in my peripheral vision.

"Go, go," Coach yelled, and the crowd seemed to yell right along with him as I kept running. *Twenty... ten...*

A hulk of a player broke free from the pack and dove for me, his fingers wrapping around my ankle as I tried to leap out of the way. He managed to get a decent grip, yanking me hard until I was no longer moving forward, but falling.

Cradling the ball to my body, I waited for the impact. The *whoosh* of air from my lungs and *clang* of pain as my body hit the ground. Players dove on top of me like a house of cards collapsing as I fought with everything I had to keep the ball in my hands.

"Okay, okay, let him up, let him up." The referee yelled as I tried to roll onto my back and get air into my burning lungs. But right as I moved, something crumpled into my kidneys. A fist. A grunt spilled from me as I cussed under my breath, fiery hot agony lancing through my back.

"You're going down, Wilder," someone hissed before the sea of bodies cleared.

"Nix, you all good?" Kye stood over me with the rest of our offense. He helped me up again, but this time, I winced.

"What happened?"

"Nothing," I said, scanning the field for my attacker, but it could have been any one of them. They all glared at me with utter disdain.

Assholes.

"You sure?"

"Don't worry about it. I can handle these bunch of pussies."

"That's what worries me." He gave me a tight smile. "Forty yards, that's more like it."

"Damn right it is." I high fived him and jogged back into position ready to finish what we'd started.

MY RISKY PLAY put us tied going into the fourth quarter. There wasn't a single part of me that didn't hurt. But I refused to quit. We could win this, and when we did, I'd take great pleasure in shoving it in Denby's face.

"Okay, huddle round." Coach beckoned us in. "You've fought hard, given how dirty they're playing. There's only a minute to go and I need you all to keep your heads, you hear me?" His heavy gaze landed on me. "Nix,

I know they've got you pinned down and they're expecting you to try and run. Keep your cool and keep pushing and I think we can do it."

"Damn right, we can," Hench said.

"Win or lose, I want you to know I'm proud of how you've handled yourself tonight. It's never easy playing here, for any of us." He ran his eyes over each of us. "Don't let them push you too far now the end is in sight."

"Forty-four is gunning for Nix, Coach. The shit he's saying—"

"You block that shit out and focus on the task at hand. They want a reaction. They want to prove to everyone here that you're a bunch of lawless degenerates. But that's not who you are. I know that and you know that, so get the hell out on that field and show them. Hawks on three."

Our voices rang out over the noise of the crowd. The bleachers were mostly full of DA supporters, but our section had held their own, amped up by the cheer squad and their school spirit.

I jogged over to the scrimmage line and got into position. Forty-four flashed me a feral grin, pointing two fingers at his eyes and then me. *I'm watching you.*

He could watch me all he wanted. I didn't plan on losing this game, no matter what the fuck they came at me with.

I didn't call a play, everyone knew their task, their responsibilities. It was fourth and goal and there was only one way this ended, with the ball in the end zone and six points on the scoreboard.

I found Kye on my left flank and nodded. Ten yards.

That's all that was stopping us from victory. We just had to push through them.

The air crackled around me, skittering over my skin like lightning.

'I'm coming for you,' Forty-four mouthed, trying to get under my skin. But I fought my natural instinct to respond, to retaliate. Harleigh was in the crowd. The last thing I wanted was her to witness me and a DA player going at it. Even if the beast inside me roared at his blatant threat.

"Hut," Gunner called and I caught the ball with ease, my fingers grasping the leather tightly.

Everything happened in slow motion. Kye ran straight for the end zone as I threw the ball into his trajectory. A blur of red and white jerseys dove at him but he leaped into the air, just getting his fingers onto the ball, enough to snatch it into his body and slam it onto the ground.

"Touchdoooooown," the announcer yelled and our section of the bleachers went wild.

"Fuck, yes." The guys clapped me on the shoulder as they headed to celebrate with Kye. I jogged over, laughing at the state of Kye as he rode cowboy on the back of Gunner's back.

"That's how it's done, baby." He pointed at me. "That's how it's fucking done."

"Fuck yeah it—"

A Devils player shoulder-checked me as he walked by, and I staggered back. "Watch where you're going, asshole," I called, and he spun around.

Forty-four. I hadn't even noticed, riding the high of the win.

"Or what? What are you going to do, Wilder? You're nothing but a piece of trailer trash scum." He stepped up to me until we were toe-to-toe, chest-to-chest. "You might have skill on the field, but do you really think anyone is going to give a guy like you a shot? Joe Wilder's son. Scum of the fucking Earth. No wonder your girl jumped ship and shacked up with Nate Miller."

Before I knew what was happening, I'd fisted his jersey and yanked him toward me. "Say that again," I seethed, my body trembling with rage.

"You heard me, Wilder. You're nothing but—"

"Walk away, Nix," Zane jogged over to me and laid his hand on my shoulder. "Walk the fuck away. He isn't even worth it."

"Oh look, Zane Washington to the rescue."

My eyes narrowed to thin slits as I glared at him, past him to his friends. Denby was there watching, a smug expression on his face as if he was waiting for me to fuck up.

He wanted this. He'd orchestrated this. The constant taunts and discreet jabs, the way his defense marked my every move on the field. He was baiting me, trying to push me to do something stupid.

"Nix, don't do this, man."

"Do it, Wilder. You know you want to. Hit me." The guy smirked. "Show me and my guys just how much of a tough guy you are."

I shoved him hard and backed the fuck up.

"Walk it off," Zane said.

"We know she's here, you know. Your little pet." I froze, fury licking up my spine. "Maybe if Denby plays his cards right, Miller will let him have a taste. See what all the fuss is about. We've all heard the stories about girls from The Row."

Zane grabbed me before I could get to the motherfucker. "Be cool, Nix. Be fucking cool," he growled in my ear. The rest of the team ran over, shielding me from forty-four, Denby, and the rest of the Devils.

"He's dead," I yelled, kicking the ground, sending grass and mud flying everywhere. "He's fucking dead."

"Nix, get the hell over here." Coach Farringdon whipped his ball cap off and threw his arm around my shoulder. "What the hell happened out there?"

I unclipped my helmet and pulled it off, tucking it under my arm. "He said some things…"

"I don't care if he called your stepmom a dirty whore, I told you to stand the fuck down tonight."

"He's still in one piece, isn't he?" I glared back at him, and his lip twitched.

"Yeah, I guess he is. I was going to congratulate you on keeping your cool tonight, but you came close to ruining it all, real damn close, son."

"Yeah…" I loosened a breath. "He hit a nerve."

"If you want to play for the Albany Falcons one day, you need to learn to control that temper of yours."

"I know." Fuck, I knew that. But it wasn't easy when your default setting was attack as the best form of defense.

When you constantly got judged for where you came

from and how you lived, it changed you. Made you harder around the edges. Like a neglected animal ready to lash out.

At least, that's how it had always been for me.

Coach gripped my shoulder and squeezed. "We got the win, Nix. That'll hit them where it hurts most." He winked. "Now go celebrate with the team. You deserve it."

15

HARLEIGH

I CHEWED MY THUMB WATCHING NIX FIST THE DEVILS player's jersey and yank him closer.

"Oh, shit," Nate breathed.

"Walk away, Nix," I murmured. "Walk away."

"If he wanted to hurt him, the douchebag would already be crying on the ground," Chloe said, dropping her chin on my shoulder. "He's in control. See."

Nix shoved the guy and let Zane usher him away, but the guy said something else. Something that had Nix lunging for him. Zane caught him around the waist, hauling him away as the rest of the team descended, forming a physical barrier between their quarterback and the Devils instigator.

Coach Farringdon beckoned Nix over and the two of them moved away from everyone else.

It had been a hard game to watch. Every time Nix got sacked or tackled, my heart stopped. And I was almost certain I'd seen a DA player punch him in the back earlier.

They'd been gunning for him the entire game. Nate and Chloe had tried to reassure me that it was only because he was the best player on the field, but I wasn't so sure. There had always been a certain level of rivalry and hatred between Nix and Marc Denby, but tonight seemed different. It felt… personal.

As the teams slowly began to disappear off the field, the bleachers started to empty. But we stayed behind, letting the crowds clear.

"So, what did you think?" Nate asked me.

"I've never really been a huge football fan."

"Seriously? I would have thought with you and Nix being close that you'd be a groupie."

"Yeah, well, I'm not."

I'd watched some of his games, but it didn't excite me the way it did most people. Not to mention the fact it had always meant watching the cheerleaders fawn all over him. At least tonight Cherri had kept her hands to herself.

The Hawks cheer squad was still on the field, chatting and laughing and taking celebratory selfies. Cherri looked the part, her ample curves wrapped in Hawk magenta and black, the pleated skirt skimming the top of her thighs. Her dark-blonde hair was scraped back in a sleek ponytail, two thick curls framing her face. She oozed sex appeal and much like Angela and her squad, had spent most of the game working the crowd into a frenzy.

Too many times I'd witnessed her congratulate Nix

on a win with a kiss. But not tonight. Tonight, she'd barely looked twice at him.

As if she felt me watching, her head whipped over, her heavily made up eyes finding mine. Her easy breezy expression dropped, replaced with sheer contempt. My stomach dipped and I glanced at my toes, needing to escape her venom.

"Friend of yours?" Nate asked.

"Is she still looking over here?"

"No, they're leaving."

Relief rolled through me and I peeked up at him. "Not a friend."

"You don't say, you've gone as white as a sheet."

"Cherri Jardin is…" *Sexy. Popular. Sexually experienced. Everything I'm not.*

"Darling Hill High's equivalent to Angela?" Celeste asked and Chloe nodded.

"You could say that."

"We should go," I said, wanting nothing more than to disappear. First Angela, now Cherri.

"Don't let her get to you," Chloe said as we filed out of the bleachers and headed down the steps. The plan was to head to the gas station at the edge of town to meet Nix and the guys, since we couldn't exactly meet up here.

Unsurprisingly, Max and Nate's brother took off, barely sparing us a goodbye.

"That wasn't weird at all," Celeste grumbled.

I still didn't quite understand why Nix had asked Max to sit near us, but he had, and I guess that meant something.

We reached the parking lot only to find Marc waiting

for us. He stepped forward and smirked. "You would have looked better in my jersey." His eyes walked the length of me, slowly dragging back up.

"Don't you have a party to get to?" Nate said, and I didn't miss the way he moved closer, his arm brushing mine.

"Come on, cous, I gotta know. Does she fuck as good as she—"

"Asshole," Nate spat.

"At least we know what side you're really on. Although I guess I shouldn't have been surprised you decided to shack up with Little Miss Trailer Trash."

"Go to hell, Marc."

It occurred to me then that Marc really thought there was something going on between me and Nate.

I didn't know how to feel about that. But I didn't say anything.

"You know, Harleigh, if you want to experience what it's like to be with a real man, I'm right here, baby."

Chloe snorted at that.

"Something funny?" Marc cut her with a scathing look.

"Nothing you—"

"What do you want, Marc?" I stepped forward, trying to de-escalate things.

"You think you're so fucking—"

"Yo, Denby," Max called, appearing from nowhere.

"That you, Rowe?"

"Good game, man." Max sauntered up to Marc as if they were best friends. "Too bad the Hawks got the win."

"Barely." Marc grumbled.

"You headed to Ange's party?"

"Fuck yeah."

"Nice, guess we'll see you there." Max nudged Toby.

"Jesus, I feel sorry for you, related to those two." He glanced over at me and Celeste.

"It is what it is." Max met my irritated gaze and discreetly flicked his head to our cars.

What was he—

An escape.

Max was giving us an escape.

"Come on," I said to Nate, as Max and Toby asked him a question about the game.

We hovered near the cars, making no move to get in.

"He is such a grade-A ass," Chloe said. "What's his and Nate's deal?"

"They're cousins," I said. "But it's complicated."

"Cousins? No shit." A strange expression passed over her face as she looked at Nate. His eyes lifted to hers, but he looked away. She cleared her throat. "We should go, the guys will be pissed if we're not there."

Code for: Nix would be pissed.

"Actually, Celeste and I are going to call it a night," Miles said.

"We are?" She gawked at him.

"Well, yeah, I thought we could—" He leaned in and whispered the rest of his plan to her. From the way her cheeks turned red it wasn't difficult to work out what he wanted to do.

"We could all hang out for a bit," she said, giving me an apologetic smile.

"Babe, come on," Miles groaned. "I want to spend time with *you*."

Indecision flickered over her face and the air turned thick with tension.

"You two go, we'll be fine," I said, making the decision for her.

"You're sure?"

"Chloe and Nate will keep me company."

"We will?" Nate's ears perked up. "I was actually going to call it a night too."

"What?" Chloe barked. "I mean, I assumed you'd hang out with us for a bit." It was her turn to blush.

He looked to me, and I shrugged. "I guess I can."

"Excellent." She clapped.

We said goodbye to Celeste and Miles, and I grabbed my bag from the trunk of her SUV. She didn't look wholly pleased with not coming with us, but maybe this would give her and Miles a chance to figure things out.

"Ladies," Nate said, bleeping open his car. He held the door for Chloe and she slipped inside.

His eyes caught mine over the roof and he smiled.

"What?" I asked.

"Life sure has gotten a whole lot more interesting with you around."

Before I could ask what the hell that meant, he ducked into the car.

"You ready?" Chloe asked me, and with a swarm of butterflies in my stomach, I nodded.

"WHERE ARE THEY?" I glanced up and down the street again, nervous energy buzzing inside me.

We'd been here almost fifteen minutes, and there was no sign of them. Not to mention the fact that Nix wasn't answering his cell phone. Neither was Kye or Zane.

"Something's happened," I said, a sinking feeling in my chest.

"Maybe we should— oh, here they are." Chloe pointed to the familiar headlights, and Nix's car came into view.

But the second he climbed out, I gasped. "What happened?"

He limped over to me and I slid my arm around his waist, pressing a hand to his chest. "Nix?"

"Fuckers jumped us."

"Wh-what?"

"Yeah, in the parking lot."

"Oh my God, did you tell someone? Coach? Security? The police?"

"We handled it."

Nate snorted and I glared at him. "Sorry," he mumbled. "You need somebody to look at that?"

Nix's arm hung at his side protectively, but he shook his head. "I need some Tylenol, a smoke, and my girl." He dropped a kiss on my head. "I know we said we'd hang out, but I—"

"Whatever you need," I said.

"You guys can come," Nix offered. "Jessa left snacks."

"I… uh, I don't want to impose." Nate rubbed the back of his neck.

"Not scared of being caught hanging out in The Row, are you?" Zane's brow arched with accusation.

"That's not… no."

"Come, don't come," Nix murmured, "but I really need to get home."

He was hurt, worse than he was letting on.

"Maybe you should get checked out?" I whispered, and his mouth curved.

"Worried about me, B?"

"Always."

"Come on, let's roll. Kye's driving," Nix said.

"I can ride with you, if you want," Chloe offered Nate. "Show you the way."

"I… uh…" He looked to me for what, I didn't know. A get out clause? Permission?

He didn't need my permission.

I shrugged and he said, "Yeah, okay."

"Great." Chloe beamed, lacing her arm through his. "We'll park at ours and then walk over."

"Yeah, because Miller's ride will look so much more at home on your driveway." Zane rolled his eyes and she narrowed hers right back.

"I'll just be over here, pretending my baby sister isn't trying to mack on Miller," Kye groaned, before climbing into Nix's car.

"As long as he isn't trying to mack on my girl, it's all good." Nix hugged me closer.

"You're a changed man." Zane gave him a bemused smirk as he got in the passenger seat, leaving me and Nix to get in the back.

A pained groan rumbled from his chest, making my heart stutter.

"I can't believe those assholes jumped you."

"Check out little Harleigh Wren's potty mouth." A grin slashed Zane's mouth as he twisted around to look at me.

"I'm not the same girl I was back then," I said quietly, stroking Nix's arm.

"No, I'm getting that." Zane's expression darkened but I didn't have time to analyze it because the car spluttered to life.

"Sounds like she needs a tune-up."

"There's nothing wrong with her," Nix murmured, tucking his face into my shoulder. "Wake me when we get there," he said.

Within seconds his breathing evened out and his body went heavy beside me.

Zane met my gaze again and I asked, "How bad was it?"

Tension bracketed his mouth. "It could have been worse, but those fuckers held me and Kye back while they—"

"Z, man. He wouldn't want her to know that."

"Well, yeah, maybe she should."

"Zane," my voice cracked. "Do you have a problem with me?"

"No… fuck, B, it's not that. I'm just worried."

"Because I'm back." A heavy weight plunked in my stomach.

He ran a hand down his face and let out an exasperated breath as Kye drove toward The Row.

"Look, I'm happy you're back. I am. I just don't know where all this ends. You're… one of them now—"

"I'm not."

"Aren't you? You live there, in that house. You go to their school. Hang out with their kids."

Breathe, just breathe, Harleigh.

I tried counting backward from ten. When that didn't work, I tried twenty. Desperately fighting the rush of tears burning the backs of my eyes.

"I know it isn't your fault. Fuck, I know that. But things are different now, you're different. And Nix has a chance at getting out of here. He can't afford to blow that. Not when he's so close…"

I wanted to run. To push Nix off me and shoulder the door open and escape. Everything Zane was saying made sense, but my heart couldn't accept it.

I couldn't accept it.

Nix had options. Before I came along he had real options, and now that I was back… I shut those thoughts down. I couldn't spiral, not here.

Not while Nix was asleep and Zane was looking at me like this was all my fault.

NIX

"NIX, WAKE UP."

The angel called to me, her touch as soft as silk as she ran her fingers over my brow.

"Hmm," I murmured, leaning into her hand, needing more.

"Wake up, Nix. We're here."

Here?

What the fuck?

"Dude, let's go!"

My eyes flew open to find Zane smirking at me and Harleigh gazing at me with guilt-filled eyes.

"Sorry," she whispered. "I tried to do it the nice way."

"It's okay." I grabbed her hand and lifted it to my mouth, kissing her knuckles.

"Pussy," Zane grumbled before climbing out of the car.

Harleigh tensed beside me.

"What's wrong?" I asked.

"Nothing." She smiled, but it didn't reach her eyes. "We should get you inside."

The trailer was bathed in shadows as Kye opened the back door to my car and offered me a hand. "Go easy," he said.

My ribs hurt like a bitch and my kidneys didn't feel much better. When the masked group had jumped us as we walked to my car, I'd known straightaway who it was.

Denby and his friends. Pretty sure forty-four was the one who hit me while Denby watched on, lording it over me and his crew like some rich boy pussy who didn't want to get his hands dirty.

I should have known they would be plotting something beyond the bullshit they pulled at the game. But I was just relieved they'd left Harleigh out of it.

Kye pulled my arm around his shoulder and took my weight as I limped toward the trailer, Harleigh trailing after us.

I hated that she'd seen me like this, but my need for her won out over my pride and dignity. Even if my injuries had ruined my plans for tonight.

She was here, in my space, and that was the most important thing.

Zane unlocked the door with my keys and let us inside. Before I could stop myself, I found myself saying, "It isn't much," to Harleigh.

"Nix..." Her hand drifted to her throat. "I've been in here before."

"I remember."

I did.

Every single time she'd stepped foot through the door. Her visits had become few and far between as we'd gotten older. She and my old man didn't exactly see eye to eye, and she found it difficult to be around the man who repeatedly hurt me.

Kye helped me into one of the armchairs. "Beer, pain meds, or a smoke first?"

"I think there's some Tylenol in that cabinet." I pointed to the kitchenette, and patted the roll of the arm, crooking my fingers at Harleigh.

She came willingly, perching on my knee. But I slid my arm around her waist and tucked her into my body.

"It feels weird to be here," she said.

"Yeah, I live here and I fucking hate the place."

"Nix…" Harleigh twisted slightly to look at me, her big green eyes alight with pity.

"Don't do that, B. Don't feel sorry for me."

"It's not that." She dropped her gaze, toying with the rope pull of my hoodie. "I just hate that I wasn't there for you the last nine months."

Sliding my hand under her hair, I gripped the back of her neck, forcing her to look at me. "But you're here now."

That same uneasy expression from earlier fell over her. Before I could ask her about it, the door swung open and Chloe and Nate came inside.

"Hey," I said to him as he stood awkwardly by the door. "Come inside, make yourself at home. It isn't much but it's home, you know."

Except, it wasn't. Not really.

"Do you want a drink?" Chloe asked Nate.

"There's beer in the refrigerator," I said.

"I brought a little something too." Nate rifled through his pocket and pulled out a small baggy.

"Nice. Light her up."

Someone turned on Jessa's radio and chilled beats filled the trailer. This was all I needed, my friends and my girl. And maybe a half hour in Buster's ring with Denby and his punk ass friends. But I'd deal with them later. Right now, I needed something to take the edge off.

Nate lit up the blunt, sucking the end until the cherry burned red. He exhaled a wispy stream of smoke and offered it to me. I glanced at Harleigh and she shrugged.

She'd seen me get high before, but she'd never indulged back then.

"You want a hit?" I asked her.

"I..."

"Relax, B. Either you do, or you don't."

She rolled her lips together, giving me a small nod.

"Come here then, pretty girl." I slid my hand to her jaw, gently squeezing her cheeks as I inhaled the end of the blunt, letting the bitter smoke fill my lungs. Harleigh watched, entranced, her eyes wide and alert as I leaned in and brought my lips right to hers, exhaling the smoke into her mouth.

Her eyelashes fluttered as the hit rolled through her and when she'd exhaled, I kissed her, slow and deep, letting my tongue tangle with hers, not giving a fuck that we had an audience.

"I've never done that before," she whispered.

"Good," I said. "I want your firsts, B. Every single one."

Fuck, it was so easy to get lost in her. In the way she made me feel.

Even beaten and bruised, every inch of me aching and sore, Harleigh made me feel ten feet tall.

I slumped back against the chair and took another couple of hits on the blunt before Kye leaned over and plucked it from my mouth. "Greedy fucker."

"Get your own," I said.

"There's plenty more where that came from," Nate said, picking out another blunt from the baggie.

"Can I—"

"No! No fucking way." Kye glared at his sister. "If Mom knew you were getting high…"

"You always get high!"

"It's different. I'm a guy, and well, it's just different."

"That's some misogynistic bullshit right there."

"I agree with Clo on this one, sorry guys." Harleigh smiled.

"Just let her have a smoke," I said. "It's not like she can get into too much trouble walking from here to your place."

"A couple of hits, that's it. I mean it, Clo, or so help me fucking God. And no shotgunning it off Miller."

"Whoa, man." Nate held up his hands. "Don't drag me into this."

Zane brought me a beer and some Tylenol. "Probably could have used something stronger."

"Nah, I'll be okay." I didn't want to be totally out of it tonight.

He didn't look convinced but flopped down on the end of the couch next to Chloe.

"Your parents are out of town?" Nate asked.

"Old man and stepmom," I corrected. "And yeah, something like that. Got the place to myself all weekend." My hand slid up Harleigh's thigh and she drew in a sharp breath. Even now, she was still so fucking coy and innocent.

"I'm so fucking happy you beat the Devils," Nate said. "The look on Marc's face was priceless."

"Yeah, well, he made sure to get us back for it," Zane said, taking a deep hit on his blunt.

The four of them fell into easy conversation as the trailer slowly filled with a smoky haze. The pain pills combined with the good weed, beer, and Harleigh's presence was like the best fucking drug in the world. My body felt loose, my mind drifting to a better future, a better fucking life. Me and Harleigh and a cute little apartment in the city. Days spent attending college classes and evenings spent studying, lots and lots of naked studying. Yeah, I liked the sound of that. Harleigh would work at some quirky coffee shop while I rose through the ranks of the Albany Falcons.

We wouldn't have much money, no handouts from mom or dad or family, just love and laughter and each other.

Jesus, I was really fucking high.

Because that couldn't ever be our life, could it?

I let out a heavy sigh and Harleigh plucked the blunt from my fingers, bringing it to her own mouth. Sucking in a deep hit, she lowered her mouth to mine, a whisper of a kiss, and exhaled long and slow.

Someone cleared their throat, but I didn't take my eyes off her, I couldn't.

"I fucking love you, B," I whispered, keeping my voice low and steady. Wanting her to know I meant every word. Every fucking syllable.

"This is fun." She giggled, taking another hit, until the cherry burned out.

"My girl likes to get high, huh?"

"It helps." She shrugged. "A guy in Albany Hills managed to get his stash past security and then bribed one of the cleaners to smuggle it in every month."

"Daddy Dearest know he sent you to a fucking place like that?"

She flinched and I felt like a giant asshole.

"Shit, B, I didn't—"

"It's okay. I guess my therapist would say I replaced one coping mechanism with another but getting high was my lifeline some days."

Silence.

Silence echoed around us, and I realized we weren't alone and everyone was listening.

"Up you go, B," I said, needing her all to myself. She slid off my lap and stood before helping me up.

"Help yourself to Jessa's cookies. I think there's a frozen pizza in there, beer, soda… just don't set the place on fire." I leveled Zane and Nate with a stern look. "And lock up when you leave."

"Yeah, yeah, we got it, get out of here."

"See you tomorrow."

Kye saluted while Zane and Nate gave us a small nod.

My glazed eyes lingered on Miller. "Thanks, yeah, for tonight." *For everything*, I wanted to say but couldn't.

As much as I hated it, he'd been there for Harleigh when I hadn't been.

I owed him.

And while I was man enough to admit it to myself, I wasn't quite ready to say it out loud.

"Night, guys," Harleigh said, a little sheepish as she tucked herself into my side, practically holding me up.

"You know, I had big plans for tonight," I said as we reached my room.

For a second, it occurred to me that maybe I should have tried to book a room somewhere. Mine wasn't exactly romantic. But this was me and it was Birdie and it had never been about anything else.

She wouldn't care.

So why didn't I want to open the bedroom door?

"Nix?"

"I'm sorry that it isn't—"

"Stop." She pressed her finger against my mouth. "I don't need anything except you, and maybe your bed. I feel kind of funny."

I dropped a kiss on her head and pulled her into my room.

"Light switch, Nix. I can barely see."

"No, leave it," I said. "Lie with me in the dark, Birdie."

We stumbled over to the bed, and Harleigh hooked her trembling fingers in my jeans. "Let me help you."

I swallowed roughly as she pushed my jersey up my bruised body. "Tell me if it hurts."

"It doesn't," I said. Even if it was agony, I wouldn't

have stopped her. Because watching Harleigh find her confidence was everything.

Every-fucking-thing.

"Lift your arms," she whispered, and I managed to bite back the pain in my voice to help her pull my hoodie off.

"I want to check over your injuries."

"I'll live. Just get naked and be with me, B. That's all I need."

Her soft laughter wrapped around me like a blanket.

"I'm nervous," she admitted.

"Don't be. It's just you and me, Birdie."

I brushed my hand along her collarbone and pushed the hair off her shoulder. Her breath caught, a shiver running through her.

"Get naked, B, now," I drawled, my heart crashing violently against my chest.

Part of me wanted to hit the light switch and look at her. But there was something about being in the dark that felt right. Not because we wanted to hide or blend with the shadows but because we understood.

We got it.

"Nix?"

"Yeah, B."

"You do it," she breathed. "I want you to do it."

17

HARLEIGH

I COULDN'T STOP TREMBLING AS NIX SLOWLY UNDRESSED me. How he could see well enough in the dark was beyond me, but from the way his fingers moved expertly over my body, he seemed to be having little issue.

"Much better," he said, brushing his fingertips down my stomach.

"You still have your jeans on."

"If you want them off, take them off, B."

My blood heated at the challenge in his words. It wasn't an order; I knew if I didn't want to go any further, he would pull me down on the bed, wrap me into his arms, and let me sleep.

But I didn't want to stop, and I didn't want to sleep, despite how high I was. My hands went to his waistband and I popped the button, shoving my hands inside and pushing them down his hips. It required a little help from Nix but we got there.

"I wish I could see you." I sighed.

"Here." He took my hand in his, stretching my pointer finger and tracing it along his abs, the narrow dip of his obliques. Nix mapped his body with my hand, letting me feel every dip and groove, every rock hard muscle, the slightly blemished skin denoting his tattoos.

Closing my eyes, I pictured him. Strong and tall and ripped and beautiful.

Nix had always been the most beautiful boy I'd ever seen.

He rested our joined hands on his chest, right over his heart. "This is yours, B. It always has been. Promise me you'll take care of it."

"I promise." The words caught in my throat.

"I don't have much, but no one will ever love you the way I do. You're my girl. My best friend. My forever." He ran his thumb along my jaw, letting it linger on my bottom lip. I couldn't breathe, couldn't force air into my lungs because he'd stolen it all.

"Lie with me, B."

"Okay."

Nix pulled the sheets back and climbed into bed, shuffling toward the wall to give me enough space to get in beside him.

"One day it won't be like this," he said. "One day, we'll have our own place, a better place."

His words made my heart race.

I wanted that—God, I wanted it so badly. But Zane's warning from earlier refused to leave my mind.

"Come here," Nix draped his arm over my hip and yanked me closer. "I don't bite."

Face to face, we lay there in the dark, breathing each other's air. The faint din of the music drifted into the room, mimicking the erratic beat of my heart.

Nix traced the lines of my face, ghosting his fingertips over my cheeks, my nose, and brows. "I can't believe you're here," he whispered, burying his hand in my hair and guiding my face down to him.

His kiss started off uncertain, lazy and unhurried. Our tongues tangled, licking and tasting. It had a drugging effect, lulling me into utter serenity. But it quickly became something else entirely. Nix moved closer, pulling me flush with his body so that every inch of him was pressed up against every inch of me. He slid one of his legs between mine and I whimpered, feeling him hard and ready at the apex of my thighs.

He kissed me harder, all teeth and tongue and total lack of restraint until I felt like I was burning up. "Fuck, B," he hissed, hooking my leg higher over his hip so that he could grind into me. Nothing but the thin layers of our underwear separated us.

"Slow… we can take it slow," he mumbled to himself.

But this didn't feel like taking things slow, it felt like tumbling headfirst into things. Fast and wild and unstoppable.

And I wanted that—I wanted him again.

"Nix," I moaned, trying to pull his weight onto me. "I need—"

"Fuck," he grunted, and not in a good way.

I instantly let go, apologizing.

"Shh, B. It's not your fault. Fuck." He flipped onto his

back, sucking in a pained breath. "This was not at all how I saw tonight going."

"What can I do?" I asked, silently willing my heart to calm down.

"You being here is enough, I promise." He reached for my hand, tangling our fingers together.

I nestled into his side, listening to the steady rise and fall of his chest. For a second, I thought he'd fallen asleep again. But then he said, "Will you tell me about that day?"

"Wh-what do you want to know?"

"All of it, B. I need to know all of it."

"I…" Fear knocked the air from my lungs. "I'm not ready."

"Okay." Disappointment clung to his words, cooling the air around us. I didn't want it to be like this. I wanted the heat back, the fire.

Tugging his hand with mine, I brushed it down his stomach and over the bulge in his boxer briefs.

"Birdie…"

"Show me," I forced the words past my lips. "Show me how you like it."

Fingers still twined together with his, I tugged at the waistband of Nix's boxers and he lifted his hips, letting me push them down. I could just make out the shadow of his hard length.

"Fist it," he said thickly, and I closed our fingers around him.

"Now what?"

I knew what to do, I wasn't stupid. But there was something so incredibly hot about letting him guide me.

"Pump up and down, slow at first, putting a little

twist on the upstroke." I did right as he asked and he breathed, "Yeah, just like that. Fuck."

A thrill went through me. I liked hearing his ragged breaths, feeling him tense beneath me.

"A little harder." He closed his fingers tighter around mine, guiding me. "Like this. Fuck, B, don't stop."

He started thrusting in our joined hands as we pumped him faster, harder.

"I want to taste you," the words tumbled out before I knew what they meant.

"Shit, B, you don't have to—"

"I want to."

"You sure?"

I nodded, moving down the bed slightly, and leaning over him. Nix threaded his hand into my hair as I grasped his dick again, lowering my mouth to the tip.

My body hummed with nerves. I'd never done this before, but I'd imagined it with Nix. Only ever with Nix.

I flicked my tongue out, flattening it against him and dragging it upward. He drew in a sharp breath, hissing between his teeth as I slowly sank my mouth down on him.

"Fuuuuck, B, fuck." His grip in my hair tightened, but it was possessive rather than painful, making my stomach curl with lust.

With zero experience, I did what felt natural, licking and sucking, using my hand to slowly pump the base.

Nix gathered all my hair and wrapped it around his fist, the heat of his stare almost too much as I drove him wild.

"I'm close," he groaned. "You don't have to—"

But I did.

I wanted all of him.

Every last bit.

Nix's hips lifted, his legs tensing as he came, sexy little moans falling from his lips. I wanted to see him, to see his brows drawn together and the look of ecstasy on his face. I wanted to imprint it to memory, to keep it forever.

I swallowed, surprised at how natural it felt.

His hand slipped free of my hair and came to cup my cheek. "You are fucking amazing," he praised me.

Moving back beside him, he leaned in and kissed me, tasting himself on my tongue. But it didn't seem to bother him in the least.

"I wish I got some of your firsts too." A soft sigh left me, my old friend insecurity rearing her ugly head.

Nix curved his hand around the side of my neck and held me. "You get the most important one, B. My heart. No one has ever come close to touching it. How could they when it's always belonged to you?"

"Nix, I…"

"Shh. I get it. And I fucking hate that we wasted so much time. But we're here now. We're here, B, and I'm never letting you go again. I can't. I won't. Because losing you last year, it was like losing a part of myself. I can't exist without you, Harleigh Wren Maguire. You're the other half to my soul."

Nix dropped his head to mine, inhaling a shaky breath. We lay there, still and silent, nothing but the sound of our beating hearts and his declaration between us.

"Nix, I…."

I realized then, he'd fallen asleep.

I brushed the hair from his eyes, marveling at how soft his skin felt under my fingertips. My beautiful broken boy who carried the weight of so much on his shoulders. I feared that one day, it would crush him. The expectation, the disappointment, and heartache.

Nix was a fighter, a survivor. He had always been so strong. But what if Zane was right? What if he was losing himself in the process? And now I was back, and things were so uncertain regarding our future, I didn't want to hurt him again.

But I couldn't walk away, I wouldn't.

Because how did you walk away from the one thing you needed more than anything? The thing you loved most in the entire world.

Our love was fragile, precarious, and new. But it was also strong, unyielding, and consuming. It had survived the worst nine months of my life.

I had to believe it was all for a reason. That our love was bigger than circumstance.

That it would survive anything.

Even a world that wanted to chew us up and spit us out.

I woke to flutters in my stomach. "Wh-what?"

"Shh, Birdie." A voice rumbled. Right. Over. *There.*

Nix had me pinned to the bed, one of his arms anchoring me in place as he licked me. A slow drag of his tongue that made me cry out.

"Sweet baby Jesus," I breathed.

"Good morning to you too." He chuckled, spreading me open with his fingers and licking me deeper.

Heat flooded me, light streaming in through the blinds and illuminating my flushed skin.

"You look like an angel," he murmured, flattening his tongue against my clit.

"Nix, God…" I slid my fingers into his hair as my other hand fisted the sheet.

My legs were already trembling, shaking with pleasure as he ate me.

Nix pulled away, gazing up at me as he slowly pressed two fingers inside me. My eyes fluttered closed, too overwhelmed at the sensations wreaking havoc on my body.

"Eyes on me, Birdie. I want to watch you fly."

The second I locked eyes on him, Nix smiled. And it was so adorable, full of so much vulnerability, that I melted.

"Does that feel good?" He curved his fingers deep at the same time as he lowered his mouth back to my clit and sucked.

"Oh my God," I breathed, slowly splintering apart. It was too much. Too freaking good. The way his tongue and fingers moved together in perfect synchrony.

"Nix, I'm—" I cried out as an intense wave of pleasure crashed over me, dragging me under. I couldn't think, couldn't breathe as warmth enveloped me.

When Nix crawled up my body, resting his weight on his elbows, I was still breathless. "Hi." He leaned in, rubbing his nose along my jaw and dropping a kiss to my lips.

"Hi."

"I like this," he said. "Waking up with you. Watching you come apart like that."

"It was very… nice." I swallowed, trying to catch my breath.

"Nice?" His brow quirked up. "Seemed like it was a little more than nice to me, B."

Looping my arms around his neck, I smirked. "It was okay."

"Okay, huh? Guess I'll have to spend some time practicing then. Figuring out what you like." His voice turned molten, deep and gravelly.

"I think I can get on board with that."

"Yeah?" His mouth twitched. "Good to know."

"How are you feeling?"

His expression slipped a little. "I'll be okay, B. You don't have to worry—"

"Don't say that. I do worry, I'll always worry. This season is important to you."

"You're important to me."

"The two aren't mutually exclusive, Nix. You can have football and still have me. Albany U is your chance, your shot at getting out of here."

His eyes narrowed. "Did someone say something to you?"

I couldn't lie, not when there had been so many lies already between us.

"He only cares—"

"Zane."

"He's worried, we all are. This thing with Marc Denby, your dad—"

The heat in his eyes guttered out. "I can handle my old man."

"I didn't say you couldn't."

Nix rolled off me and laid down, letting out a heavy sigh. I turned to face him and waited, sensing he needed space.

But when he finally spoke, they were the last words I was expecting.

18

NIX

"Good old Joe wants me gone after graduation."

Harleigh's brows furrowed and she blinked a couple of times, disbelief glittering in her eyes. She knew exactly what I meant; she just couldn't process it.

It takes a while, Birdie. Trust me.

"What do you mean he wants you gone?"

"It means that once high school is over, I am officially homeless."

"He can't do that."

Strained laughter spilled from my lips. "You've met my old man. I'm pretty sure he can do whatever the fuck he wants."

"What about Jessa? Surely she doesn't—"

"She doesn't know yet."

"Nix, you have to tell her."

"Why? She's never going to leave him, B. I realize that

now. Maybe part of me has always known it. And I hate it, because one day her loyalty to him will kill her."

The words shredded something inside me. Deep, visceral lashes I felt all the way down to my soul.

"She's not your responsibility, Nix."

She wasn't, but still.

"She's the closest thing I've ever had to a mom, B." My heart clenched. "How can I just walk away knowing what her life is like with him? What kind of person does that make me if I leave to chase my dreams?"

Dreams that had never felt achievable until recently.

Harleigh palmed my cheek, closing the space between us. "You've always been her protector, Nix. But who protects you, huh? Maybe if she saw you go after your dreams, if she saw you get out of this place, it would give her the confidence to leave him."

"I just don't know how to do it. She deserves better."

"And so do you, and me, and Zane, and every kid living in The Row. We all deserve better, but nobody is going to come along to fix things for us. Life doesn't work that way. But you have a shot, Nix." Her eyes pleaded with me. "A real shot at getting out of here."

"And what about you, B? What's your plan after graduation?"

"I..." She hesitated, her eyes darting away from me. I captured her chin, forcing her to look at me. "I haven't thought about it."

"Wrong answer." My jaw ticced. "It's you and me, B. I need you with me. If it's Albany U or somewhere else, I need you right by my side."

"Nix, it's only the beginning of senior year. There's still—"

Irritation flashed inside me. But it was more than that. I wanted her to want this—me. A future together.

"There's still what, B?"

"Nine months." The words shattered around us, like a crack of lightning or the bang of gunfire.

Nine months could change everything. But so could a second or a minute or an hour. Life could change in the blink of an eye and there wasn't a damn thing you could do about it.

"It's not the same, and you know it."

"I know." Her expression softened. "I'm not saying…" She blew out a steady breath, giving a little shake of her head. "Honestly, I don't know what I'm saying. All I know is that when I look too far into the future, I get this sense of dread. Like a lead balloon settling in my chest.

"I tried to kill myself, Nix." Her voice shook, mimicking the vibrations rippling through me. "I took a razor to my wrist and—"

"Harleigh." I inhaled a sharp breath. I'd wanted to know, needed to know what had happened that day but I couldn't listen to this. Not without wanting to roar at the world for ever landing us here.

"I hurt myself, Nix. I wanted to die. But I didn't, I survived. And over time, I realized that I didn't really want to die, I just wanted it to stop. All the pain and grief and loneliness, I just needed it to stop."

"I'm so fucking sorry, B. I'm so—" Tears burned my throat as my chest caved in on itself. I couldn't speak, couldn't get out all the things I needed to say. Because learning Harleigh had hurt herself had broken something inside of me.

"Shh." She kissed me softly. "I'm not trying to make you feel guilty or upset. I just want you to understand what life has been like for me. I survived, Nix. I survived and now I have to learn how to live again. So no, I don't have plans for beyond high school yet. But it doesn't mean I don't look forward to the day I do."

"I'm moving too fast," I said, pulling away, dejection churning in my stomach.

"No, no." Harleigh dipped her head to mine, sliding her hand around the back of my neck and anchoring me there. "But I don't want you to lose focus on what you want, Nix. I want you to go after the football scholarship. I want it so much for you. The rest will figure itself out."

Her conviction felt authentic but there was something in her eyes. A flicker of uncertainty. But maybe it wasn't doubt, maybe it was just the scars of everything that had happened. She wasn't the same girl; how could she be?

I refused to believe that Harleigh couldn't heal and move on from the past. Because while the things that happened to us shaped us, they didn't have to define us.

Who the fuck was I kidding? I let every interaction with my old man define me. I tried not to, but a guy could only be told he was worthless and would never amount to anything so many times before he started to believe it. So how could I try to convince Harleigh when I didn't take my own advice?

The vibration of Harleigh's cell phone cut through the silence.

"It's probably Celeste," she said, rolling away from me to check it.

My fingers danced up and down her spine, feeling the expanse of smooth creamy skin. She was so fragile, yet strong. So fucking strong. Like glass. She could endure a lot, but apply too much pressure and she would crack.

"Everything okay?" I asked, as she laid back down, tucking herself in the crook of my arm.

"Yeah, she just wanted me to know that Michael and Sabrina are going for brunch."

"Is that a good thing?"

She shrugged. "Means they readily bought our lie, I guess."

"You know, we could tell him and deal with the consequences." It would be a total shitshow, but I'd do it for her.

"No." The blood drained from Harleigh's face. "Not yet."

"Okay, whatever you want. I need to take a leak." Pushing the sheets off, I slowly sat up. Every inch of me still hurt but it wasn't as intense as last night.

"Nix…" She gasped, her eyes fixed on my body, the mottled bruises along my ribs and kidneys.

"It's not as bad as it looks."

"How can you say that? They assaulted you."

"It wasn't anything I haven't endured ten times before. I'm a quick healer." My body was used to a little pain, liked it even.

Grabbing some shorts, I yanked them on and padded into my tiny bathroom. I needed a second. Being around Harleigh was overpowering sometimes, my body desperate to feel hers beneath me, on top of me, wrapped around me like silk. But it wasn't always physical, being around her was intense on a lot of different levels.

Splashing my face with some cold water, I made quick work of things before going back into my bedroom.

When the door opened and my eyes landed on her, half-naked sprawled in my bed, all the doubts and frustration melted away. Because she was here, and regardless of what the future held—or what Harleigh thought the future held—she was mine. And I'd spend every second of every day proving it to her if that's what it took.

We could make this work, we had to.

"I can feel you watching me, you know." She glanced over at me, a faint smile tracing her mouth.

"Is that so?" I prowled toward her. "What does it feel like?"

"Like your fingers dancing over my skin or lips or tongue."

"Tongue, huh?" I smirked, drinking her in. Letting my eyes roam over every single inch of her. My gaze snagged on the scar on her wrist though and some of the heat stirring inside me cooled.

"Don't do that," she whispered.

"What is it you think I'm doing?"

"Blaming yourself, blaming me... I don't know. But whatever you're thinking, it won't change anything. We can't go back, Nix, we can only look forward."

"I thought you said you can't look forward."

Her eyes narrowed with irritation. "You know what I mean."

My knees hit the mattress and I crawled over her, hovering on my forearms. "I do." I kissed the tip of her nose.

Harleigh slid her hands up my chest and locked them over my shoulders. "I love you, Nix. Nothing that happened and nothing that happens in the future will ever change that. You are, and always will be, the boy who stole my heart."

Fuck.

I didn't deserve her. Her honest words. The trust in her eyes. Her gorgeous fragile body. Her broken jagged heart. But I was a selfish motherfucker because I couldn't let her go.

Tracing the seam of her lips with my tongue, I kissed her. A silent promise to the future I wanted for us. For her.

"Nix," she breathed, pulling me closer. My body fell on top of hers, the kiss turning frantic. Needy and desperate. I sucked on her bottom lip, dragging it between my teeth, making her whimper. That sound... fuck, that sound was like my own personal symphony.

"What do you want, B?" I drawled as she lifted her hips, rubbing herself against my rock hard dick.

"You, I want—"

"Nix, sweetheart, are you home?"

Birdie's eyes went wide as I stilled above her.

"What the fuck are they doing back?" I fumed, rolling off Harleigh.

She clutched the sheet to her body, staring at me with utter shock. "What should I do?"

"I… uh." I dragged a hand down my face, trying to think. Fuck.

Fuck.

This could not be happening.

"Get dressed. I'll go distract them."

"And then what? I can't exactly climb out the window."

"I guess you'll have to come out and say hello." I shrugged.

"Ugh." She flipped back down and covered her face with her hands.

"Look, we'll say hello and then get the fuck out of here. I'll take you for breakfast or something."

"Eat." Bitter laughter spilled from her lips. "You think I can eat right now? I feel like I'm going to puke. This was a bad idea."

"Will you stop with that bullshit?" I hissed, anger shooting through me.

"Nix, I didn't—"

"No, B. I get that it's hard. I get that you want to keep this on the down-low, but stop acting as if anything about us, about this"—I wagged my finger from myself to her and back again—"is a fucking mistake."

Grabbing my hoodie, I pulled it on over my head and got the fuck out of there before I said something I might regret.

Voices floated down the hall, and the knot in my stomach twisted and tightened as I forced myself toward them.

"I thought you weren't— what the fuck?" I gawked at my old man in absolute disbelief. "What the hell happened to you?"

His face was a patchwork of cuts and bruises. Dried blood crusted along his brow and bottom lip.

"It's nothing," he grunted, swatting Jessa away as she tried to come at him with a damp towel.

"Let me guess, business didn't go to plan?"

"Nix," Jessa warned, shaking her head.

"Fuck." I blew out a weary breath, looking up at the ceiling. Just when I thought things couldn't get any worse, a new level of fucked up showed itself.

"You don't look so good yourself," he grunted.

"I had a game, remember?"

"Some game," he winced as Jessa managed to wrestle the towel to his cheek. "Will you back the fuck up, woman. I said I'm fine."

"Stubborn fool." She threw it in the sink and threw up her hands. "They could have killed you, Joe."

"Yeah, maybe they should have, because when Vince—"

"Vince? Oh hell no, tell me you didn't go down there running a job for him?"

"What's it to—"

"Umm, hello."

"Harleigh, honey, is that you?" Jessa rushed over to her as she stood in the hall. "It's so good to see—"

My old man's eyes flared as he ground out, "What the fuck is she doing here?"

19

HARLEIGH

"WHAT THE FUCK IS SHE DOING HERE?"

His cold, callous words clanged through me.

"Joe," Jessa gasped, still gripping my shoulder. "Don't be so rude."

"It's okay," I forced out, staring at the ground, wishing it would swallow me whole. "I'm just leaving."

"Like hell you are," Nix hissed. "Birdie is with me. I want her here. Don't fucking speak to her like that."

"Or what, kid? What the fuck are *you* going to do about it?"

A ripple went through the air as father and son glared at each other. It wasn't the first time I'd witnessed Joe Wilder's wrath or his obvious disdain for his son, his own flesh and blood. But I'd forgotten how much it hurt seeing it firsthand.

"Joe, please." Jessa moved toward him. "Why don't I make us all some breakfast and we can—"

"For the love of God, woman, will you just stop your fussing." He threw his hand up in the air and caught her smack in the face.

The *crack* of the impact reverberated through the room and I yelled, "Jessa," as she stumbled back, blood exploding from her nose.

"Shit, baby, fuck, I didn't—" He tried to reach for her, but she darted out of the way, grabbing the damp towel and pressing it to her face.

"Jessa, baby, let me—"

Nix stepped between them, shielding her. "You need to leave."

"Like fuck I am. This is my place, kid. If you want to go, there's the door."

Nix closed the distance between them. "I said, you need to leave." The icy tone to his words made me shudder.

Jessa's pained sobs filled the trailer and I managed to slip around Joe and Nix to get to her. "Come on," I whispered, taking her arm in mine, "let's get you cleaned up."

Guiding her over to the couch, I took the towel from her trembling hands and leaned in to inspect the damage. "Does it feel broken?"

"I-I don't think so. I don't— Nix, no!" I glanced up in time to see Nix grab his father by the collar of his t-shirt and shove him toward the door. Joe cussed, clearly in agony as he staggered into the wall.

"Jessa, baby, it was an accident. I didn't mean—"

"Just go, please," she cried.

"You heard her," Nix seethed. "And don't come back

until you've figured out how to fix this."

Heart in my throat, I watched as Joe glared at Nix, hatred burning in eyes like the heat of a thousand suns. I'd never understood why he hated Nix so much, but the bitterness between them had only grown over the years.

Joe cast Jessa a guilty look, but it didn't stop him from grabbing his jacket off the coatrack and slipping out of the trailer.

"Fuck." Nix punched the wall and I screamed.

"Go to him," Jessa said, elbowing me. "Something tells me he needs you more than I do right now."

I nodded, completely numb as I got up and went to him. Nix pulled me into his arms, burying his face in the crook of my shoulder.

And I was sure I felt the wetness of tears there.

"She's resting," Nix said, pulling the door closed on Joe and Jessa's bedroom.

"Will you let me look at your hand now?"

"I already told you, B, I'll live."

"Nix..."

"Fine."

Motioning for him to sit on one of the stools, I grabbed the first aid kit we'd used to clean up Jessa's bloody nose and lifted his hand gently into mine.

It had been intense, holding him while he broke down on me, only to have him pull away a minute later, wearing a blank expression. He'd gotten good at hiding his emotions—too good—and it made me wonder how bad things had been while I was away.

Nix hissed through his teeth as I ran my finger over his split knuckles, the skin there scarred and angry from old injuries.

"Fine, huh?" A smirk tugged at my lips.

He rolled his eyes, snagging my fingers and bringing them to his mouth. "I'm sorry that our weekend got ruined."

"You don't have to apologize, Nix."

"I just wanted it to be perfect. I wanted us to have space to be together without all the drama and bullshit."

I cupped his cheek, leaning in close as I said, "Perfect is overrated."

"Yeah, I guess it is."

"It could have been worse, they could have walked in on us… you know."

"No, I don't think I do." His mouth trailed along my jaw to my ear. "Maybe you should tell me, just to be sure."

"Nix…" It came out a breathy moan as his fingers walked along the curve of my neck and slid into my hair. A whimper built in my throat and he let out a frustrated sigh.

"Shit, we can't. Not now, not with Jessa down the hall."

"Yeah."

He kissed me. Once. Twice. Sliding his lips over mine with easy familiarity as if we'd been doing it forever. I loved that. How easy it felt. How right.

"Do you think she'll be okay?" I asked.

"No." His brows knitted. "But she made her choice."

He said the words, but I could still see the doubt in his eyes. He didn't want to leave Jessa here, and I loved him all the more for it. But you couldn't always save someone. Sometimes they had to want to save themselves.

I knew that better than most people.

"What will you do, about your dad?"

"What I always do, avoid him, and try to protect her as much as I can. Figure out a way to make some cash." I arched a brow at that and he chuckled. "A legitimate way, B. Maybe Bryson will let me clean down at the gym, or work with some of the younger kids or something."

"Is that a good idea, working there?"

"It's not like I have my pick of jobs. Who's going to give a tatted guy from The Row a shot?"

"You won't know if you don't try."

"Yeah, okay." He captured my lips in a bruising kiss that stole my breath and left my knees weak. "Rain check for this weekend?"

"Yeah. You should stay with Jessa. Do you think Kye or Zane will give me a ride back?"

"Yeah, they can borrow my car." He pulled out his cell phone and started texting them.

"I'll get my things," I said, my stomach already tumbling at the thought of going back to Old Darling Hill.

I wanted to be here with Nix.

"Kye's going to drive you. Chloe will probably tag along."

"Okay." I went to walk away but he snagged my wrist.

"One day, B, one day life will be different."

"I HAVE A FAVOR TO ASK," Chloe whispered as Kye drove us back across town. She flicked her eyes to the rearview mirror and back to me. "Will you give me Nate's number?"

"Do you think that's a good idea?"

"I've had worse ideas." She grinned. "I like him, he's… interesting. There's something layered about him."

"Did you ask him for his number?"

"With big brother glaring at me all night? What do you think?"

"I should probably ask him first," I said. "I don't want to make things weird."

"Ask who, Kye?"

"Nate, stupid."

Chloe poked her tongue out at me just as Kye piped up, "What are you two whispering about?"

"Sex."

"What the fuck, Clo? I don't need to be hearing my little sister and my best friend's girl talk about sex. Ew."

She gave me a knowing smirk. "Why do you think we're whispering?"

He muttered something under his breath. We'd already crossed into Old Darling Hill which set me on edge. They couldn't drive me up to the house, so we'd decided they would drop me off at Miles's house so I could ride back with Celeste.

"Are we going to see you soon?" she asked as Kye turned into the affluent neighborhood. The rows and rows of beautiful houses with their immaculate lawns and expensive cars in the driveway was worlds apart from The Row. But it felt nothing like home.

"Fancy," Kye said, rolling to a stop a few houses down from the Mulligans' place.

"Thanks for the ride. Can I ask a favor?"

He nodded.

"Can you check in on Nix later? I'm worried."

"You and me both, B." Kye gave me a tight smile. "You and me both."

"I'll text you later," Chloe said, as I grabbed my bag and climbed out.

I texted Celeste.

Me: I'm here.

Celeste: Miles doesn't bite, you can come inside.

Me: I don't think that's a good idea. Meet you at your car?

I WANTED to get back and decompress.

Celeste: Give me five. xo

STICKING to the trees and shrubs lining the Mulligans' driveway, I hovered by Celeste's Range Rover. Part of me wondered if I should have stayed with Nix and Jessa. If Joe returned angry, or worse: drunk and angry, who knew what might happen.

God, it didn't bear thinking about. The anger that had exploded from Nix when Joe had inadvertently hit Jessa was a side of him I'd never seen before. And I didn't doubt that was what Zane was talking about. Nix was different. An unpredictable storm. And I'd done that.

Me.

Even though I hadn't meant to, I had.

My chest tightened, my breaths coming in short, sharp bursts. It was too much, like a band around my ribs, slowly crushing the air from my lungs.

Breathe, Harleigh. Breathe.

But I couldn't breathe. I couldn't stop thinking about earlier, about the state of Joe's face, the conversation I'd overheard, the way Jessa's nose had exploded with blood. It was a stark reminder that Nix's life had moved on while I was gone. And if this morning was anything to go by, it had only gotten worse in my absence.

"Harleigh?"

I almost jumped out of my skin at the sound of Celeste's voice.

She frowned, her expression falling. "You're not okay." She reached for me, but I held up my hand, dragging in a deep breath.

"Can we just go?"

"Of course." Grabbing the passenger door, she opened

it and I hauled myself inside, dropping my head back against the leather headrest.

"Can I do anything?" Celeste asked, climbing into her seat.

"No, I'll be okay."

"I'm here, Harleigh. If you need to stop or go to the ER or—"

"I'm fine," I snapped through gritted teeth, digging my nails into my palms.

At least, I would be just as soon as we got back to the house and I locked myself in my bedroom.

It was silly really, to think that because I'd had a few panic attack free days that it wasn't still there, lurking, waiting to strike. This wasn't something I would just get over. It was a part of me now, always there under the surface, like a slumbering beast.

Maybe I would never be able to control it, but I could control how I responded to it.

I could take back some of the power.

I FOLLOWED Celeste into the house, completely drained.

"I think I'm going to head straight up to my room," I said, heading for the stairs. But Sabrina's voice gave me pause.

"Girls, in the kitchen please. Now."

Not again. I squeezed my eyes closed, pinching the bridge of my nose.

"Come on," Celeste said. "It's probably nothing."

If this morning had taught me anything, it was that luck really wasn't on my side.

Begrudgingly, I trailed after her.

"Late night?" Sabrina cocked a brow as she cut into a piece of melon.

"I told you we were staying at Miles's."

"You did." She lifted her coffee mug to her thin lips and took a sip before placing it gently down on the plate. "But I had an interesting chat with Sandra Dempsey last night, you know, the Mulligans' neighbor, and she seemed to think that it was only you at the Mulligans'." Sabrina pinned her daughter with an unforgiving look. "She said you"—her gaze swung to mine—"were definitely not present."

"I already told you, Mom," Max said. "She was with her boyfriend."

"M-my what?" I glared at Max, my entire body trembling.

How could he?

After everything with Nix and Bryson, how could he sell me out like that?

"Is it true?" Sabrina's expression gave nothing away, but it was hardly a surprise given her face barely moved thanks to all the cosmetic enhancement she and her friends got.

"That you and the Miller boy are dating?" Her mouth twisted with disgust.

I gawked at her, trying to figure out the right answer here. If I said no, it might lead to more questions. And if I said, yes... I didn't want to think about what Nix would do.

"I—"

"Just fess up, Harleigh." Max smirked. "Enough people saw the two of you shacked up last night at the game."

"We were not—"

"You should have seen them, Mom. They couldn't keep their hands off each other."

Her expression darkened, disapproval heavy in her eyes. "Yes, well. I already expressed my concern over the two of you fornicating."

"Oh my God, Mom." Celeste smothered a laugh. "Who says that anymore?"

Sabrina got up and dabbed the corner of her mouth with the napkin. "Nate Miller is a complicated young man. Someone might even argue that he's unstable. If you're going to pursue this… this thing with him, I suggest you talk to your therapist about it first. Maybe she can advise you what a dreadful idea it is."

With that piece of stellar advice, Sabrina stormed from the kitchen, leaving me and Celeste gawking at Max.

"What the hell was that?" she spat the words.

Max got up and shoved his hands into his shorts. "You can thank me later."

"Thank you?" I recoiled. "I should be—"

"Now Mommy and Daddy will think you're dating Miller, which means you'll have a cover story. I'm sure Nate will play along since he's such a fan of yours."

"You're helping me?" I gawked at him.

"We have an arrangement. You helped me, I thought I'd return the favor."

I glanced at Celeste and she shrugged. "Don't look at

me, half the time I have no idea what's going on in that head of his."

"I've got shit to do." He headed for the hall, glancing back at the last second. "But like I said, you can thank me later."

Max disappeared and I stood there, dumbfounded.

"So wait, is he like on your side now? Because if he is, that's just weird." Celeste frowned.

My lips thinned as I murmured. "So weird."

20

NIX

"What the hell happened to you?" Coach said the second I entered the locker room.

"Would you believe me if I said I fell out of bed?"

His brows hit his hairline. "Nice try, son. Just tell me if I need to pay that son of a bitch Bryson Shaw another visit."

"I can confirm you don't. I haven't stepped foot in the ring again." Technically, it wasn't a straight up lie. I hadn't fought for Bryson again.

"Good, keep it that way. We've got a big game Friday against Hennington and I need you one-hundred percent ready. Rumor has it the scout from Albany U might come down and see you."

Fuck.

"I'm ready, Coach," I forced out.

"Good, that's what I like to hear." Coach Farringdon

scanned the room before moving in closer. "Is everything with your old man—"

"I appreciate the concern, Coach, I do." My teeth ground together. "But I can handle it."

"That's what worries me, son." He clapped me on the shoulder and disappeared off into his office.

"What was all that about?" Zane came over and slung his bag down.

"He's worried about me."

"Must be nice to be Coach's pet." The fucker smirked, and I flipped him off. "How's Jessa?"

"You know how it is." She was putting on a bright smile, baking a shit ton of cookies, and acting like everything was hunky-fucking-dory. The only positive about it all was my old man was acting a little sheepish. Last night over dinner, he'd even gone so far as to ask how the game went.

I wasn't stupid enough to think his change of attitude would last, but I was glad for Jessa that he could muster up a bit of human decency.

"We still need to figure out what we're gonna do about Denby and his crew."

"Maybe we should let it go," I said, bracing myself for his response.

"Let it go? Are you fucking insane? They jumped us and beat the shit out of you. I say we—"

"Z, man, I said let it go." I blew out a frustrated breath. I couldn't afford to escalate this thing with Denby. Not while he had daily unfettered access to Harleigh. I wouldn't risk her like that.

"Why the fuck… Birdie." Understanding flashed in his eyes. "You think he'll go after her."

"I can't risk it."

"Man, I fucking hate this." He yanked off his t-shirt and began changing into his pants and jersey. "There's still a long way to go until graduation, Nix."

Like I didn't already know.

We were barely a month into the semester and things had gone to shit. But getting Harleigh back, that outweighed all the bullshit. I just needed her safe, protected. I needed her to heal, I wanted to heal her. Or at least, help.

But her attending DA and me being here was a big fucking problem. One I didn't know how to fix.

I understood her reluctance to go public, to step out of the shadows with me. It didn't mean I had to like it though.

Shoving my feet into my cleats, I tied the laces and glanced up at Zane. "Coach said the scouts might be at Friday's game."

"Yeah, and what did you say?"

"I want a shot, Z."

"About fucking time." He held his fist out and I bumped it. "You deserve good things, Nix. If you stay in The Row"—something dark edged into his expression —"it'll bleed you dry."

"AGAIN," I said to Max as he stayed light on his feet, jabbing the air. One two. One one two. He had good technique. *Natural* technique. And for as much as I hated to admit it, I was starting to see what Bryson had seen in him that first time I'd brought him here.

"Breather, I need a breather." His body slumped and he inhaled a ragged breath.

"Not getting tired on me already, are you?" I smirked, grabbing a bottle of water and throwing it at him. He caught it and chugged half the thing down in one.

"Ready to tell me yet why you're really here?"

He cut me with a cold look.

"Fine." I shrugged. "But sometimes it's good to talk."

"I didn't come here to bond," he hissed.

"Good, let's go again then."

"How much does it pay?" I cocked a brow and he added, "Fighting for Bryson?"

"Depends on how good you are and whether or not you win. But that's not something you need to worry about anytime soon."

"You fought for him before you were a senior."

"Because I'm special."

"More like an arrogant asshole," he muttered under his breath.

"Trust me when I say, you don't want to get tangled up in that side of things. I only did it because I needed to. Something tells me you're not hard up for some cash."

"Yeah, I guess you would think that."

"What the fuck does that mean?"

"Forget it." He flexed his hands, shaking off our conversation. But it lingered in my mind as we went again. Max was... a strange one. He gave off that cocky rich kid vibe, but when he was here, hitting the bag or pads, he was someone else entirely.

"Have you talked to Harleigh?"

His question caught me off guard. "Yeah, we've talked." I'd texted her every chance I had.

"Did she say anything about the other morning?"

"No." My spine stiffened. "Why?"

"My mom was asking questions about where she was all night. She's like a dog with a bone when she gets something into her head. So, I uh… I…"

"What did you do, Max?"

"I nudged her into thinking Harleigh was with Nate."

Okay. That didn't sound so scandalous. They'd been hanging out before things with me and her—

"Wait a minute, when you say *with* Nate, what exactly do you mean?"

"I figured it's the perfect cover. If they think she's dating him, they won't be asking questions all the time."

Dating him.

Dating him?

"She didn't say anything."

My stomach dropped into my fucking toes. When was she going to let me in? It was like she was keeping me at arm's length. One step forward, two back. Was she trying to protect me? Shield me from the complications in her life? Or was it more than that?

"I figured she wouldn't." Max gave me a sympathetic smile, and I hated it. Hated that he—the half-brother who had tormented and bargained with her—seemed to have my girlfriend more figured out than I did.

"I guess they'll find Miller a more suitable guy for

her."

Max snorted. "Un-fucking-likely. Miller is more messed up than Harleigh."

"Watch it," I snapped, indicating for him to change up his leading hand. But then I snagged on his other words. "What do you mean he's more messed up than Harleigh?"

Max shrugged, landing an impressive left hook. "Some shit with his sister."

"Miller has a sister?"

"Had." Max said as if it was no big deal, referring to someone, a person, in the past tense.

What the fuck had happened to this kid?

"She killed herself about ten years ago."

"Fuck." I dropped the pad and Max stopped jabbing.

"Yeah. The Millers are very tight-lipped about it. It was a long time ago and Nate and Toby were only kids. I've been best friends with Toby for most of my life and he's only ever mentioned her once."

"That's… I don't know what to say."

"Now you know why Nate took such a shine to Harleigh. He's broken just like her."

Just like her.

The words ripped through me, cold and hollow.

She knew, Harleigh knew. I didn't doubt it for a second. Max was right. It was why they hung out. It was why Miller had taken her under his wing. They shared something.

Something that I could never understand.

"You okay?" Max frowned.

"Yeah, let's call it a night."

"Shit, Wilder, I didn't mean to—"

"It's all good." I waved him off, slipping the pads off and dumping them on the pile along the mirrored wall.

"Don't hold it against me, yeah?" He unwrapped his hands.

I studied him. He seemed genuine. But what the fuck did I know?

Just when I thought things were finally falling into place, someone always went and dropped another bomb. It was like walking across a minefield.

Relax, asshole. Harleigh loves you. She wants you.

But there would always be this thing between us. Something I couldn't understand. Something I hadn't been around to help her deal with. It was the single defining moment in our relationship, and I hadn't been there.

"I need to get out of here," I said.

"Same." Max pulled his cell phone from his bag. "Me and Toby are meeting a couple of girls downtown."

"Word of advice," Kye said, sauntering over to us. "Wrap it before you tap it." He slung his arm around Max's shoulder, but caught my stare and frowned. "Everything good here?"

"Yeah. Max has places to be and I need…"

I didn't know what the fuck I needed.

"Same time Wednesday?"

I nodded at Max and he took off.

"Do I even want to know?" Kye watched him walk away before settling his eyes on me.

"Did you know Miller's older sister killed herself?"

"The fuck?" He paled. "So that's why he and B struck up—"

"Don't."

"You're not actually freaking out about this? I thought things were good between the two of you?"

"Sometimes they are. But it's new, Kye. Really fucking new."

"It's Birdie. She's been your girl forever."

"Not like this. It's different. And after everything that happened… what if—" I stopped the thoughts, refusing to give them steam.

Kye's expression grew serious. "Talk to me, Nix. Where's your head at?"

"What if she only thinks she wants to be with me because it's what she always wanted… before everything happened."

"Nah, no way. Not possible. The two of you belong together. You know, I always wondered why you never went there with her. It was obvious you loved her."

"I've always loved her." Possibly since that very first day I'd talked to her when I'd found her sitting on her porch crying.

I was too young back then to know what love was, but I'd felt something. This innate need to protect her and watch over her.

It was the only thing I'd always had absolute faith in, her.

Harleigh Wren.

My Birdie.

She'd always been mine, one way or another. Friend, confidante, the girl in my dreams. Other girls came and went, but Birdie was my one constant. My foundation. My roots.

"Look, Nix, don't do this to yourself. Don't get hung up on the what-ifs. What happened, happened. You can't change that. All you can do is embrace it and find a way to learn to live with it."

Harleigh had said something similar.

"She loves you, man. You. Something tells me she never stopped. Nate, Max, Marc, her father, they're all inconsequential. She's eighteen in a few weeks. You could run off to bumfuck nowhere and marry her if you wanted to."

"Are you done?" A faint smile lifted the corner of my mouth.

"I was just getting to the good part." He grinned.

"Where's Z at?" I asked, noticing he'd never turned up for our usual training session.

"His gran wasn't feeling so good so he stayed there."

"Shit, is she okay?"

"She's getting worse," he said, pain flickering across his expression.

"Damn." Mrs. Washington was a fighter. One of the strongest people I knew, but sometimes strength wasn't enough. Sometimes disease ate at you from the inside, ravaging your body and mind.

Zane would stay with her to the bitter end and nurse her in her final days. Hopefully they had time though, because losing his gran—the woman who had raised him —would destroy him.

I guess we had that in common.

Losing the women we loved more than anything would one day ruin us.

21

HARLEIGH

"Hello, girlfriend." Nate grinned and I rolled my eyes.

"Please don't say that in public."

"Hold up, I'm confused." He fell in step beside me as we headed for class. "Aren't we supposed to give the illusion we're dating?"

"I didn't agree to this," I said.

"But Max said—"

"Max?" I ground to a halt and turned my full wrath on him. "Max put you up to this?"

"He said… and I thought… wait," Nate grew flustered, "you didn't agree to this?"

I let out a heavy sigh. "No, I didn't. But I didn't exactly deny it either."

God, why hadn't I denied it? The last thing I needed was everyone thinking me and Nate were together. But

Max had a point, it did provide me with a legitimate cover story.

It felt wrong though. Unfair to Nate and Nix.

Definitely Nix.

Which is why I hadn't told him yet. I didn't want to make something out of nothing.

Except, it didn't feel like nothing.

"Well, it's no big deal. I'm happy to help out."

"Why?" The word fell from my lips, plunking between us like a stone in the ocean.

He dipped his hands in his pockets and shrugged. "Do I need a reason?"

"Nate…"

"Because I couldn't help Penny, but I can help you, okay? I can do something. Besides, Wilder," he lowered his voice, "seems like a good guy. I don't have a scheme or some ulterior motive. I just want to help."

"You're really okay with this?"

"I wouldn't offer if I wasn't."

"Okay, thank you," I conceded. "While we're talking favors, I have something else to ask you, but I'm not sure you'll want to say yes."

"Let me guess, Chloe…"

"She asked me for your number."

His mouth tightened as he ran a hand through his hair. "She's a nice girl, but I'm not sure—"

"Say no more. I'll let her down gently."

Damn. Chloe was going to be disappointed. But maybe it was for the best given that Nate's family were just as uptight and entrenched in the traditions and expectations of Old Darling Hill than Michael and Sabrina.

I still couldn't shake the awkward conversation I'd had with her Saturday. Not that there had really been a conversation. Sabrina didn't converse, she talked at you. Michael had been nowhere to be seen all weekend, so I had yet to hear his thoughts about my 'fake' new relationship with Nate. But if it kept them from asking questions about Nix, I could endure it.

"It's not her, it's me. I'm just not ready to—"

"You don't need to explain yourself to me."

Some days I still didn't feel ready to be out here, in the big wide world, learning how to live again.

At Albany Hills it had been all about survival. About directing those dark, dark thoughts onto something more positive. There had been so many days when I'd wanted to quit. Therapy. Meds… *Life*. But I'd survived. I'd healed enough to function outside the safety net of Albany Hills.

But every day was a struggle. Some days, it was like trudging up a never-ending mountain, and no matter how hard you pushed, there was no end in sight.

Having Celeste, Miles, and Nate here, and Nix, Chloe and the guys there, it all helped. But it wasn't a magical solution. It didn't fix those parts inside me, parts that only I had the ability to mend.

Nate gave me a small uncertain smile. "I've never met anyone like you, Harleigh."

"I hope that's a good thing." I tried to keep it light, friendly. But things had a habit of turning intense whenever Nate was around.

"I should probably get to class," I said, needing some space.

"Yeah, sure. Sorry. I'll see you later, Harleigh."

"Bye." I lifted my hand in a small wave.

"He's like a lost puppy," Celeste appeared. "Adorable. And you're so lucky he's all yours." She gave me a wry smile.

"About that... Do you think it's a bad idea, going along with it?"

"You mean, in case you end up in some dramatic love triangle?"

"Celeste!"

"What? A girl can dream." She shrugged, her eyes twinkling as if she was fantasizing about that very thing.

It didn't take much to figure out who she imagined would be the two guys fighting over her.

"I don't want anyone to get hurt," I said.

Nate. I didn't want Nate to get hurt. Because whatever happened, the ending would always be the same. I was with Nix.

I loved Nix.

Even on the days where I doubted everything, where my inner critical voice was so loud, I couldn't hear anything else, I still loved him.

Because it had always been him.

We meandered down the hall, Celeste's arm laced in mine. "Have you spoken to Miles?" I asked.

Because this was normal girl talk.

This was safe, appropriate, normal.

"We had a nice time Saturday night." They'd gone on a date to the drive-in movies in the next town over. "But

I... I don't know." Torment swirled in her eyes as she glanced at me.

"You shouldn't string him along." It wouldn't end well, and he deserved more.

"I wouldn't." My brow lifted, and she let out a resigned sigh. "He's my best friend. I don't want to damage that."

That I understood.

The lines between Nix and I had been blurred for me for a long time. But there were different kinds of love. The kind of love that warmed you and made your heart beat in a strong, steady rhythm, and then there was the kind of love that consumed you. Made you burn and your heart beat like a wild thing inside you.

Celeste loved Miles, I didn't doubt that, but maybe it wasn't the right kind of love to sustain a relationship.

"Being seventeen is hard." She laid her head on my shoulder. "But I'm glad I have you in my life, Harleigh."

Her words, as innocent as they were, sucker punched me in the stomach. It wasn't a dig or a backhanded comment, she was being one hundred percent genuine because that's who Celeste was. Good and kind and full of compassion and second chances. But that little voice inside my head twisted her words, whispering something else entirely.

"Hey, I know." She pulled on my arm a little. "We should go out, just the two of us. We could invite Chloe too, if you wanted. I've never had girlfriends before. It's nice."

"What would we do?"

"I don't know," she shrugged. "Go to the spa and get

facials and manicures maybe?" My face screwed up at that and she snickered. "We could go bowling?"

"At Strike One? The guys would find out and gate-crash."

"A party. We could go to a party."

"Umm, no." I pressed my lips together.

"Okay, what about… oh I know, we could go to open mic night at The Coffee Spot, that cute little coffee shop downtown with the bookstore inside. They do live events on the weekend."

"Hmm, that could be fun, I guess."

She grinned. "It'll be great. I'll ask Chloe. We could go Saturday."

"Okay. But no boys."

"Deal."

"You didn't have to give me a ride home," I said to Nate. "I could have—"

"Would you stop? It's fine." He smiled over at me. "Wilder?" His eyes dropped to the phone in my hand.

"Yeah." I quickly texted Nix back.

Me: Hope practice goes well.

When I looked up again, I frowned. "Nate, this isn't the way to the house."

"Confession time. I'm not taking you to the house."

"You're not?" Fear spread through me as I curled my fingers into the seat.

"Nix called me."

"He did?" I gawked at him, disbelief coursing through me. "But he has practice."

"Not today."

"Okay, this is weird. Isn't it weird for you?" Nate was driving me to meet my boyfriend.

He chuckled. "It's all good."

I folded my hands in my lap, trying to focus on something—*anything*—except the violent beat of my heart.

"You good over there?"

"Fine." I inhaled deeply, counting the perfectly symmetrical trees lining the sidewalk. *One. Two. Four. Six. Eight—*

"Harleigh, it's just Nix."

Just Nix.

But it wasn't just Nix. It was lying to Michael and Sabrina. Keeping Max's secret. Avoiding Marc and Angela. Pretending to be Nate's girlfriend. Not having a plan for post-graduation.

It was all of those things, and I was slowly drowning under the weight of them.

And the kicker was, the one person I'd always been able to trust implicitly, to confide in, was now the person I wanted to shield from the truth.

I was a mess. A giant knot of warring emotions tangled and twisting inside me as I tried to keep my head above water every day.

And I didn't want Nix to know.

I didn't want anyone to know.

It was like sailing on turbulent, unpredictable seas. Sometimes there were great lulls where you drifted only to be swept up by angry unrelenting waves.

It was exhausting.

Being me. Playing a part. Telling everyone—telling myself—I was fine.

"Do you want me to take you home?"

A small, bitter laugh escaped.

Home.

The Rowe-Delacorte estate wasn't my home.

It never would be.

"No, you went to all this trouble. It's fine."

I wanted to see Nix, of course I did. But I was worried —terrified he might see the cracks. The shadows in my eyes.

Terrified of what he would say about Nate and our fake relationship.

Closing my eyes, I touched my head to the cool glass and inhaled a shuddering breath.

"Harleigh, if you're not—"

"I said I'm fine," I snapped, refusing to look at him.

"Yeah, okay." He blew out a strained breath that sounded an awful lot like, 'We both know you're not.'

"THE MILL," I said as Nate's car rumbled along the dirt road.

"Hey, I'm just the driver." He winked, trying to lighten the mood. But the knot in my stomach was unforgiving.

Nix came into view, sitting on the hood of his car. The second he saw us, he stood up and started walking toward us. Nate's car rolled to a stop and he glanced at me. "See you later."

"What will you do?"

"Actually, I'm going to meet Kye and Zane."

"You are?"

"Yeah, I think he probably told them to keep an eye on me. But I don't mind. They're good guys."

"You don't mind being here?"

"You sound surprised." He shrugged. "I told you once before that I'd probably fit in better in The Row than I do in Old Darling Hill."

"Nate, I—"

Nix yanked my door open and the air whooshed from my lungs. "Hi," I breathed.

"Hi." He offered me his hand and gently pulled me from the car before dipping his head back inside.

"Thanks, man. I appreciate it."

"Any time, text me when it's time."

"Will do." Nix closed the door and tapped the roof, his other arm looping around my waist.

When Nate drove off, Nix pulled me into his arms and gazed down at me. "Hi, Birdie."

"Hi, Nix."

"Something you want to tell me?" His expression was guarded, tripping my heart into a free fall.

A sticky trail of guilt snaked through as I choked out, "I can explain."

"I get it," he said. "Miller gets their approval. He's the obvious choice." His finger pushed the stray hairs out of my eyes before stroking down my cheek. "The right choice."

"Nix, that isn't—"

"It's okay, B." He dipped his head, kissing my forehead. "I get it. Don't like it much, but I get it. Come on, I want to show you something."

He took my hand and tugged me toward the abandoned building.

It was the same as before. The atmosphere thick and musty, the sliver of light illuminating the particles of dirt and debris floating in the air. Except when we reached the office we'd been in before, it had been cleaned out of all the ramshackle old furniture and made… homely.

Nix watched me from the doorway as I took it all in. The small couch, draped in a worn but clean throw. The small mattress in the corner of the room covered in blankets. An older than old television, and a floor lamp, neither of them connected to a power source yet.

"What is all this?" I asked, looking at him over my shoulder.

"This." He came to me, sliding his arms around my waist and tucking his chin into my neck. "Is ours. Somewhere we can be together without worrying about my old man or your family."

"I… you did this, for me?" Emotion clogged my throat.

"For us." Nix kissed my cheek. "Things have been intense, I get that. And I know you're not ready to defend our relationship to the world, but I need to know we're together on this, B. I need to know—"

Spinning in his arms, I threw my own around his neck and kissed him. *Thank you,* every slide of my lips said. *Thank you, thank you, thank you.*

Nix answered with his tongue. Long, lazy licks that made my toes curl. *It's ours,* he seemed to say. *Yours. Somewhere we can just be.*

It was perfect. Even if the rational part of my brain knew it was just another temporary fix, a Band-Aid on the wound that we'd eventually have to deal with.

We couldn't live here. But we could come here. We could love and laugh here.

"Maybe I can bring some things from the house," I said, pulling away from him. "To make it more comfortable."

Nix stared at me, a faint smile tracing his mouth.

"Blankets, some snacks, oh and I think Michael and Sabrina have a small generator in the garage. They won't notice it—"

"Whoa, B, calm down. It isn't a permanent thing; it's just somewhere we can come and—"

"I know that." I rolled my eyes. "I'm just excited."

It was ours.

Ours.

A few little touches here and there and it would be like our very own place. I could picture it now, meeting Nix after school, asking him how his day was while I made us both cup noodles. We could go for walks and watch reruns of old TV shows and talk about everything and nothing.

"This is… Nix, this is perfect," I said, beaming.

I was so wrapped up in it, I didn't notice the way his expression tightened.

I didn't notice his happiness morph into concern.

I didn't notice it at all.

22

NIX

As I took in the relief in Harleigh's eyes, the simmering gratitude, I was hit with the thought that this was a bad fucking idea.

It was supposed to be a temporary answer to our predicament, not a permanent solution. But here she was planning the décor.

I didn't want to feed her anxiety, nurture it. I'd thought by doing this for her, it would show her how much I wanted us to make it work. But instead, it felt like I'd just offered her the keys to a kingdom where we didn't have to go out in public, or face her father or mine.

A kingdom where we could hide our relationship like a dirty little secret.

Fuck.

I was out of my depth here.

When I'd learned about Nate from Max, my first

instinct had been to call her up and demand answers. But Nate had been there for her, he'd been on our side. Maybe it was time I trusted his intentions. I couldn't keep her safe at DA or across the res. But maybe he could.

It was a sacrifice I was willing to make if it meant I got more time with her until we could figure out our next steps.

"This is… Nix, this is perfect."

My heart sank.

Perfect. That sounded hella permanent.

"It's just a temporary fix," I said, cupping her face. "Until we tell them."

"Y-yeah." She didn't meet my eyes and it fucking stung.

But I wouldn't push. Not here. Not when the clock was ticking on our stolen time together.

"Come here." I brushed my lips over hers, eliciting a soft whimper from deep inside her.

Kissing Harleigh set my body on fire. Heat swarmed in my chest, low in my stomach. It was primal, some baser instinct that was equal parts smug and as relieved as fuck that I was the only guy who got to experience this. Her. Whimpering and needy.

"We go as far as you want, okay?"

She broke the kiss long enough to nod, to take one of my hands and press it against her chest. Jesus Christ, her curves were sinful. The fact that she was so unaware of how beautiful she was only made it sweeter.

"Is this okay?" I dropped my hands to the hem of her t-shirt, and she nodded, her pupils blown with lust.

I hadn't brought her here for this, but I wanted her. I wanted her so fucking much. And maybe a part of me wanted to forget too. Wanted to forget that although Harleigh was mine, there were still any number of things that could take her away from me.

She slipped her hands under my hoodie, her touch branding me. Searing me to the fucking bone. How had I ever denied myself this? Her?

I couldn't ever imagine not having this, not feeling this again.

"I dream of this, you know?" I brought my mouth to her ear and whispered, "Kissing every inch of your skin, painting your body with my tongue, tasting you."

"Nix." A breathless moan rolled through her, full of eager anticipation.

Sliding my hand up her spine, I gripped her nape and gazed at her. "You're mine, Harleigh Wren Maguire. Whatever happens, whoever tries to come between us, you're mine."

"Show me," she breathed the words onto my lips, sealing them with a kiss. "Show me, Nix."

Emotion tumbled through me. I wanted to show her the world, wanted to make her see herself the way I saw her. I wanted to erase every shred of doubt and insecurity from her mind.

My hoodie came off next, her pants, my sweats. I brushed a hand down her stomach, sweeping it over the curve of her hip. "So fucking beautiful," I rasped, my throat bobbing, disbelief still lingering in my mind that I got to have this. Her.

"Show me," she whispered. Begging me with her eyes.

Grabbing her ass, I lifted her up my body until she locked her ankles around my waist. "Hold on," I said, walking to the mattress and lowering to my knees. Harleigh shrieked, laughter chasing the sound. I laid her down, leaving her legs hooked around my body. "Look at you."

Pure lust coursed through my veins. But it was laced with love. With the sheer and utter adoration I felt for her.

"Nix..." Her skin was flushed, gentle vibrations still rolling through her.

"You're nervous."

"How many times do I have to tell you, you've always made me nervous."

"Maybe I should flip the tables and let you take control. Then you can go at your pace." The idea of her on top of me, riding me was enough to make me shudder.

"I..." She hesitated, innocence swirling with the desire in her eyes.

"It's okay." I leaned down, kissing her. "We can work up to that."

"Oh God," she cried out as I sank into her, letting her feel exactly what she did to me.

"You like that, B?" Rocking my hips a little, I let my dick nudge against her warm, wet heat.

"Yes, yes..."

Amused laughter bubbled in my chest as I ran my nose along her jaw, nipping her bottom lip. "Wouldn't you prefer the real thing?"

Harleigh nodded, her eyes heavy lidded and glassy. Slipping her legs from around my waist, I rocked back on my haunches and hooked my fingers into the waistband of her black cotton panties.

"Just a second," I said, ready to grab my jeans and fish a condom from my wallet.

"Wait." Harleigh grabbed me. "I-I want to feel you.

Fuck.

"Yeah?" The word came out hoarse.

"Yeah."

I couldn't get out of my boxers fast enough. Then I was on her, kissing her, running my hands over her gorgeous curves, making her moan my name.

Nix. Nix. Nix.

"Are you ready for me?" I slipped a hand between our bodies and dipped two fingers into her.

"Ah." She turned her face into my arm, the one braced at the side of her head as I crooked my fingers inside her and rubbed.

"Nix, it's… God…" Her body arched into my touch, writhing, seeking more.

I kissed her again, licking the seam of her lips. Her jaw. The corner of her mouth.

I couldn't get enough.

"More," she panted, head thrown back in pleasure as she rode my hand, taking what she needed.

"Wait. I want to feel you," I said, replacing my fingers with my dick. With one smooth stroke that made us both moan, I slid home.

My forearm trembled as I held my weight above her

while my other hand found her clit, and Harleigh shattered around me. Clenching me, pulling me further into her body.

"F-fuck," I choked out. She felt too good. I wasn't sure I could last. And I needed to fucking last.

"Wrap your legs around me," I urged, easing slowly out of her, then I slammed back home.

"God, Nix, it feels…" Harleigh moaned again. The sound fisting my heart the way her pussy gripped my dick.

"I know, I know." I kissed her, my tongue mirroring the slow roll of my hips, the deep, intense drag of me against her tight walls.

Sweat rolled down my back, the air thick with sex and endorphins. I rocked harder, sliding my hand under her ass, and tilting her onto me, letting me go deeper. Dipping my head, I flicked my tongue over her nipple, closing my mouth around the peaked bud. Harleigh cried out, her body trembling beneath me.

I trailed my lips and teeth and tongue up her neck, nipping and sucking, marking her. It was a reckless move, but I couldn't resist. I wanted everyone to know she was mine. That she belonged to me, even if they would never truly know whose mark she wore.

"Fuck, Birdie… *fuck*." I went harder, chasing the release barreling down my spine. She kissed me, dragging her teeth over my bottom lip and biting down. It was enough to send me over the edge and I came hard, her name punching from my lips.

"I love you," I breathed, dropping my head to hers.

Harleigh wrapped her arms tighter, anchoring us together. "I'm happy, Nix. You make me happy."

I wanted to believe her, I wanted so fucking much to believe her.

So why did the pit in my stomach grow wider instead of shrinking at her words? Her soft, honest declaration.

I made her happy, sure.

But was it enough?

"I WISH we didn't have to leave," Harleigh sighed, brushing her fingertips over the whorls of ink snaking around my bicep.

"We can come back. That's kind of the point."

She smiled. "Where did you even get all this stuff?"

"From the Carters' storage shed. They had a ton of stuff lying around."

"And Mrs. Carter didn't mind?"

"Didn't you know I'm her favorite Wilder?"

"Nix." Her smile grew uncertain. "You didn't tell her—"

"Relax, I didn't tell her any more than she needed to know. Besides, I figured I can come out here if things with my old man get too much."

"What?" She pushed up on her elbow and stared down at me. "You mean like live out here?"

Shit, it was the wrong thing to say. I didn't want her to worry more than she already was. I also didn't want her to think that I wanted to be out here without her.

The lines I had to walk with her were so fucking

razor thin that sometimes I felt clueless. I could command a team of football players, deliver intricate plays, and plan game strategy. Yet half the time I couldn't figure out what my girlfriend was thinking.

And it cut me up inside.

But I had to go at her pace, had to take whatever scraps she decided to throw my way. It was going to take time.

I had time.

We both did.

"No, I don't mean live out here." I leaned up to kiss the corner of her mouth. "But it wouldn't hurt to have somewhere to go."

"You could go to Kye's or Zane's."

"Yeah, I know. But it isn't a permanent solution if—" I stopped myself.

"If what?"

"If things get too bad to stay."

"God, I hate this." Her expression fell. "I hate it so much. I guess I thought… I'd hoped that things had gotten better between you. But they haven't, have they?" She touched her head to mine, inhaling deeply.

"No, B. They haven't." Something cracked inside me.

I didn't let myself think about it often because there was no fucking point in crying over spilt milk. But sometimes, the thought creeped in.

What was wrong with me?

What made me so unlovable that neither of my parents wanted me? I wasn't a bad kid. Sure, I'd become a bit of a handful as I'd got older. But what teenage boy living in The Row didn't?

"You deserve better, Nix." She laid her hand on my cheek and smiled, but it didn't reach her eyes. "You always did."

"Yeah, well, I don't need them." *I don't need anyone except you and my friends.* "I have something to ask you, and I know you're not going to want to do it, but just hear me out, okay?"

"Okay."

"Coach said the scouts from Albany U might come to Friday's game and I want you there, B. I fucking need you there."

"I-I can't Nix." She paled. "I can't go back there."

"You can go with Chloe. You can sneak in and watch from under the bleachers. I'll get the groundskeeper to put a couple of chairs under there."

"Nix…"

"I need you there, B. This is a big fucking deal to me." One I still wasn't sure I was ready for. "But I can't do it without you."

Maybe I was pushing too hard, too soon, but it wasn't like I was asking her to sit front and center in the bleachers surrounded by my classmates. Chloe could sneak her in and out unnoticed. Lyle, the groundskeeper, would help me if I asked.

"You really want me there?"

"I do. Promise me you'll try."

"I…"

"Say it, Birdie." I kissed her, sliding my hand along the curve of her neck, distracting her. And yeah, maybe manipulating her a little. But I liked to think of it as gentle coercion.

I needed her there.

I needed her full stop.

"Say it."

She pulled back, breathless and starry-eyed and whispered, "I promise."

23

HARLEIGH

"Harleigh, a word please." Michael's request made me falter as I helped myself to breakfast.

I'd assumed he had already left for the morning.

Obviously, he hadn't.

"I'm actually busy," I said, my hand tightening around the spoon as I refused to look at him.

"Harleigh, please, it's important."

With a heavy sigh, I turned around. "What?"

"The secretary from Albany Hills called."

My blood ran cold.

"No, no, don't be alarmed, it isn't anything to be concerned about. They wondered if you'd tried to contact Dr. Katy at all? It appears she's taking an unexpected sabbatical, and they're aware some of her patients might not have been informed."

"Is she okay?"

"She is, but she's dealing with some things and needs to take some time off."

"She didn't call me to let me know." A sinking feeling went through me.

"No, it would appear she left quite suddenly."

So that's why she'd never returned my call.

"What happens now?" I asked.

"You'll be assigned a new lead therapist. Someone will contact you soon."

"Okay." I turned back to my bowl of cereal.

"Do you… want to talk about anything? I know I'm not a substitute for Dr. Katy's years of training and expertise, but I have a good—"

"What are you doing?" I whirled back around and cut him with an icy stare.

"Excuse me?" He clutched his tie, loosening it slightly; the way he did whenever he felt uncomfortable.

"Why are you doing this? Pretending you care?"

"Harleigh, I do care. You're my daugh—"

"Don't say it. Don't you *dare* say it. I might be your flesh and blood, but I am not your daughter."

I know what you did.

I know what you did.

I know what you did.

The words played on a loop in my mind. I wanted to roar at him. To grab the nearest sharp object and hurl it at him. I didn't care that my therapists would deem that *inappropriate behavior*, the kind of behavior that could land you in a padded cell or stuck with a sedation needle like a wild animal.

He'd banished me there once, would he do it again? If

I lashed out, called him on his secrets, his lies and betrayal?

"Harleigh, come on now. I know things haven't been easy—"

"Easy? You think any of this has been easy? You pulled me from my home and brought me here to appease your guilt, to soothe your conscience. Don't try to spin it into something it's not. If she hadn't died that night you never would have inserted yourself into my life."

"That's not true, I tried… I tried." Frustration bled into his expression.

"What did you say?" My blood ran cold.

"Over the years, I tried to see you. But Trina, she always made things so difficult."

"Keep her name out of your mouth," I snarled. "She died because of you. You killed her. You."

The blood drained from his face, and strangely, it was the most human I'd ever seen him look. "I made mistakes, yes." He cleared his throat, visibly uncomfortable.

Good.

I wanted him uncomfortable. I wanted him squirming around in his over-expensive tailored suit.

"But you really can't hold me responsible—"

"It must be so easy for you, *Dad*," I spat the word, "to sit here in your mansion telling yourself that it wasn't your fault. That you weren't responsible for her illness. I bet you even pitied her, her dependency on alcohol. Of course, that couldn't be your fault either, right?"

I inhaled a ragged breath, fighting the urge to just tell him I knew. To call him out on his single worst betrayal. But if I did it, if I crossed that line, there would be no going back, and the truth was, I was scared. Scared of what the truth would do to me once it was out in the open.

So I bit my tongue and shoved *those* words down, refusing to give them purchase. The day would come when we would have it out, but I needed more time.

"What is going on here?" Sabrina appeared, glancing between me and her husband. "Michael?"

"It's nothing, sweetheart."

"It doesn't look like nothing. I heard shouting." Her cool gaze fixed on me. "Harleigh?"

"Nothing." I pasted on a saccharine sweet smile. "Just having a father-daughter chat."

"It didn't sound—"

"Everything's fine, I promise." He draped his arm around her shoulder and pulled her close.

I didn't know Sabrina, not really. She'd made as much effort to get to know me as I had her. But he loved her. In his own way, Michael loved her, and it cut me up inside to watch them together. The life they'd built, the family they'd raised, while me and Mom were left to rot in The Row.

I tried to see you.

His words echoed through my mind, refusing to dissipate.

Did it really change anything? He was Michael Rowe, one of the wealthiest, most revered men in Hudson Valley. If he'd wanted to see me, he could have found a way to make it happen. Besides, I would never blame the woman he practically threw out of town. Even if she had failed me as well.

Tears burned the backs of my eyes like acid.

"You know, Harleigh." Sabrina clicked her tongue, disapproval rippling off her immaculate presence. "Most girls would be grateful to be here, yet your attitude really is quite something. Now I know you've had a hard time, I understand that. And after the blip last winter—"

"Blip… the *blip*?" Strangled laughter spilled from my lips. "I'm sorry, I didn't realize trying to slit your wrists amounted to a blip."

Sabrina sucked in a sharp breath while Michael said, "Harleigh, that is enough."

"Enough what, Dad? Enough anxiety? Enough manic depressive thoughts? Do you think I like being like this? That I wake up in the morning with a smile on my face because I get to spend yet another day overanalyzing every little detail about my life? I mean, it is pretty special attending a private school where everyone hates you and thinks you're nothing but trailer trash scum. I'm sorry if I didn't express enough gratitude. How fucking rude of me."

My chest heaved with the weight of the words, the crippling truth laid bare before them. Sabrina looked horrified, utterly speechless as she stared at me, the stepdaughter she'd never wanted or cared about.

But it was Michael's expression that unnerved me. The guilt etched into his crinkled eyes as if he knew exactly what had happened and his role in it. He looked… sad.

And I hated it.

I hated that they got to stand there, poised and pretty with their perfect lives, their perfect little family, while I fell apart, bleeding out all over their expensive kitchen floor tiles.

"Go to your room," Sabrina said with deadly calm.

"Excuse me?"

"I said, go to your room."

"Sabrina—"

"No, Michael." She shrugged my father's arm off and stepped forward, her eyes filled with disdain. "She does not get to disrespect us like that in our own goddamn home. A home we have opened up to her. Now go to your room and stay there until it's time for school."

I realized it then.

Sabrina hated me.

She hated what I stood for, what I reminded her of. She hated that I was her husband's illegitimate child from a relationship deemed inappropriate by the elite of Old Darling Hill. She hated that I was here, in her house, messing up her idealized version of life. But more than anything she hated that I'd brought this... this chaos to their doorstep.

The fight inside me sputtered out like a candle in the wind.

I'd thought she was just indifferent. Cold with everyone and anyone who wasn't part of her inner circle. But it was more than that. She censored herself around me.

"Morning." Celeste breezed into the kitchen, grounding to a halt when she sensed the thick tension. "What's the matter?"

"Nothing." Sabrina managed a smile for her daughter.

Her kind, intelligent flesh and blood. "Harleigh was just leaving."

Leaving...

The word clanged through me.

"Yeah, excuse me." I shoved past them all, the edges of my vision blurring.

"Harleigh, wait—" Celeste called after me, but I was already gone, staggering down the hall as I tried to suck in deep, greedy lungfuls of air.

The precarious threads of my resolve, my inner strength, began to fray, tearing open like a piece of fabric stretched to its limits.

I couldn't breathe. Couldn't get oxygen in fast enough. The walls around me began to close in, making me pant with fear as I grabbed the stair rail and hoisted myself up. Up, up, up. I kept climbing, gasping for every breath, tears streaming down my face. I was almost at the top when my vision turned black, my heart beating too fast.

I lost my footing and tripped, flying forward, right into a solid body.

"Shit, Harleigh?" Strong hands steadied me as I blinked up at Max. "Should I call Dad?"

"N-no," I choked out. "Just... help me back to my room. Please."

"I..." He hesitated, dragging a hand down his face. "Yeah, okay. Come on."

But Max didn't take me to my room, he guided me into his, and sat me on his bed. I dropped my head between my legs, breathing slow and deep, forcing my heart rate down.

"Can I, uh, get you anything?" He didn't sound thrilled to have me here, in his space. But I couldn't find it in myself to care.

"Water," I choked out.

Max walked off and I looked up to find him opening a small minibar. Of course he had a minibar in his room.

The thought was so random, so preposterous, that a garbled laugh bubbled up my throat. He stared at me. "Are you all right?"

"No, I don't think I am."

"Here." He handed me the bottle of water and dropped down beside me. "Want to talk about it?"

I shook my head, uncapping the lid and chugging the entire thing down. "Thanks." I wiped my mouth with the back of my hand and drew in a shuddering breath. "Your mom is a bitch."

He laughed. Max Rowe-Delacorte laughed and I found myself laughing right alongside him.

"Can't argue there."

"She hates me." I sank my hand into the soft coverlet beneath me.

"She hates everyone."

"Not like this. I saw it, in her eyes. She thinks I'm trailer trash just like everyone else."

"Harleigh—" His breath caught, and I glanced up at him, frowning. "I... have something to tell you."

"I'm listening."

"Shit, yeah, okay." Guilt etched into his expression. "So I... uh, I sent you that text message."

"What text—" I gasped. "It was you."

"It was a shitty thing to do, but I was so fucking angry and I do dumb shit when I'm angry."

"You sent it." I shouldn't have been surprised. It was Max—he'd never liked me. But it didn't stop my stomach free-falling.

"I heard what happened, at Nate's house. I tried to tell you before, but I'm not good at… at this. For what it's worth, I'm sorry."

"Why are you telling me now?"

"Because I get it now. I get it."

I didn't know what he meant, but I didn't have time to ask because Celeste burst into his room. "There you are. I've been looking everywhere. What happened?" She glanced between us, settling her murderous expression on Max.

"Max helped me," I said, throwing him a bone.

"He did?" She gawked.

"Yeah." I glanced up at him and smiled. To my surprise he gave me a flicker of a smile back.

"He did."

"Okay, somebody's going to have to explain things to me, because I'm confused."

"The genius, confused?" Max laughed.

"Did you just… crack a joke?"

"What?" He shrugged. "Stranger things have happened."

"What is happening right now? It's like I've walked in on *The Twilight Zone*. Are you two like friends now or something?"

"No," I said.

At the same time as Max murmured, "Or something."

24

NIX

"Okay, nobody needs to see that first thing in the morning," Kye covered his eyes, fake retching as we passed Hench and Cherri practically dry fucking up against the gym wall.

"Get a fucking room," Zane called out to them, and Hench flipped him off behind her back, not bothering to break the kiss. If you could call it that; it looked like he was eating her whole. Gross.

"Any regrets?" Zane mocked while punching my shoulder.

"Only that I ever touched her in the first place."

They both chuckled as we made our way down the hall toward the locker room. "So did B like the place?" Kye asked.

"Yeah, maybe a little too much."

"What do you mean?"

"She seemed... relieved. Like now we have somewhere to be together, we don't need to deal with all the shit circling us."

"Ah." Pity shone in his eyes. "Well, it can't be easy for her. She lives there, and her old man is the only family she has—"

"She has me." I snapped.

"Yeah, and you're one argument from being thrown out on your ass. You have no job. No scholarship—"

"*Yet*. He has no scholarship yet." Zane's brow lifted.

"I need some cash." They both looked at me and I rolled my eyes. "Legitimate cash."

"Time to think about your gleaming résumé. Star quarterback. Son of The Row's local dealer and acquirer of the darker things in life." Kye smirked. "Bryson Shaw's undefeated champ. What else?" He stroked his chin in contemplation.

"Asshole," I mumbled, shouldering the door to the locker room.

Their laughter followed me as I headed for my usual spot on the benches. Kye was right. I needed to get my house in order if I was going to be able to support B if things went to shit with her father.

I needed a job—some cash of my own. But between school and the team and stealing what little time I had with Harleigh, it didn't leave much in the way of spare time.

I hadn't wanted to tangle myself up with Bryson any more than necessary, but maybe it was the only option. I didn't want to fight for him, but I could offer my services elsewhere. Keeping the gym clean and tidy, offering some sessions with the younger kids. It was worth a shot. So long as it didn't come with any conditions.

My cell phone bleeped and I frowned at the number.

"What is it?"

"Harleigh's asking about plans for the game tomorrow night."

"Why the long face? That's a good thing, isn't it?"

"I don't know. She wants to know if there's a party at the res after."

"Little Birdie grew up, Nix." Kye chuckled. "You can't keep her caged up forever. Z's right, this is a good thing. Maybe you got it wrong last night, maybe she's more ready to go public than you think."

I very much doubted that. Which meant something had happened.

I texted her back.

Me: Is everything okay?

B: I thought you'd be happy I wanted to be there...

Me: I am but why the sudden change of heart?

B: Because I'm tired, Nix. I'm tired of always feeling like this.

Me: Do you need me to come get you? We can blow off school and go hang out at the mill?

B: We can't do that. Besides, you have practice to get ready for your big game tomorrow.

Fuck. I wanted to call her, I wanted to hear her voice and know she was okay. But Coach chose that moment to enter the room.

"Look alive, ladies. I want your asses out on the field in five."

"Shit," I murmured, weighing up my options. But before I could make a decision, another text came through.

B: Don't worry about me, I'm fine, I swear. I just had a bad morning. I'll tell you all about it later.

I lowered my cell phone behind my bag.

Me: You're sure?

B: I'm sure. xo

"She okay?" Zane asked, looking concerned.

"I don't know."

"We need to get out on the field or Coach will tear us a new one," Kye said.

"You two go, I'll be right there."

Even though it fucking pained me to do it, I pulled up another message thread.

Me: I need you to keep an eye on Harleigh for me.

THE REPLY CAME A SECOND LATER.

Miller: You got it.

PRACTICE WAS A SHITSHOW. I was unfocused, thinking about Harleigh. Thinking about last night, her moans and little sighs as I fucked her. Trying to figure out how it was possible to be on cloud fucking nine while bracing yourself for the impending storm rolling your way. Because that's what being with her was like, a constant roller-coaster of emotion. Highs so high I felt like I was flying, and lows so low I wasn't sure I'd ever fucking claw my way back to the surface.

"Let's hope you get your shit together for tomorrow's game, son." Coach cut me with a scathing look. He knew why my head wasn't in it and I didn't blame him for being concerned. Because she was a distraction.

The best and worst kind.

Coach disappeared into his office, his twang of disappointment lingering in the air around me.

"He's right, you know. This is exactly what I was worried—"

"Leave it, Z." I ran a tense hand over my face.

"What. I'm just saying that you can't afford to screw this up. She said she was okay."

"And how many times have you told me and Kye you're fine? That the shit with your gran is under control? How many times have I said I'm okay after limping into the locker room after another argument with my old man? It's a bullshit answer and you know it."

They both stared at me with stunned expressions.

"You really think something is wrong?"

"Nothing about any of this is right," I said, slinging my bag over my shoulder and barging past them.

"Nix, man, come on, we didn't mean—"

But I was gone, storming out of the locker room and into the balmy morning air.

I pulled out my cell phone, a bolt of jealousy shooting through me at the sight of Nate's name.

MILLER: **She's okay. A little crabbier than usual, but I don't think you need to stage an intervention just yet.**

. . .

Code for: Don't do anything stupid that'll only piss her off even more.

Me: Keep me updated and don't tell her about this.

Miller: Sure. Does that make me your dirty little secret though because I've got to say, Wilder, that's all kinds of fucked up.

A faint smile played on my lips. Miller was a weird one. But he'd helped me out more than once now.

I couldn't stop thinking about what Max had told me though, about his sister. That was some tragic shit, but it explained his savior complex where Harleigh was concerned.

Me: Just text me if anything changes.

He texted back a thumbs up emoji.

Pocketing my cell, I dropped down on the bench, inhaling a ragged breath. If Harleigh was spiraling… fuck, I didn't know how to help her. How to be the guy she needed me to be. I'd read some stuff on depression and anxiety, tried to understand what she was going through. But I also knew it was a deeply personal experience, and what triggered one person, didn't necessarily trigger another. I figured it was like looking through cracked glass. The visual impairment was the same, but everyone's perception of the scene beyond it was different.

Until Harleigh opened up more and shared her experience, I was stumbling along in the dark, hoping like hell I got it right with her.

***

"CAN I HAVE A WORD?"

Bryson beckoned me into his office and I slipped inside, closing the door behind me.

"Didn't expect to see you here at this time." He glanced at the clock on the wall.

"School got out thirty minutes ago."

"Didn't make it to senior year." He sat back in his chair. "What can I do for you, Nix?"

"I… uh, I need a job." I ran my hand over my thigh, trying to stop my leg from jostling.

"A job, you say? Well, I can probably put you back on the rota, and—"

"No, I don't mean fighting. I mean something legitimate."

"Legitimate?" He cocked a brow. "Didn't have you down as the kind of guy who'd wanna clean the johns or make the coffee." Deep laughter rumbled in his chest.

I didn't laugh though, and his brows pinched. "You're serious?"

"I am."

"I see."

"Well, I don't have much in the way of legitimate work right now. Pendall sees to the cleaning and repairs and we have Jodie on front of house." If you could call the small desk in the foyer front of house. "I'm not sure what else—"

"I could work with the younger kids, help train them?"

"Like you're working with the Rowe kid?"

I shrugged. "I guess."

"Gotta have permits for that kind of thing, Nix. I'd be breaking all kinds of laws if I take you on as a trainer." His lip curled. "How about I cut you a deal? I'll take you on as my assistant. You can do a bit of this and a bit of that. And you go into the rotation once a month."

"Brys, come on. You know Coach won't—"

He stroked his jaw. "Football season is over in, what, less than three months? And that's if you make the playoffs."

"We'll make it," I said.

He smirked. "I like your confidence. Okay, how about you're my back up during football season. And then when it's over, you go on the regular rotation."

"One fight a month after the season is over?"

"And the job's yours."

"I need a minimum of ten hours a week. Twelve dollars an hour." That would be nearly five hundred dollars a month. It wasn't much, but it was a start.

"Ten dollars an hour, but I can probably find twelve to fifteen hours a week."

"Done."

"Welcome to the team, kid. Speak to Jodie about ordering you a couple of branded tank tops and getting you set up with a roster. Something tells me the local kids will all want to learn from the infamous Phoenix Wilder." He winked, and a chill ran down my spine.

Although I guessed if all else failed—if Albany U decided not to waste their time with a guy like me—I could always follow in Bryson's footsteps.

There was a desperate fucking thought.

"When do I start?"

"No time like the present." He pressed his palms against the desk and stood.

"Right now?"

"Unless you have other plans?"

I'd wanted to try to see Harleigh. Her handful of text messages this afternoon had been brief. But Nate had reassured me more than once that she was okay.

Cranky but okay.

"No, no plans."

"Excellent. Throw your shit in my locker and I'll give you the grand tour."

"I'll be one minute," I said, digging my cell out of my pocket. As I headed for the locker at the back of Bryson's office, I quickly texted Harleigh.

Me: Something came up, but I'll call you later, okay? I love you, B. Always. xo

"Good to go?" Bryson asked, a hint of impatience coating his words.

"Yeah." I zipped up my bag and threw it into the bottom of the locker and followed him into the hall, and into my new job.

25

HARLEIGH

"Hey, Harleigh, wait up." Max jogged up beside me, slowing his pace to match mine. "You're walking home?"

I shrugged. "Celeste left with Miles. They offered me a ride, but I thought I'd walk."

I hadn't wanted her to look too closely, not after this morning.

All day, I'd felt like I was walking on a knife's edge. Nate had followed me around school like a lost puppy. After the second time, he'd asked me if I was okay and I'd bitten his head off. He'd backed off, but I knew he was worried.

I was worried.

Something had splintered this morning during my confrontation with Michael and Sabrina. Not that you could really call it a confrontation.

"Are you okay? After… you know?"

"I'm fine."

"Aren't we all," he muttered.

I cut him a sideways glance and asked, "What are you doing, Max? Surely you could have gotten a ride with Toby."

"I could, but I saw you and figured I'd check if you were okay."

"Why? We're not friends. You hate me, remember. I'm nothing but a *trailer trash whore.*"

He flinched. "I was an ass."

"Yeah, you were."

"It wasn't even about you, not really. I just needed someone to aim my anger at."

"Lucky me," I scoffed.

He ran a hand down his face and let out a heavy sigh. "I know I don't deserve—"

"Nothing. You don't deserve a damn thing from me, least of all forgiveness."

All the name calling and taunts. The text message that had triggered me that night. Max had made it perfectly clear what he thought about me.

I didn't owe him forgiveness—I didn't owe him anything.

And yet…

"You're right, I don't," he said quietly. "But you know what it's like, right? To live with the pain and anger. The betrayal." The apology in his eyes guttered out, and his tone… it was sad. Laced with hurt.

"Max, did something happen—"

"It doesn't matter." He forced a smile. "I was an asshole. I'm still an asshole. Probably always will be. But I shouldn't have pushed you so hard."

"Okay." My brows knitted together.

He was talking in riddles and I didn't have enough energy to try to solve them. I didn't like him—the feeling was mutual there—but I couldn't deny something had changed between us. And he had helped me this morning, and before with Sabrina, and before at the game.

"So we're good?"

"You really care if we're good or not?" I inclined my head studying him.

"I guess not." He shoved his hands in his pockets and shrugged. "But I realized something, Harleigh. You're not my enemy."

"I'm not?"

"No." He kicked a stone, sending it flying across the sidewalk.

It was half on my mind to ask him who the enemy was if it wasn't me, but I couldn't find the words.

This whole conversation had been weird, and I didn't have the headspace to take on someone else's troubles.

"Are you seeing Nix tonight?" he asked me, and I shook my head.

"He's busy."

"Doing what?"

"He said he had some stuff to take care of."

"Cryptic."

Cryptic indeed. But I was trying not to think about *what* he could be doing or *who* he was with.

Nix was popular at Darling Hill High. Everyone wanted to hang out with the Hawks star quarterback. Maybe something came up. A team thing… a guys' thing.

I shut down *those* thoughts. Overthinking it wouldn't end well, not with how irritated I'd been all day.

Nix had a life outside of me. He had school, the team, responsibilities. I didn't expect him to just give those up for me, and I didn't want him to. But anxiety was a bitch, twisting and turning things into something they weren't.

"I like him," Max said. "I didn't think I would, but there's something real about him." I murmured some unintelligible reply and Max went on, "Wouldn't have put the two of you together, but I guess—"

"What do you mean?" I asked, already knowing his answer.

"Wilder is so confident and sure of himself and you're… not. No offense."

"None taken." My lips thinned, my stomach churning.

Did he honestly think I didn't know how different Nix and I were? Of course I knew. It's what made all of this so hard.

Nix could go off to college and make something of himself. With a little determination and drive, he could chase his dreams and achieve them. I, on the other hand, could barely get through the day.

When it came down to it, I was just another burden for him to shoulder.

Silence swirled around us, filling the space between us as we headed for the estate.

"Can I ask you something?" I said. "Two things actually."

Max nodded. "Sure."

"Firstly, how did you know… about me and Nix?"

"Ah, that." He ran a hand down his face. "That night you went to Nate's, I was there."

"You were—*what?*"

"Toby, he lets me stay over sometimes. When I need to get out of the house. I have a key to their pool house. I saw you all."

"That's… I don't know what to say. Does Nate know? Their parents?"

"Not officially, no. So I'd appreciate it if you didn't mention it to him."

"Another favor?" I asked, a little incredulous.

"Consider us even." He motioned to the bottle of water in my hands.

"Okay, second question." Because this conversation was getting stranger by the second, and I had too many questions. Questions I knew Max wouldn't answer yet, maybe never.

"What do you think would happen if Michael and Sabrina found out… about me and Nix?"

His expression hardened, his eyes simmering with something that made dread sluice down my spine. "If you love him, really love him, Harleigh… don't do it. Don't tell them. Not yet."

"But if they find out?" Because it would come out eventually.

He inhaled a sharp breath. "If I were you," he warned. "I'd hope like hell they don't."

I didn't go back to the house, I couldn't.

The second it had come into view, I'd frozen. Max must have noticed my hesitation, whatever emotion simmered in my eyes, because he took one look at my expression and told me he'd cover for me so long as I didn't disappear.

Disappear.

There was a thought.

I'd spent years feeling invisible. Around The Row, walking the halls at school, even in my trailer. I'd been the girl few people saw or cared about. It was different here. People watched. They watched, they judged, and they gossiped.

Was this what it had been like for my mom when she'd fallen in love with the wrong man?

A man she could never have.

I'd never get to ask her now. I'd never have the chance to truly understand what it was like for her back then. To ask her why she'd never let Michael see me.

Part of me got it. Understood why she hadn't let him into my life. But I wasn't a child now. I could make my own decisions.

I let my fingers drift over the branches of the low hanging trees. I hadn't wandered far, the estate still visible in the distance. But I couldn't go back there yet. Not until I'd calmed down. I felt unstable, my thoughts erratic and disordered.

Mom.

Michael.

Sabrina.

Max.

Nate.

Nix.

Mom.

Michael.

Nix.

Sabrina.

Nix.

Michael.

Nix.

Nix.

Nix.

It always, *always* came back to him. The invisible tether binding us, refusing to let me forget. But the more I thought about it, the more I let myself look at things, truly look at my life and the future, the more certain I was that I couldn't hold Nix back.

I needed him to pursue the scholarship—for both of us—even if I didn't end up going with him. He had to do it.

He had to.

I didn't realize I was crying until a big fat tear dripped off my face, landing on my t-shirt and saturating the thin material.

Wiping my eyes with the heels of my palms, I sucked in a sharp breath. Dr. Katy said crying was a good thing. That it helped reduce stress hormones. But I didn't like it. I'd spent too many years crying with little or no positive outcome. Crying because I was sad or lonely or scared. Crying because my mom didn't turn up for show and tell at school or yet another parent teacher conference.

Crying took me back to those memories, to that

desperate, desolate place where I was just a girl who wanted her mom to care. And knew she never would.

I gripped the fence and tipped my face to the sky, letting the balmy air wash over me. *You're okay, Harleigh. You're okay... you're okay.* But I didn't feel okay.

I was tired of it all. So freaking tired. At least before when I'd been a quiet, meek girl, I hadn't questioned everything. My own mind hadn't constantly worked against me, whispering dark evil things.

My heart cinched, that familiar hollow feeling spreading through me.

Nix filled the void. Just as Celeste and Chloe and Nate did. Friends—they were my friends. And Nix was so much more than that. No words could even begin to describe what he meant to me. But it was temporary. Precarious and fragile. A Band-Aid on a wound I feared would never heal.

The tears came harder, faster as emotion crashed over me. Anger. Sadness. Love. Desperation. Hopelessness... Hope.

It was exhausting to feel so much and nothing at all. To be overwhelmed and somehow numb all at the same time.

I needed to confront Michael. If I ever truly wanted to move forward, I needed to face the truth. I needed to call him out on everything and admit that Nix was a part of my life again.

But I wasn't ready.

For all that it meant, all that it would change.

My cell phone vibrated but I ignored it. I didn't want

to speak to anyone right now. Sobs wracked my body as I embraced the memories, all the pain and anguish.

I could still remember that night like it was yesterday. How smooth and cold the razor felt in my fingers, the way it slid into my skin like butter. The blood. So much bright-red blood, dripping down my hand like the tears dripping down my cheeks.

But I'd survived.

That was what I held onto. When the days got too hard and the nights were endlessly dark, I clung to the good things. The little things.

To the hazy dreams I'd once had.

Because if I let them slip away…

"I'm here, B." Strong arms wrapped around me, and Nix dipped his chin to my shoulder, hugging me tight. "I'm right here."

"N-Nix?" His name was a whisper on my lips.

"I'm here," he said, kissing my cheek, letting his mouth linger. "I'm here."

"How did you know I was out here?" A shiver went through me.

"I told you, B. I'll always find you." I gazed up at him and he smiled. "Always."

26

NIX

HARLEIGH'S EYES FLUTTERED CLOSED AS I HELD HER. SO tightly I wasn't sure I would ever let her go.

When Max's text had come through, I'd made my excuses and left Buster's, running at least two red lights to get here.

Harleigh needed me.

And there wasn't anywhere else I'd rather be.

She turned in my arms, sliding her hands up my chest as she gazed up at me. "You're here."

"I'm here." I brushed the hair stuck to her damp cheeks away and traced my fingers down the planes of her face. "Do you want to talk about it?"

"I-I don't know what to say."

"That's okay."

"How did you know? Really?"

"Max texted me."

"He did?"

I nodded. "I asked him to keep an eye on you."

"Why?"

"Because you're my girl, and it fucking kills me that I can't be here for you."

She pulled away, drying her eyes on her sleeves. "I didn't want you to see me like this."

"Shh, B." I kissed her forehead. "You should have called me. I knew something was wrong. I fucking knew it."

"Nix, I…"

Harleigh's cell phone started ringing, cutting the tension around us. "It's probably Celeste." She dug it out of her pocket and nodded.

"You should answer her. She'll be worried."

"I'll text her." Harleigh began typing furiously, and then her eyes drifted to mine. Fuck, the lost expression on her face slayed me.

"Come on," I said. "Let's get out of here."

She glanced back toward her father's estate and irritation skittered up my spine.

"I can take you ba—"

"No, no. I don't want to be there." Her eyes silently pleaded with me.

"Come on." Wrapping my arm around her shoulder, I led Harleigh back to my car. I'd parked it out of sight as much as I could, wanting to save her anymore trouble.

"In you go." I yanked open the passenger door and eased her inside.

She seemed so sad… so empty and detached. It scared the fuck out of me.

Raking a hand through my hair, I blew out a strained

breath as I rounded my car and climbed in. "You good?" I asked her, and she nodded, gnawing the end of her thumb.

I didn't believe her, but we couldn't stay out here. Not so close to her father's estate.

So I fired up the engine, pulled a U-turn and headed straight out of Old Darling Hill with only one place in mind.

THE MILL WAS the same as the last time we'd been here, except things felt more strained between us. Harleigh had barely said two words on the ride over, staring out of the window like a statue.

It was unnerving to see her so quiet and still.

I pulled over by the building and cut the engine. "B, look at me," I said softly.

It was enough to coax her out of her trance and she blinked up at me. "Yeah?"

"Do you want to go inside?"

"O-okay." She nodded and I studied her for a second, but she seemed to look right past me. Through me.

Shouldering the door, I went around to her side and helped her out. She gripped my hand tightly as we walked toward the building. I didn't like it: the silence, the utter feeling of helplessness coursing through me. I wanted to help her—to *fix* her—but as I was quickly learning, it wasn't that simple.

Usually when I had a problem, I sorted it with words or actions, or sometimes even my fists. But Harleigh's demons weren't some living, breathing thing I could fight for her. Some monster I could slay.

The second we reached the office and slipped inside, my heart rate kicked up a gear. The last time we'd been here, I'd had her naked and under me, and it was really fucking hard not to let my mind wander to that night.

"Tell me what you need, B. What can I do?"

"Just… lie with me." She sounded so drained, so empty. It was like a bullet through my heart.

We laid down and I pulled her into my arms, resting my chin on her head as she rested her cheek on my chest.

"I'm sorry," she said. "That I'm not normal. That I don't—"

"Stop. Stop right there." I gently gripped her chin, tilting her face up to mine. "You have nothing to apologize for. Not a damn thing."

Harleigh's lip wobbled but she fought against the tears threatening to fall, swallowing them down.

"Shh, B. Don't cry. Please, don't cry." I leaned in, kissing the end of her nose. Her eyelids flickered closed, and I kissed those too, sliding my mouth over her clammy skin.

Harleigh inhaled a ragged breath, her entire body shuddering.

"I got you," I whispered, my voice breaking. "I got you."

Slowly, Harleigh's breathing evened out and I realized she'd fallen asleep.

What the fuck had happened?

I managed to dig my cell phone out of my pocket and one-handedly texted Max.

Me: What the hell happened?

**Max: She got into it this morning with my mom
and dad...**

SHIT.

I should have known it would be something to do
with Michael. I would have known if she'd told me.

Gazing down at her, I ground my teeth together,
trying to make some of the tension dissipate.

Harleigh didn't need to protect me from this. Didn't
she realize I'd walk over burning hot coals if it meant
protecting her. Standing at her side.

She let out a small whimper, nestling closer. I smiled.
Even in her dreams she reached for me. That's what I
wanted; that's how it was supposed to be.

Another text came through.

Max: Is she okay?

Me: Honestly, I don't know.

Max: If you need anything...

Me: I can handle it.

I STILL HADN'T FIGURED Max out, but he seemed genuinely concerned.

And I didn't know if it was a good thing...

Or a bad thing.

TWO HOURS, twenty-three minutes, and ten seconds. That's how long I lay there, holding her.

My arm was dead, my neck ached, and I was slowly losing feeling in my toes, but she was worth it.

She was worth every long second.

"N-Nix?" she murmured, rousing beside me.

"Hey," I said with a faint smile. "How are you feeling?"

"Embarrassed." She flushed. "I'm so sorry I—"

"What did I tell you, B? No apologies. Not now, not ever." I swept my thumb along her cheek. "You should have told me." She frowned, so I added, "About Michael and Sabrina."

"I... I didn't know how."

Because for nine months she'd believed I'd abandoned her. For nine months, Harleigh had believed she was all alone in the world.

"Do you want to talk about it?" I asked.

"I'd rather not. And not because I don't trust you or I don't want to share things with you, Nix. I do. I swear. I just... it makes me so angry. I'm scared of what could happen if I... if I let myself keep reliving it."

Tears welled in her eyes again, and I leaned down,

cupping her face and kissing each brow. A violent shudder rolled through her as Harleigh gripped my hoodie.

"You came for me," she whispered.

"Well yeah, you're my girl, B." *I'll always come for you.*

Silence settled between us, but it was lighter now. Strained but lighter. The need to fix this, to fix her still burned through me, gnawing my bones like acid. But there was no magic cure, no quick antidote for this. It was a part of who she was. Just another part for me to love, to understand and cherish.

Because all of Harleigh's parts, even the broken ones, made her who she was today. And there wasn't a single inch of her I didn't adore.

"How are you feeling? About the game?"

I gazed down at her. "It's just a game, Harleigh." *You're more important.*

"We both know that's not true, Nix. It's your chance to get out of this place. This life." Exhaustion clung to her words making them heavy.

"Can I tell you something?" I whispered.

Harleigh turned to me, putting us face to face. "Anything." She smiled. A small uncertain smile, but it was enough.

Enough that I said, "Going to college... leaving The Row... playing for Albany U... it all fucking terrifies me."

"It does?" No judgment shone in her eyes, only mild surprise.

"Yeah. It freaks me the fuck out."

"But you're so good, Nix."

"Here. I'm good here. But it's college, B. What if I don't fit in there? What if I'm not good enough?"

What if I was the boy with the sad life story? The outcast? The charity case?

She leaned up, touching her head to mine and inhaled a shaky breath. "Isn't it better to have tried than to always wonder what if?"

A small chuckle left my lips. "You make it sound so easy."

"You're good enough, Nix." Her eyes drilled into mine, the flecks of dark green hypnotic. "And you're worthy. You deserve this. You deserve a shot at something good, something better."

"You do too, you know? You deserve the world." And I wanted to give it to her.

"I can't see that far yet." She dropped her gaze, leaving a cold chill in my veins.

"Birdie, look at me." I angled her face to mine. "If you can't see it yet, I'll see it for the both of us."

"You promise?"

"I promise. Can I… kiss you?"

Harleigh nodded and my heart stuttered in my chest. Leaning in, I brushed my lips over hers, tracing them with my tongue. "Open up for me, B. Let me in," I murmured, sliding my fingers into her hair, anchoring us together.

We kissed and kissed and kissed. We kissed until my lungs ached and my dick strained painfully behind my sweats. But I didn't push her for more and Harleigh seemed content to get lost in the way our tongues tangled: slow indolent licks chased by teeth and lips and breathless moans.

"Nix," she whispered, pressing her body closer. Tears rolled down her cheeks, dripping between us.

"Don't cry, B." *Please don't cry.* My heart splintered as I dried her eyes and kissed her some more.

"I don't want to be like this… I don't want—"

I kissed her harder, drowning out the words, the roar of blood between my ears.

She was perfect.

Harleigh Wren.

My Birdie.

Mine.

Mine.

Mine.

I just needed her to believe it, to understand that this —*us*—was real. It was worth fighting for.

She was worth it.

"I love you, B." I breathed the words onto her lips. Murmuring them over and over until there was no way on earth she couldn't believe them.

Harleigh broke the kiss and stared at me. Eyes glossy and weary. "I love you too," she whispered.

Her words sank into me, filling the cracks, smoothing the sharp and jagged edges inside me. Her love had always been my salvation.

But as she kissed me again, I couldn't ignore the ball of dread deep inside me.

That maybe love wasn't enough.

A CAR RUMBLED outside alerting us to Celeste's arrival.

"She got here quick," I grumbled.

I'd wanted to be the one to take Harleigh back, but she'd insisted that Celeste come. To protect me? To avoid the giant fucking elephant in the room? I didn't know. But it irritated me that I wasn't the one driving her home.

"We should go," Harleigh said, trying to pull out of my embrace. I tugged her back to me though, pulling her between my legs.

"You sure you're good?" I cupped the back of her neck and searched her eyes.

She nodded. "Thank you for coming for me and for—"

"Harleigh? Nix?" Celeste's voice echoed through the building.

"In here," Harleigh called, and I bristled, a spike of jealousy shooting through me.

This was our space. *Ours*. I wasn't sure I wanted to share it with anyone. Least of all Celeste.

"Oh my God," she said, coming inside. "This is... so freaking cute." But the second her gaze landed on her sister, the blood drained from her cheeks. "Oh, Harleigh."

Celeste pulled Harleigh into her arms and out of mine. I ran a hand down my face, trying to rein in the urge to pull her back. To wrap my arm around her and dismiss Celeste.

Harleigh needed friends. She needed people in her life. People who could be there when I couldn't and Celeste was *family*. Even if it turned me inside out that I had to rely on others to do what I couldn't, I had to try to accept that.

"I'm okay," Harleigh said, stepping out of Celeste's embrace.

"I've been so worried. When Max called—"

"He called you?" Harleigh balked.

"Weird, right? I don't know what you did to him." Celeste looked at me. "But it's like he's had a personality transplant."

I shrugged. "So long as he's on our side, he's good with me."

She studied me and murmured, "Interesting. You ready to go?" Celeste laced her arm through Harleigh's.

"Yeah." Bewitching green eyes settled on me. "I'll see you tomorrow?"

"Listen, you don't have to come to the game. There's no pressure."

"I'll be there." Something flickered across her face.

"Yeah?"

"Yeah." Harleigh smiled, and this time it wasn't shy or uncertain, but full of determination.

Of fight.

My girl was still in there, fighting, pushing herself.

"Bye, Nix," she whispered.

"Bye, B."

I watched as she and Celeste left. She didn't spare me a second glance back and it wrecked something inside me. But then she burst into the room and flung her arms around my neck, kissing the shit out of me.

"I love you, Phoenix Wilder," she breathed. "Always."

My heart swelled so big I thought it might explode right out of my chest.

I gripped her tight, burying my face in the crook of her neck, breathing her in.

I love you too, Harleigh Wren Maguire.

Always.

27

HARLEIGH

"You're sure you're okay?" Nix asked me for the third time today.

It was Friday.

Game day.

One of the most important days of Nix's life, and I'd almost messed it all up.

All day, butterflies had fluttered in my stomach, making my skin vibrate. If someone asked me to recite today's classes, I wouldn't have been able to tell them a single thing. All I could think about, all I could focus on, was holding myself together enough to support Nix.

Celeste didn't think it was a good idea. Nate neither. But I needed to be there. I needed to dig deep and go.

It was all arranged. Chloe would meet me and Celeste at the back entrance once most of the crowd was seated, and then we would sneak under the bleachers and watch from there.

It wasn't ideal, not when Nix deserved to have someone in the stands watching him, cheering him on. But it was the compromise I could handle. Would handle, for him.

"I told you twice already," I chuckled, "I'm fine."

"B, you don't have to protect me, I can handle the truth…"

"Don't you have a game to prepare for? Coach will tear you a new one if you're late."

"You're really coming?"

"Yes, I'll be right there. I promise."

"Okay." He let out a steady breath but all I heard was the relief there. "I'm not making a huge fucking mistake, am I?"

"Why would you even say that, Nix?"

"Because it's college, B. A scholarship. Guys like me—"

"Guys like you deserve a chance. They deserve a shot at a better future."

"Fuck, I love you. You know that, right? No matter what happens tonight at the game or when people find out… it won't change how I feel about you."

His words rumbled through me like thunder in the distance.

"I know. Now go. You have like ten minutes to get there."

"Shit, yeah, okay. I'll see you later."

"Good luck," I said, my stomach churning. "And Nix?"

"Yeah, B?"

"I love you."

His breath caught and my smile grew.

"Love you too."

He hung up and I clutched my cell phone in my hand.

I'd agreed to go to the game, but only if he agreed to go celebrate with the guys for a little while after. He hadn't wanted to say yes, but little did he know, I had a plan.

A reckless, terrifying plan.

But I hadn't been lying the other day when I told him I was tired of everything. The lies, deceits, and half-truths.

The betrayal.

Last night, lying in Nix's arms, listening to him confess his fears, had made me realize something. It made me realize that being afraid was okay. That not being able to control everything was okay. Being scared didn't make you weak. It was what you did with that fear that determined what kind of person you were.

You could drown in it, let it suffocate and ruin you. Or you could fight against the tide and face it head on.

And anything worth having was worth fighting for.

Friendship.

Success.

Happiness.

Love.

None of it came easy and there would always be slip ups along the way. Because life was messy and hard and it hurt sometimes.

But I was still here, and in my own way, I was fighting.

Every single day I got out of bed, I was fighting.

A knock sounded on my door. "Harleigh," Celeste called. "We need to leave soon."

"Almost ready." I glanced at myself in the mirror.

The girl staring back at me was beautiful. She was strong. She was fearless. And yeah, maybe she was a little bit broken, but it was our scars that made us unique. That reminded us of where we'd been and how far we'd come.

Celeste shoved her head around the door and grinned. "I'm so proud of you."

I frowned. "Thanks, I think."

"I'm serious." She came inside and closed the door. "You didn't let yourself slip."

"I'm not sure about that…"

"I can't claim to know what it's like for you, Harleigh, but I witnessed it. I was there. And I've watched you battle every day to get to where you are now. I know Mom and Dad both said some things—"

"Don't." My voice shook.

"Sorry, I didn't mean… I know it's hard. But you stood up to them and it didn't break you. Be proud of that. Be proud of yourself. I am." Celeste wrapped me into her arms. "You're strong, Harleigh. Stronger than you give yourself credit for. And I don't know what will happen tomorrow or the day after that, but I've been thinking." She pulled away to look at me. "I think you should tell them."

"Celeste—"

"Just hear me out, okay? It's real, Harleigh. What you and Nix have, it's real. And he's never going to let you go, not again. I've seen the way he is around you. The longer you keep it a secret, the harder it's going to be to tell them."

"He threatened Nix, Celeste." I gawked at her with disbelief.

"I know, but it was different then. You weren't yourself and I honestly think he was trying to protect you. From Nix and from yourself."

I tried to see you.

His words continued to haunt me.

"Maybe if you explained… maybe if he saw the two of you together—"

"I-I can't do this right now. I need to focus on the game." On Nix.

Thinking about my father, about the tense conversation we'd had the other day unnerved me. And I needed all the strength I could get if I was going to walk into Darling Hill High and watch the Hawks.

"Of course." She gave me an apologetic smile. "We can talk about it another time."

Another time.

Never. I *never* wanted to talk about it.

But Celeste was right, I had to face him one day.

Nix wasn't my dirty little secret, he wasn't. It wasn't about that. But he deserved more. He deserved to be loved out in the open. To be adored and cherished and made to feel worthy. But I was so scared of what going public would mean for us. Terrified that the pressure, the judgment that would no doubt come, would crack my already fragile shell. And if it did… would Nix want to stick around to piece me back together?

You know he would. He promised.

"Harleigh?"

I blinked at Celeste, panic swelling in the pit of my stomach.

"It's time," she said. "Let's go watch your boy kick some ass." She beamed, and I wished more than anything, that I could feel even a speck of her enthusiasm.

"OH MY GOD, OH MY— *YES*!" Chloe held out her hand and Celeste high fived it, the two of them completely in their element.

Even from our shadowy little corner under the bleachers, it hadn't dampened their mood. But I was too tense to celebrate. Every time Nix got the ball, those few precious seconds where he decided what to do— pass or run—I held my breath, gripping the chair beneath me.

He was a thing to behold. An unforgiving storm that the opposing defense couldn't break. If they knocked him down, he got straight back up. Strong, sturdy, and one-hundred-and-ten percent focused. I didn't think too hard about the fact he'd looked for me before kick-off. Searching the dark recess under the raucous crowd. The second our eyes had collided, it was like time had stopped.

The same way my heart had.

Only, time had restarted but I wasn't entirely sure my heart would beat again until the final whistle blew.

"They've got this." Chloe clutched my arm, grinning. "Your boy did good."

"So good," Celeste added as we sat poised to watch their final play.

Blood pounded in my ears, the leading rhythm to the rising cacophony of the crowd.

"I feel sick," I said to no one in particular.

"They've got the win," Chloe said. "You don't need to worry."

But I couldn't help it. Because every time I saw a group of blue and yellow players racing toward Nix, the knot in my stomach twisted violently.

The Hawks moved into their positions along the scrimmage line, but I only had eyes for Nix. He looked so fine in his tight white pants and the magenta and black jersey. He began yelling plays, trying to stupefy the opposition.

Somewhere above us was a scout from Albany U, watching. Assessing. Weighing Nix's future in the palm of his hands.

Nix had played with everything he had. Commanded his team and held the crowd on a breath's edge. He had it. Whatever it was, Nix had it in spades, and sitting there, I knew I was watching a star being born.

"Go. *GO!*" Chloe yelled, yanking me from my reverie. I hadn't even realized the whistle had blown, too lost in what-ifs and maybes.

"Yes, yes... go... run. RUN!" Celeste was practically bouncing in her seat, the crowd above us cheering on their star quarterback.

"Touchdooooooown," the announcer bellowed through the PA system and the place exploded, making me flinch.

The team jogged straight for Nix, jumping on him,

and jostling him as they celebrated. But he fought them all off, his eyes frantically searching for me.

Without thinking, I stood and began walking to the edge of the bleachers. My heart was a wild beating thing in my chest. Nix was already halfway to me when he spotted me. He paused at the edge of the field and slowly pulled his helmet off, shaking the sweat from his hair. The corners of my mouth tipped up as I watched him watch me. He didn't move another inch, waiting. Giving me the choice.

Stay in the shadows or walk into the light.

But I needed to do this—I needed him to know I was here and that I supported him and believed in him.

I believed him in so freaking much.

The second I moved, he moved too, the two of us crashing into one another as he picked me up and kissed me. "You're here," he breathed.

"I'm here. And you were good, Nix. You were so damn good." I clung onto him, not daring to look anywhere but at him.

"You're shaking," he said, leaning back to look at me.

"I…" Heat flooded my cheeks as I realized people were watching us. Not everyone because of the angle of where I stood but enough to make my skin crawl.

Nix noticed and moved into the exit a little, giving us limited privacy.

"You came." Awe coated his words.

"I promised I would."

"Nix, son," Coach Farringdon appeared on our periphery. "Miss Maguire," he acknowledged me with a tight nod. "Nix, the scout wants to talk to you."

Nix didn't take his eyes off me as he said, "Yeah, okay."

"Go," I urged when he made no move to put me down. "You need to go."

"Later," he whispered. "You and me and—"

"Let's go, Wilder," Coach barked, heading back to his team.

"I think he's mad," I whispered.

"Don't give a shit." Nix kissed me again before lowering me to the ground. "I'll call you as soon as we get done."

I nodded, not trusting myself to speak, sinking back into the safety of the shadows.

'I love you,' he mouthed, waiting.

"I swear to God, Wilder. Get—"

"Coming, Coach." With a cocky smirk, Nix jogged away.

Chloe and Celeste each laced their arm through one of mine and Celeste shrieked, "That. Was. Epic."

"She's right, Harleigh," Chloe added. "I didn't know you had it in you."

Neither did I.

But the night wasn't over yet…

And I still had one thing left to do.

28

NIX

"NIX, REMEMBER DARRAH O'KEEFE?"

I dragged my sweaty palm down my thigh and held it out. "Hello, sir. It's nice to see you again."

"You looked impressive out there tonight, Nix. Exactly the kind of talent we're looking to bring into our program."

"I... t-thanks." I stuttered over the giant fucking lump in my throat and Coach glared at me as if to say, 'Don't fuck this up.'

"Coach Farringdon seems to think you've had a change of heart regarding your future." Darrah regarded me, his heavy gaze making me wish the ground would open and swallow me up.

"I... uh, yeah. I think so."

"Think so? This isn't high school football, Phoenix. Albany U is a Division 1 school with a program a lot of guys would chew my arm off for a shot at."

"I know, I'm sorry, sir. I just… I didn't ever expect to have this kind of opportunity." I ran a hand through my hair and down the back of my neck, wishing like hell that Harleigh was here.

But she'd come. She came and she met me halfway. It was more than I could have ever hoped for.

She came.

I let the lingering feel of her touch ground me. The way she'd clung to me as if I was her life raft as much as she was mine.

Harleigh was always with me, even when she wasn't.

Inhaling a deep breath, I collected my thoughts and cleared my throat. "Sorry, sir. What I meant to say was…"

I could do this.

I'd earned this.

My old man. Jessa. My shitty childhood. Michael Rowe. The world's opinion of a guy like me. It didn't mean anything. Not unless I let it.

"You're good enough, Nix." Her eyes drilled into mine, the flecks of dark green hypnotic. "And you're worthy. You deserve this. You deserve a shot at something good, something better."

Harleigh's words echoed inside me as I said, "What I meant to say was I'm honored you're thinking of me, sir."

Coach Farringdon nodded his approval, clapping Darrah on the shoulder. "You saw his skill on the field, but what you don't get to see is the fact that this kid always shows up. No matter what is going on in his life, he leaves all the bullshit at the door and gets the job done."

"Glad to hear it." Darrah smiled. "We'll be in touch,

Nix. Arrange for you to come up to Albany real soon and meet the team."

"Wow, that would be… wow."

Holy shit. Was this really happening?

Coach had always told me it was a possibility; that Albany had made inquiries about me before now, but I hadn't wanted to believe it. Hadn't *dared* let myself believe it.

But this was real. It was real and I had a shot, an honest-to-God shot, and I didn't know what the fuck to do with that.

"Don't look so shocked, son," Coach said, a glint of pride in his eyes. "You deserve this, Nix."

You deserve it.

Three little words I'd always had a real hard time believing. But maybe it was time I started.

Albany U was my ticket out of here. It was my ticket to a better life for me and Harleigh.

Fuck.

It was more than I could ever have hoped for.

I just had to want it.

I just had to reach out and take it.

***

"Nix, that's amazing. I'm so proud of you."

I knew Harleigh was smiling, it was in every softly spoken syllable, every vowel.

"I'm thinking of blowing off the thing with the guys and coming to meet you now. I want us to celebrate together."

"You can't do that," she rushed out. "They're expecting you to be there."

"Jeez, don't sound so desperate to see me or anything."

She chuckled, the sound soothing some of the dejection I felt at her easy dismissal. "I can't wait to see you, but you should celebrate with them too. It's only an hour or two."

"One, tops," I grumbled, throwing the rest of my things into my bag. The locker room was almost empty, the frenzied crowd already moved on to the party down at the res.

To them it was just another night. Another excuse to get fucked and get fucked up. But to me and my guys, it meant more.

"You're sure I can't persuade you to meet me now?" My lips quirked thinking about all the ways she could help me celebrate. Preferably naked and underneath me.

"Two hours."

"B," I warned, a lick of frustration rolling up my spine.

"You don't have to sacrifice your time with me," she said. "I'm hanging out with Chloe and Celeste."

"You're having fun?"

"I am actually. Tonight has been good for me."

"Yeah?" I smiled. It was all I wanted. Her, happy.

"Go, spend some time with the guys. I'll see you later."

"You're sure?"

"Positive. Now go. Before they—"

"Yo, Wilder," Kye said right on cue. His face appeared around the door, and he grinned. "Are we gonna get the hell out of here? This tequila won't drink itself."

"Tequila?" I balked. "I thought I said to grab some beers."

"You did, but we're celebrating."

I grabbed my bag and joined him. "I can't get trashed, I'm meeting Harleigh later."

"Relax, *Dad*." He slung his arm around my shoulder and guided me down the hall. "I'll make sure you get to your girl in one piece."

"No funny business, Carter." I cocked my brow at him. "I mean it."

"Seriously, Nix. You're gonna be a Falcon. This is huge fucking news. Even if you don't get fucked up, I am." He leaped in front of me and gripped the back of my neck, staring me dead in the eye. "You're going to college, man. Fucking college."

"They haven't made the offer yet."

"No, but we all know they will. You've got it, Nix. You've got what it takes to get out of here and go all the way. And I'm proud of you. I'm so fucking proud."

"Alright, *Mom*." I shoved him away, laughing off the tense moment. "Grab a tissue. I think you have a tear right"—I reached for his face—"there."

"Fuck you, Wilder. Fuck. You. I'm over here trying to be all serious and shit and you're acting like it's a joke."

"What's a joke?" Zane hopped off the hood of my car as we burst through the doors.

"Kye's acting like a proud mama bear," I teased, and he flipped me off, grumbling something about not bothering to support me next time.

"Did he have a moment?" Zane smirked.

"Fuck you, assholes, I'll keep the tequila to myself." He

ducked inside the back seat of my car and Zane and I climbed in the front.

"You sure you want to head to the res?" Zane asked me, and I shrugged, jamming the key into the ignition.

"Harleigh wants me to celebrate with you guys."

"She should be there," Kye said.

"She's not ready."

"She seemed pretty ready earlier after the game." Zane snorted, and I pinned him with a hard look. "Relax, I'm joking. It was good to see her step out of the shadows for once."

"Yeah." My lips twitched. It had been pretty fucking epic, not that many people had seen us. And the few that had, knew me better than to make a big deal out of it.

Fuck, I just wanted to see her. Not go and party with the team.

"One hour," I said, firing up the car. "You get one hour and then I'm out of there."

THE PARTY WAS in full swing by the time we arrived. A loud chorus of cheers filled the air as we weaved our way through the crowd. Hench, Gunner, and a few of the other guys from the team descended on me and before I knew it, someone had a cup of some disgusting concoction in my hand.

"Fuck that," I said, staring at the funky looking drink.

"Come on, Wilder. We're celebrating. It's not every day a Hawk lands himself a D1 scholarship."

"I haven't got it yet."

"You're a sure thing," someone shouted. "At least, that's what all the girls say."

The crowd snickered and I scowled.

"From what I saw earlier," Hench chimed in. "Wilder is officially off the market. The question is, who was the little hottie waiting on the sidelines for him? Huh?" His eyes flashed to mine, and he smirked.

"Fuck off," I mouthed at him. He chuckled, draining his beer.

"Well, don't just stand there, Wilder," Gunner grinned. "Drink it."

"*Drink it, drink it,*" they all began to chant. I glanced at Zane and Kye for a little back up, but the two of them only smirked.

Traitorous fuckers.

"One hour," I pinned them with a dark look before bringing the cup to my lips and downing it in one.

"Motherfucker," I hissed, the liquor burning the whole way down. Everyone cheered, and someone thrust a beer into my hands, so I washed away the bitter taste.

"No more surprises," I said to no one in particular, but the crowd was already dispersing.

We headed for our regular spot by the bonfire, and I sank into one of the chairs, sipping on my beer.

"You want?" Zane waved a blunt in front of me, and I shook my head.

"Light it up," Kye said. "I'll smoke and drink his share."

"Greedy fucker," I murmured, digging out my cell and checking it for a message from Harleigh.

"Seriously? We only just got here." Zane rolled his eyes.

"One day, Z. I swear to God, bro. One day a girl is going to swoop in and knock you on your ass and I'm going to love every second of it."

"Never gonna happen."

"Famous last words," Kye drawled, taking a deep hit on the blunt. "You sure you don't want a—"

"I'm good." I wasn't here to get wasted and high. I was here to show my face, spend some time with my guys, and then get the fuck back to my girl.

Pulling up our chat history, I typed out a new message.

Me: Fifty minutes and counting.

JESUS, I was whipped. And I gave the sum total of zero fucks about it.

I waited for her witty reply, but it never came.

"She's with the girls. Stop being so overbearing," Zane grumbled.

"I'm not—"

He leveled me with a look that said, 'You sure about that?'

"Duty calls." Kye drained his beer and leaped up.

"Duty—let me guess, the blonde," I said, spotting the girl who had caught his eye.

"You would be correct. See you two fuckers later. Z, look after our guy."

"I'm surprised his dick hasn't fallen off," Zane said the second Kye was out of earshot.

"At least he's putting his to good use," I countered, and he narrowed his eyes at me.

"I get pussy."

"Didn't say you didn't." My lips curved.

"Whatever, asshole. I'm going to grab some more beer." He got up and disappeared into the sea of bodies. I checked my cell phone again, my vision blurring a little. I rubbed my eyes, trying to stave off the effects of the alcohol.

What the fuck had been in that drink?

"Everything okay?" a soft voice said, and I glanced up to find Cherri looming over me.

"Hey," I said.

"Good game tonight."

"Thanks."

"Is it true? What they're saying about Albany U?"

"If it works out."

"That's great news, Nix."

She went to move around me, but her foot caught mine and she tripped. I just managed to grab her before she went flying.

Cherri landed with a little *oomph*, right in my lap, and wrapped her arms around my neck. "My hero." She grinned.

"Cher," I warned, my hands settling on her hips, ready to move her off my lap.

"Come on, Nix. I just want to congratulate you. Is that so bad?" Her eyes dipped to my mouth, one of her hands running up my chest.

"Cherri." I sucked in a sharp breath, my head a little cloudy. "Don't do this."

"Do what?" She gazed at me. Big bright eyes full of seduction and sin. "It's only a little celebration kiss." Leaning closer, she pinned me to the chair. "What's the worst that can happen?"

29

HARLEIGH

The music thrummed through me like a second heartbeat as I followed Chloe through the crowd. Some people stared, trying to piece together where they knew me from. No doubt wondering if they were seeing a ghost. But most of them ignored me, too interested in their conversations, their drinks and drugs, the boy or girl all over them.

It was always overwhelming being here. One of them yet not.

I'd forgotten just how out of place I'd always felt amongst my classmates, especially here.

"This is wild," Celeste yelled over the music, squeezing my hand with a mix of reassurance and excitement. I doubted she'd ever been to a party like this in Old Darling Hill.

"Maybe you should have texted him." She leaned in closer as we fought our way through the sea of people.

"I wanted to surprise him."

It had seemed like a good idea at the time, but now I wasn't so sure.

"Oh my God, is that Kye?" She flicked her head over to a quieter spot where sure enough Kye was making out with some blonde girl, his hand shoved under her skirt.

"Don't tell Chloe," I whispered, but she swung around. "Don't tell Chlo— oh my God, my eyes. My fucking eyes. Make it stop… make it—"

We pounced on her, covering her eyes and pulling her away, our laughter drowned out by the noise.

This wasn't so bad, being here with them. Knowing I was about to be with Nix.

I couldn't wait to see his face when he spotted me. Especially after I'd heard the disappointment in his voice earlier.

"Oh shit," Chloe drew to a stop, and we slammed into her.

"What's—" The air sucked clean from my lungs as I spotted them.

Cherri Jardin curled on Nix's lap, their faces pressed close together.

It was like a slow-motion car crash. You knew what was coming, but you couldn't look away. My hand flew out, clutching Celeste's arm as Cherri dipped her face, brushing her lips against his. Kissing him.

She was *kissing* him.

And he just sat there. His hands on her hips, her hand on his chest, the other locked around his neck.

"Oh my God." Bile rushed up my throat, burning.

"Harleigh," someone said. But I stumbled back,

needing to get away. Needing to not see a single second more. "Harleigh, it isn't what—"

"Go," I blurted, tears stinging my eyes. "I need to go. Celeste, get me out of here, please."

She wrapped her arm around me, shielding me as she ushered me back through the crowd. "Breathe," she said. "You need to breathe."

But I couldn't breathe, I couldn't get any air into my lungs as the image of Cherri all over Nix seared into my mind.

He wouldn't…

He wouldn't betray me like that.

Yet he was right there, and she was—

I retched again, Celeste guiding me away from the party.

Someone yelled after us, but it wasn't Nix.

He didn't come.

He didn't come.

"WE'RE ALMOST HOME," Celeste said, squeezing my hand gently. She hadn't let go of me the whole ride back.

But I was numb.

Flayed open and raw, bleeding out all over her fifty-thousand-dollar car.

"You know, you need to hear him out. Chloe said—"

"It doesn't matter."

"What do you mean it doesn't matter? You love him, and he loves you, Harleigh. You know he does."

I shrugged, refusing to meet her eyes, pressing my head against the cool glass.

"Harleigh, don't do this. You know girls like Cherri, girls like Ange…"

"You're right," my voice was icy cold. "I do. And that's what I can expect if we stay together."

"What on earth do you mean?" The gates to the estate rolled open and she pulled into the driveway, cutting the engine. "Harleigh, look at me." Reluctantly, I did, and she added, "Talk to me. I'm begging you."

"You know I was never strong enough to stand at his side. Not then, and definitely not now."

"Harleigh, that's not—"

"It is." I sighed, a deep ache spreading through my chest. "I'm broken, Celeste. Maybe I'll always be broken. And Nix, he's going places. He can make it out of The Row and chase his dreams. What kind of girl would I be if I held him back with all my… my baggage."

"He loves you."

"Maybe love isn't enough."

I was pretty sure love wasn't supposed to hurt this much. To build you up only to break you down.

"You don't mean that."

"All I know is I'm tired, Celeste. I'm so freaking tired. Of always second guessing everything. Of always being the girl who hides. The girl who doesn't know how to go after what she wants. Nix deserves more. He deserves someone like Cherri—"

"Have you lost your goddamn mind?" she shrieked, silencing me. "I'm sorry, I didn't mean to shout." Guilt shone in her eyes. "But you have no idea how lucky you are, do you?"

"Lucky? You think I'm *lucky*?" A bitter laugh bubbled inside me.

"No, that's not… Look, I know you went through something awful, and I know you have a lot of stuff to work through still, but you found your way back to him, Harleigh. That has to count for something, doesn't it? Forget about Cherri and Marc and Max and Dad and Nix's dad… it isn't about them. It's about you. About what *you* want. About how *you* feel."

"I want to go inside," I said, dropping my gaze.

"Harleigh, just promise me you'll hear him out."

I barely managed a nod before pushing open the door and making a beeline for the house.

"Harleigh?" I almost walked straight into Michael. "I wasn't expecting you back so— what happened?"

"Nothing." I shouldered past him and headed for the stairs.

"Harleigh Wren—"

"Dad, leave it," Celeste said as I hurried up the stairs, their voices becoming nothing but low rumbles, lost to the ringing in my ears.

The second I reached my room, I slipped inside and slammed the door, inhaling a shuddering breath.

The tears came then.

Big ugly sobs that wrecked me from the inside out as I laid down on my bed, clutching a pillow and giving myself over to the intense emotions.

Celeste was right. I needed to hear Nix out. He wouldn't betray me like that. But the rational part of my brain couldn't withstand the onslaught of irrational thoughts. Those dark, dark whispers of betrayal and deceit.

I wasn't good enough for Nix. Not pretty or strong enough. I didn't dress like the cheerleaders or bat my eyelashes and show my cleavage. I didn't dye my hair or wear a ton of makeup. I wasn't sexy or feminine and I didn't know the art of seduction. I wasn't—

A knock at my bedroom door startled me.

"Harleigh?"

"Go away," I murmured.

"I'm coming in." The door cracked open, and Michael filled the space. "What happened?"

"I don't want to talk about it."

"That isn't your decision. If something upset you, I need to—"

"Let me guess, you want to make sure I'm not a risk to myself."

"Are you?"

Unbelievable.

That's what our relationship had been reduced to. A father checking on his unstable daughter to ascertain whether or not she was about to do something stupid.

"Don't worry, *Dad*, I'm not going to try to kill myself again, if that's what you're worried about."

"Harleigh." He had the decency to look shocked. "That isn't fair."

"Fair?" I bolted upright. "You think any of this is fair? You did this to me, you know? You broke me… You took away the one person I needed and made me believe he'd abandoned me, and I hate you for it. I'll always hate—"

"You know." The blood drained from his face.

"I know." My voice wasn't my own. "I know everything. It wasn't enough that I'd lost my mom, my home; you took him away from me and then watched me fall apart."

"Harleigh, that's not—"

"I LOVED HIM," I roared, something splintering inside me. "I loved him, and you stole him from me. I hate you. I hate you. I hate you. I HATE YOU." The pillow flew across the room, but he easily batted it away.

"Are you—"

"What on earth is happening in here?" Sabrina burst into the room, taking in the scene. Me sitting in a pool of my own tears, my chest heaving. Michael standing there, ashen, and as still as a statue.

"Sweetheart, this doesn't concern you. Go downstairs and I'll be—"

"I will not." She glared at me. "This is all your fault. Ever since you came here, things have been in disarray. You're nothing but a troublemaker, just like your moth—"

"Sabrina!" Michael hissed. "That is enough."

Silence.

Utter silence.

It was usually nice, comforting. Except now, it seeped into the cracks in my heart and made my blood run cold.

Sabrina glowered at me, silently fuming. "I want her gone," she said, swinging her gaze on Michael. "I told you this was a bad idea. Last year, I told you she would ruin things. But you wouldn't listen. And now look at us. She is single-handedly ruining this family and you're just standing by and letting it happen. Well, I won't do it. It's her or me, Michael. I won't live in Trina's shadow for another second. I won't do it."

Her words were like shrapnel, blasting toward me and slicing me open. But I didn't respond. I didn't say or do anything. I just sat there numb, watching their lives unravel around me.

Maybe I should have cared, maybe I should have offered to leave, to give them space to sort out their issues.

But I didn't.

Because Michael hadn't only destroyed her life; he'd destroyed mine.

"Sabrina, please be reasonable."

"Reasonable? *REASONABLE*?" she shrieked like a banshee.

I got up then and walked right past her.

"Where the hell do you think you're going?" she snarled at me.

But I ignored her, walking right out of the room and down the hall. Max was already hanging out of his bedroom, watching. He yanked the door wider as I reached him, and I slipped inside and laid down on his bed.

"Do you need me to call him?"

"N-no. I just… I need to not think for a second." I closed my eyes and curled up into a ball.

As the darkness swept in, I was sure I heard Max whisper, "For what it's worth, I'd choose you over her."

"Harleigh, wake up." Someone nudged me. "Harleigh, wake—"

"I'm awake." I swatted the hand away, cracking an eye open. "What do you want?"

"We have a problem." Celeste's expression was grim, and I sat up, pushing the fine hairs out of my face.

"What's—"

"You cannot go up there, young man," Michael's voice carried down the hall. "If you don't come down here this instant, I'll have no choice, but to call the—"

The door burst open, and Zane appeared, breathless and pale. "Thank fuck."

"Z-Zane?"

"That's the problem I was referring to," Celeste said. I pushed her away and swung my legs over the side of the bed.

"What happened?"

Something was wrong.

"It's Nix. He's at the hospital."

The hospital?

The ground went from under me, and I gripped the sheets to keep myself upright. "What. Happened. Zane?"

"His old man, his old man fucking happened, okay. It's bad, B. It's really fucking bad. He needs you. He needs—"

I jumped up and ran to Zane, pulling him into my arms. "He's okay. He'll be okay."

I didn't know what I was saying, but the idea that he wouldn't... I couldn't think *that.*

I refused to think that.

"Harleigh." The disapproval in Michael's voice made me flinch. "What is going on here?"

"Nix needs me," I said.

"It's the middle of the night. You can't just—"

"Watch me." I stared him down, a deep sense of resolve settling inside me.

"You heard her," Zane said, standing at my side. "I'm sorry I scaled your precious fence and beat down your door, but my best friend is lying in the hospital, and you wouldn't let me speak to B."

I cut Michael with a scathing look. "If you try to stop me, I will never, *ever* forgive you."

"Dad," Max said from his chair over by the window. I hadn't even realized he was in the room. "You should let her go."

"I don't think you're in any position to—"

"Max is right," Celeste said. "In fact, I'm going too. Come on."

"You will do no such thing, young lady."

Michael looked positively flustered and maybe on any other day I would have delighted in it. *Reveled* in it. But not today, not while I knew Nix was hurt.

Celeste stepped forward, putting herself between me and Zane, and her father. "I have always defended you. I have always tried to see things from your point of view. But you're wrong about this. Just like you were wrong when you pulled that crap with Harleigh and Nix last year. Nix is a good guy, and he loves Harleigh, and that is worth something."

He choked on air, clearing his throat as he no doubt

tried to prepare his argument. But I was done waiting for his permission.

"We need to go," I said.

"Go," he said, stepping aside. "We'll follow in our car."

"You're coming?" I gawked at him.

"I'm your father," he said, as if that was any kind of explanation. But I didn't stick around to analyze it. I grabbed Zane's hand and got the hell out of there.

30

NIX

"WHAT THE FUCK ARE YOU DOING?" I TRIED TO SHOVE Cherri away, but she was wrapped around me like a fucking koala.

"Come on, Nix." She dipped her head closer. "It was always so good between us." She trailed her hand down my chest.

"Cherri, I'm serious, get the fuck—"

Her lips crashed down on mine, her tongue plunging into my mouth. "Fucking stupid bitch." I shoved her off me and she landed on her ass, cussing me out.

I tried to stand, but the world spun, and I staggered back into the chair. "Whoa."

"What the hell, Nix?" Another voice shrieked and I strained to see but everything was spinning.

"Clo?" I blinked and blinked again trying to focus.

"What the hell are you doing with her?"

"Who?"

"Cherri, asshole."

"I'm not—"

"I am right here, you know."

"I swear to God, Cherri," Chloe sneered. "If you don't get the fuck out of here, I will—"

Kye scooped his sister up and pulled her out of the line of fire as Cherri staggered to her feet.

"Keep your feral bitch of a sister away from me, Carter. Or I'll—"

Zane appeared. "Don't say something you'll regret."

"Yeah, whatever. My work here is done anyway. Poor little Harleigh Wren sure did look crushed when she saw you all over me. That was pure luck that she turned up to witness the fall of the mighty Phoenix Wilder, but I guess the universe was on my side tonight." She smirked.

My heart stopped, sobering me.

"What did you say?" Ice trickled through my veins.

"You heard me." She sneered. "Did you really think I'd let you just cast me aside without a little payback?" Her smug laughter was like nails down a blackboard. "Oh, you did. Poor baby. I'd planned to seduce you, spread a few rumors, maybe snap a photo or two. But seeing the look on her face when she saw us... so much sweeter. Enjoy the party, assholes."

Cherri sauntered off as if she hadn't just dropped a bomb at my feet.

"Tell me she's lying," I seethed, my body trembling as I clenched my fists at my sides. "Tell me she wasn't here."

"Fuck," Zane hissed.

"Clo?" I asked.

"I'm sorry, Nix. She wanted it to be a surprise."

"Fuck." I shot up, shoving the chair so hard it flipped over. "Fuck." I kicked the damn thing for good measure, pain shooting up my foot and into my leg. "I need to go, right now. I need— whoa." Everything spun again and I stumbled on my feet.

Zane caught me, dragging me to another chair. "Sit there and don't move."

"I need to—"

"Don't. Fucking. Move. I'll get you some water."

"Nix," Chloe kneeled before me. "What happened?"

"I... I don't fucking know. She tripped and—"

"Fell into your lap?" She rolled her eyes.

"Yeah, something like that. Next thing I know, she's kissing me."

"I need to call Harleigh." Pulling out her cell phone, she pressed the screen and waited. "Shit, it's ringing out. I'll try Celeste."

But she didn't answer either.

"I'm going to text her."

"She's long gone," Kye said, wearing a frown. "I saw her, and it didn't look good."

I was out of my chair, fisting his t-shirt. "You saw her, and you didn't—"

"I tried. I fucking tried, okay? But I didn't know what was happening. I didn't know you were making out with Cherri."

"I wasn't..." Fuck, I was.

At least, that's what Harleigh thought she'd seen.

Fuck.

Fuck.

I shoved Kye away and dropped back down in the

chair, defeated. She didn't trust me. Even now, even after everything, Harleigh still didn't trust me. And maybe it wasn't her fault. Maybe it was the part of her brain she had no control over. But it didn't change the fact that she saw me with Cherri and assumed the worst. She didn't even confront me. She just left.

She ran.

She was always running from me.

"Fuck this, I'm out." I got up again and stumbled toward the cars. Chloe and Kye followed me but gave me a wide berth. I could hear them whispering, trying to decide what to do with me. But I shut them out. I shut it all out.

Harleigh had been here.

Now she was gone.

And I didn't know what the fuck to do with her anymore.

"I'M TELLING YOU, Nix, go sleep it off and tomorrow things won't seem so bad." Kye leaned over and squeezed my shoulder.

He'd volunteered to drive when it was apparent I couldn't. Whatever my teammates had put in that drink had knocked me on my ass.

Fucking idiots.

If I hadn't drunk it, maybe I wouldn't be here now. And if Harleigh hadn't tried to surprise me... Who was I kidding? If the universe wasn't dead set on fucking us over, Cherri had planned to do it anyway.

It had happened and we were here instead of being at the mill, wrapped up in each other celebrating.

"Fuck," I murmured, kicking the glove compartment.

"You need to chill the fuck out before you head home."

"What I need, is to talk to Harleigh, but since she won't answer her cell phone and you fucking idiots won't take me over there, I guess I don't have much choice—"

"You'll thank us tomorrow," Zane said.

"Not fucking likely," I grumbled, sending Harleigh another text. Her cell was switched off, but it made me feel better doing something—*anything*—to try to fix the absolute shitshow that had unfolded tonight.

The second the car pulled up outside my trailer, I shouldered the door open.

"Nix, come on, man. Maybe we should—"

"I'll see you tomorrow." I waved them off, needing to be alone.

But the second I stepped into the trailer, I sensed it.

"Jessa?" I called out, a cold ball of dread plunking in my stomach. Silence answered me and I scanned the place for any signs of her.

Nothing.

But something was wrong. I knew it. Too many times, I'd walked in on something bad happening. It was in the eerie calm, the chill in the air.

"Jessa?"

A faint cry came from her bedroom, and I blew down the hall, grabbing the handle and shouldering the door open.

"N-Nix," she squeaked.

"Shit, shit." I rushed to her side, dropping down to the floor and brushing the hair from her barely recognizable face. One side of her face was swollen to the point her eye had closed up.

"He did this?" I seethed, pure rage boiling in my veins.

She nodded, clutching my arm. "D-don't do anything… he'll… please…"

I pulled out my cell phone, but she knocked it out of my hand. "N-no EMTs or police. You can't, Nix… can't…"

I dropped my head, inhaling a sharp breath. This was fucked up. Her face looked shattered, the bruising deep and angry.

"Do you think you can move?" I asked and she nodded again.

"Okay, stay here. I'm going to pack you some things and get you out of here."

Because there was no fucking way I was going to leave her here in this state. He would kill her. One day, my old man would go a step too far and kill her. Unless I could make her see there was a way out.

I swallowed down the tears burning my throat, the backs of my eyes. Jessa needed me to be strong. She needed me to figure this out.

Rushing to their closet, I grabbed the backpack at the bottom and began filling it with her clothes. When there was enough to get her by, I texted Zane and told him to meet me outside in ten.

"We need to go," I said, bending down to wrap my arm around Jessa's waist. She cried out and it was then I noticed the way her arm lay protectively in front of her body.

After helping her to her feet, I slowly lifted her t-shirt, almost puking at the sight of her ribs. She quickly snatched her t-shirt down and wouldn't meet my heavy gaze.

"Come on," I said, barely holding onto my restraint. "Let's get you out of here." Taking most of her weight, we moved through the trailer to the living area.

Neither of us could come back. At least, not tonight. Not until we figured out some things. So I left Jessa sitting on the couch, while I grabbed a bag of my own things.

But when I stepped back into the living area, Jessa wasn't alone.

And my old man gave me a feral grin as he drawled. "Always trying to play the hero, aren't you, kid?"

My eyes flickered open, stars swimming across my vision.

Whoa, that hurts.

Everything fucking hurt.

I inhaled a sharp breath and instantly regretted it, a deep burning pain radiating inside me.

"N-Nix?"

Her voice echoed through me, fisting my heart so tightly I was sure I must be dreaming. But then she was there, looming over me, tears pooled in the corners of her eyes.

"Birdie?" I croaked, my mouth dry and lips sore.

"I'm here," she said, taking my hand. "I'm right here."

"W-what happened?"

I could remember the game. That kiss on the edge of the field after we won. But then everything grew hazy. I could vaguely remember the party—

"You were there," I said, and silent tears began to roll down her cheeks.

"I'm so sorry."

"What? You have nothing to be sorry—" My brows furrowed. "Cherri." Her name clanged through me. "I didn't… Harleigh, B, it wasn't—"

"Shh," she soothed, leaning down to brush her lips over my forehead. "It doesn't matter, none of that matters."

Other memories slammed into me. Fists and insults. Cruel barbed words and a boot to the stomach. Pain, endless swathes of pain as my old man kicked the shit out of me on the trailer floor.

"Jessa… is she?"

"She's okay. She's going to be okay."

"Thank fuck." Some of the panic subsided, but it didn't change the fact that my old man had finally snapped and almost killed her.

And me.

"God, Nix. I was so scared when Zane turned up. All I kept thinking is, I might never get to see you again and things between us were all wrong."

"I didn't kiss Cherri, B. I need you to know that."

"I know. Deep down, I knew you would never betray

me like that. But my thoughts aren't always rational, Nix. I saw the two of you together and I got spooked." Her expression darkened. "If I had only stuck around to hear you out… then maybe none of this would have happened."

"No, we're not doing that. We're not playing the blame game. The only person responsible for this is my old man." I inhaled a ragged, burning breath. "He did this. Him."

She nodded, tears welling in her eyes. "If Zane hadn't gotten to you when he did—" A garbled sob caught in her throat, and I slid my hand around the back of her neck, tugging her down to me.

"You can't think like that. I'm here, B. I'm right here. I love—"

The door opened and my friends peered inside. "About time you woke up. Faker." Kye grinned but I saw the dark shadows under his eyes.

"You look like you've seen better days," I said to him.

"Takes one to know one." He dropped onto one of the bedside chairs. "How's our boy doing, B?"

"He's good." She kissed my head and went to move away, but my grip on her hand tightened.

"Need you up here with me," I said, and she went to argue.

"Just do what he wants," Zane said. "It'll save us all the moaning."

"No one asked you to be here."

"The nurse said company is good for the soul." He smirked and I flipped him off.

Harleigh climbed up on the bed beside me and tucked

herself into my side. "I love you, Nix," she whispered, laying her hand gently on my stomach.

I picked it up and brought it to my lips, kissing her fingertips. Then I laid it over my heart. "I love you too," I whispered, gripping on so tight I never wanted to let go.

31

HARLEIGH

A CONCUSSION. BRUISED RIBS. A BROKEN NOSE AND countless cuts and bruises. Nix was a mess. But he was alive, and he was okay.

I pressed closer into his side, needing to hear the steady beat of his heart. I didn't think I'd ever been so scared as when Zane burst in Max's bedroom and told me Nix was hurt.

"How is he?" Zane and Kye came back into the room, both wearing grim expressions. They'd left earlier when the nurse came to check on Nix, insisting we give her some space to work.

I glanced up at his sleeping form and managed a small smile. "He's okay. He's been out a little while."

"And you, B?" Kye sat in one of the chairs. "How are you doing?"

"I... honestly, I don't know. If I hadn't run—"

"Don't do that to yourself. If it wasn't tonight, it would have been another night."

"We spoke to Jessa," Zane said, running a hand down his face. I'd never seen him look so scared as he had tonight. "Joe's in some hot water with Vince Colombo and it looks like things went sour."

"I know. I was there the morning they got back from NYC. I overheard some stuff…"

"She's done. Whatever Joe did." Zane stared past me, a haunted look in his eye. "He broke something in her this time."

"Yeah, probably when he tried to beat Nix half to death." Kye gritted his teeth, pain flickering in his eyes as he looked at his broken and bruised best friend.

None of us said anything.

What was there to say?

"Your old man's still here?" he asked, and I nodded.

"He's downstairs with Celeste and Max."

Celeste told me earlier that Max had insisted on coming to the hospital with Michael. But the two of them had stayed away so far. Which I was relieved about.

"What a fucking shitshow," Zane murmured. "He knew. Nix always said that one day he'd kill Jessa—or him."

A chill went through me at the severity in his tone.

Nix began to stir, moaning with pain. I stroked his forehead, whispering, "Shh, I'm here. I'm right here."

"Birdie?" His eyes fluttered open.

"Hey, how are you feeling?"

"Like I got hit by a truck."

"Do you want me to call the nurse?"

"No, I'm okay. I have everything I need right here." He lifted his hand and stroked my cheek with his thumb.

Zane made a gagging sound and muttered, "Good to know you're still as pussy-whipped as ever."

Nix flipped him off over my shoulder, and he chuckled.

"How long was I out for?"

"Not quite an hour. I thought the nurse was going to ask me to leave but she didn't."

There was a knock at the door, and we all looked up to find Michael standing there. Nix grew tense, groaning with pain. I went to climb off the bed, but he snagged my wrist, panic flaring in his eyes.

"It's okay," I whispered. "I'll get rid of him."

I didn't know how, but I wasn't leaving Nix. Michael would have to drag me out of here kicking and screaming and I knew he wouldn't appreciate me making a scene.

Before I could get to the door though, Zane was there, glaring at my father. "What the fuck do you want?"

"I came to see my daughter… and to see how Phoenix is doing."

Zane snorted at that. "Yeah, okay."

"Z, man," Nix croaked, and I grabbed him a cup of water.

Michael's heavy stare followed me as I helped Nix sit up and offered him the cup. "I'd like to talk to the two of you if possible."

"Can't you just go?" I sighed, finally meeting his gaze. "I'm not leaving him. I won't—"

"I realize that." He scrubbed his jaw, looking

positively uncomfortable. His eyes moved to Nix, and he flinched. "How are you feeling, son?"

"Me?" Disbelief coated Nix's voice. "You're asking *me* how I feel?"

"Please, can we have some privacy? It's late and you need to get some rest. It won't take long."

Nix glanced at me, and I shrugged. It was his choice.

It had to be.

"Fine."

"Nix, I don't think—"

"Come on, Z," Kye cut him off. "I need to take Chloe home, and you need to check in on your gran."

Zane hesitated, glaring at Michael like he was the devil incarnate. I clambered off the bed and went to him, gently grasping his arms. "I won't let anything happen to him, I promise." I hugged him tightly and whispered, "Thank you. Thank you for everything."

"Ah, shit, B." He hugged me back, and the two of us stood there, silently promising to always look out for Nix. The boy we both loved more than anything.

"We'll be back first thing in the morning," Kye said. "Keep an eye on our boy, B. If you need us—"

"I know, thank you," I said, stepping out of Zane's embrace. He gave Nix a small nod and pinned Michael with a dark look before leaving the room.

"I'll watch him," Kye said, as if he knew we'd both worry about him too.

He followed Zane, leaving me and Nix with my father. The three of us were silent, the air strained and thick between us.

I returned to Nix's side, taking his hand in mine.

Michael's eyes tracked the movement, our united front. He'd separated us once, I didn't plan on letting it happen again.

"May I sit?" he asked, helping himself to one of the chairs.

"What do you want, Michael?" I asked, not bothering to hide my exasperation. "It's late and Nix needs to rest."

He regarded me—the daughter he'd never wanted, the daughter he'd betrayed in so many ways—and let out a steady breath.

"I think I owe you both an apology."

Silence.

It saturated the room, the spaces between us.

But his words, those eight little words I never thought I'd hear from Michael Rowe, echoed through me.

I think I owe you both an apology.

"You can save it," Nix said. "We have nothing to say to each other."

"Nix, I—"

"No, B. I wasn't good enough for you then. I'm not going to lie here and have him tell me that because my old man is a piece of shit it changes anything. I'm not—"

"I didn't know," Michael said, clearing his throat. "I-I thought…"

"You thought what, Dad?" I pushed, anger curling my stomach.

So much pain and hurt and desperation. He'd broken me, broken me in ways I never thought possible.

"I thought I was protecting you. Life in that place is unforgiving, Harleigh. Look at what it did to your mother. Look—"

"You. *You* did that to her."

"Yes, well. It seems like I have more than one mistake to atone for. But Sabrina felt—"

"Sabrina," I spat. "Of course this would be about her. About what she wanted. About what suited her perfect little life."

"B," Nix whispered, clutching my hand to his chest. Our eyes met and he smiled. Even through the agony he smiled for me. "You don't owe him anything. Least of all your tears."

"How long?" Michael's voice cut through the tension. "How long has this been going on?"

"Excuse me?"

His heavy gaze settled on Nix. "How long has your father been hurting you?"

"My entire life."

His words, his honesty, broke me.

Michael was right. Life in The Row was unforgiving for so many. It was hard and brutal and filled with never-ending agony and pain. But there were glimmers of hope. Friendships that were forged out of pain and strife and survival. Bonds that could never be broken.

The Row had its problems, sure. But it wasn't all bad.

"I see." My father's jaw clenched. "And the woman? Your stepmom?"

"The same." Nix said, and I wondered if he knew how brave he was to admit that. How strong.

"Have you ever reported it to the authorities?"

"You're an intelligent man, Mr. Rowe. I'm sure you know that the authorities have no interest in what goes on in a place like The Row."

Michael's jaw clenched again. "I need to make a few phone calls." He stood abruptly. "I take it you don't intend on returning to your trailer while your father is on the loose?"

"I wouldn't go back there if you paid me."

"Very well. Get some rest and we'll talk tomorrow." Michael's eyes lingered on me, guilt and apology swirling there. "If you need anything—"

"I don't." *Not from you.* I bit back the retort. It had been a long night and all I wanted was to hold Nix and get some rest.

"I'm going to take Max and Celeste home, but I'm sure they'll want to stop by tomorrow."

"We'd like that," I said, and it was the truth.

"Very well. I'll tell the nurse you'll need a foldout bed brought in." With that he left.

Nix tugged my hand. "Get back up here, Birdie."

My soft laughter drifted over him as I climbed up beside him and laid my head on his chest. "That was… weird."

"That was a man who knows he fucked up, B."

"What do you mean?" I lifted my face to look at him.

"It's strange because I've hated him so much, but standing there just now, he seemed… kind of pathetic."

"Nix." I fought a smile. Because he was right. Michael had seemed a little pathetic.

Pathetic and sad.

"Part of me believes him, B. He could have whipped

you out of here and stolen you away again, but he didn't. Because he knows, he knows he fucked up. And he knows that if he fucks up again, he'll lose any shot at earning your forgiveness."

My spine stiffened. "I'll never forgive him."

"You might, one day."

"Nix, I—"

"Just hear me out, okay?" He cupped my face. "I know he's an asshole and I know he betrayed you in ways I can't even fathom, but in his own messed up way, he thought he was protecting you. He thought he was fixing his mistakes. And part of me gets that. I get that he just wanted the best for you because I want the best for you. It's why I kept you at arm's length all those years, why I never admitted how I felt..." Sincerity glittered in his eyes, hurtling a rush of emotion through me.

"You are nothing like my father," I said.

"Maybe not. But I will always do whatever it takes to protect you, B. Even if it meant hurting you. Even if it meant breaking your heart."

"Y-you... *what?*"

"I've been pushing too hard," he went on. "You're not ready—"

"Nix, I love you." Tears rolled down my cheeks. "I love you so much, I always have. But I don't want to hold you back. I don't want to ever become a burden to you."

"Never, B. You could never be that to me. You're my best friend. My ride or die. You're my home, Harleigh Wren." He kissed me, breathing the words onto my lips as he said, "All I've ever needed in this life is you."

32

NIX

"Harleigh isn't here," I said to Michael Rowe as he slipped into my room. "She left to get something to eat."

"I didn't come to see Harleigh, son. I was hoping we could talk."

I motioned to one of the empty seats.

It was mid-morning and I already felt a little better. Although I was pretty sure waking up with Harleigh curled up next to me had something to do with it.

"How are you feeling?" he asked.

"I'll be okay."

His brow lifted in a way that told me he wasn't so sure, but I didn't want or need his pity.

"I hope you don't mind that I took it upon myself to call a friend down at Darling Hill PD. He's in with Jessa right now, taking her statement, and then he'd like to talk to you, if you're up to it."

"Why?" I asked. "Why help us?"

"Because my daughter loves you very much, son. And because I am man enough to admit when I made a mistake, and something tells me I made a huge mistake where you and my daughter are concerned."

"She'll never forgive you," I said. Not out of malice, but because it was the simple truth. Michael had broken something in Harleigh, something I wasn't sure would ever heal.

Not even with time.

"And I'll have to live with that every day for the rest of my life." His lips thinned. "But it doesn't mean I won't try to fix things."

I gave him a small nod of understanding, but said, "Just so we're clear, I'll never forgive you either. But this really isn't about me."

"No, no it isn't." He let out a heavy sigh full of regret and shame. "I thought she was just grieving... I thought in time she'd get over it. I didn't know... I guess the how or the why doesn't really matter now. Harleigh hurt herself because of the decisions I made, and that's not something I'll forgive myself in a hurry for either."

"You really called in a favor with the police?"

"I did. And I have the means to make sure your father can't hurt you or Jessa again, son. All you have to do is say the word."

"W-what does that mean exactly?"

"Don't look so worried, Nix." He smiled and it was all Harleigh.

Jesus, that would take some getting used to. Especially if he was going to be in her—*our*—lives, which his presence this morning suggested he was.

"I'm referring to legitimate means. We have enough evidence to make sure Joe Wilder gets put away for a very long time."

"You'll have to catch him first." Fear snaked through me. If my old man knew we were talking to the police…

"That was the other thing I wanted to talk to you about. The police arrested your father and a Vince Colombo in the early hours of this morning.

"You're shitting me?" I bolted upright, sucking in a pained breath at the sudden movement.

"Jesus, Nix, are you—"

"Fine, I'm fine." I sank back against the stiff pillows, gritting my teeth through the pain. "You really think the charges will stand?"

"I'll make sure they do."

"Tell your cop friend I'll give a statement after he's done talking to Jessa."

"Good. You're making the right decision, son."

I wasn't sure Jessa would see it that way, but I was done. The second I'd found her broken and beaten on her bedroom floor, any tolerance I had for my old man died.

I would rather sleep on the fucking street than stay a second longer under his roof.

"I got us— oh, hello. I didn't realize you were here." Harleigh paused in the doorway, glancing between her father and me. "Is everything okay?"

Michael stood. "I'm sure Nix will fill you in. I need to go take care of some things, but I'd like to talk to you both soon."

"Okay." Harleigh came over and placed the brown

paper bag down on the trolley. "Are Max and Celeste here?" she asked.

"They are."

I didn't know if she saw the flicker of dejection in his eyes, but I did.

"I'll send them up if that's okay?"

"Yeah," I said, patting the bed. Harleigh perched on the edge, but I hooked my arm around her waist and pulled her closer, uncaring if her father was here or not.

"Okay, well, I'll check in soon."

"Sure, whatever." Harleigh dismissed him, unpacking the bag, and lining up the small haul of snacks she'd found downstairs in the cafeteria.

Michael lingered, watching her. A man who knew he'd lost something precious. Squandered it. I focused on my girl, giving him a moment of privacy to soak her up. Because maybe it's all he would ever get, and part of me couldn't help but feel sorry for the guy.

"Are you going to tell me what he wanted?" Harleigh asked me a few minutes later.

I hadn't wanted to jump right in, not when she'd insisted upon spoon-feeding me Jell-O and candy.

"He came by to tell me that my old man and Vince were arrested."

"You're serious?"

"Yep. His cop friend is in with Jessa now."

"I... I don't understand." She stared blankly at me.

"It would seem your dad wants to help."

"And you're okay with that?"

"If he can help put Joe behind bars, I'd be stupid not to let him help." I shrugged. "It doesn't mean anything more than that, B."

"Sorry, of course you should let him help. I just… it hurts, Nix. It hurts to know that he wants to help now, after everything."

"I know." I slid my hand along the side of her throat and around the back of her neck, tugging her down gently. Our breaths mingled, our lips brushing softly together. "We don't have to forgive him. We don't even have to thank him. But if he wants to help, we'd be fools not to let him."

"We?" Her brow lifted as she pulled back slightly. "There's a *we* in this scenario?"

"Too soon?"

"I kinda liked it."

"Good, because so did I." My lips quirked and I kissed her again. Slow and soft, shaping her mouth with mine. It hurt, every tiny movement, but the pain was worth it.

She was worth it.

Harleigh let out a small sigh, breaking the kiss to touch her head to mine. "What are you going to do now? You and Jessa, I mean?"

"I guess I need to talk to her." I'd been too chicken shit to go to see her yet, and then Michael had arrived to tell me she was giving a statement to the police.

"You know she loves you, right?" Harleigh smiled. "Whatever happens, she loves you, Nix."

"I know."

The ache in my chest spread, squeezing the air from my lungs.

"And you know what happened to her wasn't your fault?" Harleigh traced her fingertips over my jaw, refusing to let me cower in the face of the truth.

"I... yeah." I conceded, because she was right, it wasn't my fault. But it didn't stop me carrying a seed of guilt that I hadn't been there to stop him.

"You'll figure it out, Nix. We'll figure it out. Together."

"Nix," Jessa breathed, reaching for me. I shuffled toward the chair beside her hospital bed.

The nurse had wanted to wheel me in here, but fuck that. I could walk on my own two feet, even if my ribs felt like they might snap clean in half.

Coach was going to lose his shit when he found out the extent of my injuries, but I'd worry about that later.

"Hey," I said, taking her hand and easing myself into the chair. "How are you feeling?"

"Oh, sweetheart. I'm sorry." Tears filled her eyes. "I'm so, so sorry."

"Don't do that. Don't apologize for him. He did this... he..." I clenched my fist against my thigh, willing the anger out of my veins, my pores. "I'm just sorry I wasn't there last night—"

"Let's make a deal." A hint of a smile broke out from underneath all the swelling and bruises. "Neither of us apologize. It's over, done. He can't hurt us anymore."

Something akin to relief glittered in her one good eye. "Is Harleigh—"

"She's here," I said. "She went with her brother and sister to get coffee."

She was exhausted, but when I'd suggested she go home and get some rest she wouldn't hear of it.

"I met her father. Michael. He's very… put together."

My lips twitched at Jessa's assessment. "He's a selfish, pretentious asshole. But he came through for us."

"He did. He said we won't have to pay a penny, Nix. His legal team will handle everything."

"Yeah, I know." I rubbed my jaw, still unsure of how I felt about all of Michael's handouts. But we didn't have the money for lawyers and court hearings.

"I thought he was going to kill you." The words got stuck over the sob in her throat. "I thought—"

"I'm okay," I said, inhaling a thin breath. "I'll be okay."

But I'd come so close to *not* being okay. If Zane hadn't arrived when he had, if he hadn't pulled my old man off me and shoved him away… I probably wouldn't be sitting here now.

A shudder rippled through me, but I forced my fist open, laying my palm against my knee. He couldn't control me anymore—he couldn't hurt me.

"We'll get through this, Nix. You and me, okay? I'll get a job, figure out somewhere for us to live. I'm not sure I can go back there… I'm not—"

"Hey, hey, we'll figure it out."

She nodded. "I'm tired, Nix. I'm so damn tired."

"It's okay, close your eyes. I'll be right here, I promise."

"You're a good boy, Phoenix, and I feel so lucky that I get to call you my stepson."

She closed her eyes, but her words stayed with me long after she fell asleep.

———

"You know, this isn't a club." The nurse smiled as she checked my notes. Kye and Zane were busy fighting over the television channels while the girls were curled up on Harleigh's makeshift bed.

"We can go?" Nate suggested.

I didn't know who had been more surprised when Chloe had turned up with Miller in tow. But the two of them had barely interacted since they'd been here. Whatever. I had my own shit to worry about.

"No, it's okay. Mr. Rowe requested that we overlook your number of visitors given the circumstances."

Harleigh's brow went up at the mention of her father, but she let it go.

"So when do you think our boy can get out of here?" Kye asked.

"That's up to the doctor. But maybe tomorrow morning."

Harleigh gave me another lingering look, and I knew exactly what she was thinking. Where would I go? Because I sure as fuck wasn't going back to that hellhole.

"Come here," I mouthed, and she left Chloe and Celeste to join me on the bed. "Don't look so worried, B." Smoothing my fingers over the crinkles in her forehead, I kissed her softly.

Someone cleared their throat and I flipped off the room.

"Dude, lady present," Kye chided.

"Relax, Nurse Beth knows the deal," I said, winking at her. The woman blushed, murmuring something about teenage boys and left us to it.

"I'm surprised your newest groupie isn't here." Zane snorted.

"Max is cool," I said, and Harleigh and Celeste both pinned me with a surprised look. "What? The kid's all right."

"Until Daddy Rowe finds out about the fact you're training him at the gym and all hell breaks loose."

"That's why we aren't going to tell him that little nugget of information," Harleigh said.

"You're such a badass, B. I like it." Kye grinned his approval.

"Whatever Max's reasons are for training at Buster's are his. He can deal with the fallout." She shrugged, and I nuzzled her neck.

"Your old man won't like it," I whispered.

"My *old man* can go to hell. He's lucky I even let him in here."

"Shit, Nix. You got your hands full there."

Harleigh poked her tongue out at Kye and everyone laughed.

"It's okay, B," I said quietly, only for her. "I'm going to be okay."

She was worried. About what came next. About me and Jessa and where we were going to go. About football and the future. But it just didn't seem significant. Not when I might never have got to feel her in my arms again.

"Find something to watch or fuck off," I said to the room. "I'm tired and I want to nap."

"Damn, he's a cranky patient."

Harleigh shifted a little up the bed and slipped her arm around my shoulder so I could rest my head on her chest. "I'll be right here," she whispered.

And this time, I believed her.

33

HARLEIGH

Being in the hospital wasn't somewhere I'd ever expected to enjoy being. They were usually places of such pain and suffering. But spending the day with Nix and our friends was surprisingly nice.

The nurses only disturbed us when necessary, and Michael didn't make another appearance. And Nix was an impressively quick healer. He wouldn't be playing football anytime soon, but he was in significantly less pain and moving more freely.

"Thank fuck they've gone. I thought they were never going to leave," he muttered.

"What? I thought you liked having them here."

"I did, but I like having you all to myself more." He nuzzled my neck, kissing the skin there.

"Nix..." I breathed. "We can't, not here."

"Yeah, I know. I'm not even sure I could... perform right now." I gawked at him, my cheeks heating, and he grinned. "Fuck, you're beautiful. I can't wait to get out of here and—"

The door opened and Michael stood on the threshold again, just as he had yesterday.

My stomach sank.

"Sorry, I didn't mean to interrupt."

"You're not," Nix said. "We were just… talking."

"Talking, yes, well, I'd hoped to talk to both of you. If that's okay?"

"Sure, come in."

I didn't bother trying to move to one of the chairs. I had nothing to hide.

Not anymore.

"How are you feeling?"

"Good, better. The doctor thinks I can probably get out tomorrow."

"That's good news. Have you given any thought as to where you'll go?"

"Zane and his grandma said I can stay there until Jessa gets out and we figure out something more permanent."

"I might have a solution."

"You?" I frowned.

"I made some calls and there's a triple wide available near your friend Kye's place, I believe."

"That's nice of you and all, Mr. Rowe, but Jessa and I can't afford—"

"You don't need to afford it, son. I'd like to buy it for you."

"The fuck?" Nix paled. "What is this? Like some kind

of bribe? I end things with Harleigh and you set me and Jessa up in a new home?"

"No, that's not… Let's start again, shall we?" Michael ran a hand down his face. "Neither of you want to return to your father's trailer, and I'm almost certain you wouldn't want to move into our house, so I made some calls and found something for you both. The three of you, since I imagine Harleigh will want to stay with you occasionally."

"I-I don't understand," I finally spoke, pushing the words past the giant lump in my throat. "Why would you do this?"

"Because I can. Because I have the money and they don't. And because I want to help. I want to try and begin fixing my mistakes."

"I… I don't know what to say," I choked out and Nix hugged me tighter into his side.

"It's a nice offer, sir, but we couldn't possibly—"

"Actually, I already spoke to Jessa, and she agreed to my terms."

"Terms?"

"I don't want this to feel like charity, Nix. It's an opportunity for a fresh start, somewhere to call your own. You and Jessa can pay me the going rate for rent, but instead of pocketing the money, I will set it against the cost of the property so you'll be effectively buying it back off me, piece by piece."

I sucked in a sharp breath. "You can't—"

"I can and I will. When she left, Trina refused my help and look where it landed her." His expression softened at the mention of my mother.

"Will you ever tell me what really happened between the two of you?"

"One day, when you're ready to hear it, I'll tell you everything."

I nodded. It was enough, for now. Because he was right. I wasn't ready. Not yet.

"Nobody has to know about our arrangement, if you would prefer it that way. I have numerous shell companies that can act as your landlord."

"Whatever Jessa wants," Nix said, and although I didn't wholly like it, I understood. Michael was offering him a solution to his biggest problem. Jessa's security. Regardless of what had happened, Nix loved her like a mother, and she'd always been one of his biggest tethers to The Row. But if she was safe and looked after, he didn't have to worry anymore. He could finally be free to carve out his own path, chase his own dreams.

"Is that a yes?"

"Yeah, it's a yes." Nix slid his eyes to me, and I forced a smile. This was his decision, his life. I wouldn't stand in the way of that.

"You will always have a place with us, Harleigh. But I also spoke to Jessa about your situation… and I want you to know that if you choose to leave DA and transfer back to Darling Hill High, I won't stand in your way. The same goes for where you choose to live."

"Because Sabrina doesn't want—"

"I love my wife dearly, but you are my daughter, Harleigh, my flesh and blood. I failed you too many times already. I don't plan on making the same mistake again. You will always have a room at the house. You will always be a part of my family. But if you need space, if you need to not be with us, I understand."

"I… I need some time to think about things."

"Of course, take all the time you need." He retreated to the door. "I can't turn back time, Harleigh, and I know nothing I say or do will ever heal the hurt I caused, but I am sorry. For all of it."

Nothing. I had nothing.

Michael didn't linger, the tension in the room unbearable, even after he left.

"I did not see that coming." Nix let out a low whistle.

"No," I whispered, my eyes still fixed on the door.

"If you don't want me to—"

"No." I met his wary gaze. "You should take his offer. Jessa needs stability, and so do you."

"And you heard what he said, you can come stay with us. I definitely like the sound of that." Nix pulled me in close, ghosting his mouth over mine.

"You're really okay with all this?"

Because I couldn't process everything, let alone decide what I wanted to do.

"It's just a trailer, B. I don't care about what it looks like or where it is. All I care about is that you and Jessa are safe and happy. The rest is just a bonus."

"I can't believe my father is going to buy you a trailer."

"I can't believe your old man offered to buy me and Jessa a trailer, and then suggested you can stay with us. Doesn't he know the kinds of things I want to do to you in the dark?" Nix dragged his mouth along my jaw all the way to my ear. "Will you lie with me in the dark, Birdie?"

"Always, Nix."

Always.

"Holy shit, this place is… in dire need of some furniture. But I'm digging it," Kye said as we walked through Jessa and Nix's new trailer.

"We're bringing some of our stuff from the old place," Nix said. "But Jessa wants to go shopping together once she's out. She had a bit of cash stashed away for a rainy day."

"Which room is going to be yours, B?" Kye waggled his brows and I narrowed my eyes at him.

"I haven't decided anything yet."

"I give it two weeks, tops," Chloe said.

"We have some self-control, you know."

"No, you had self-control when you had nowhere to get it on. Now you have this place, there's no way you'll be going back across the res much."

"I…"

"Hey, it's okay." Nix dipped his mouth to my ear. "Whatever you decide, you know I'll support you."

It wasn't that I wanted to stay with Michael, I didn't. Sabrina had made her feelings about me quite clear. But I didn't want to impose on Jessa and Nix's space either. Maybe I could move between the two. Avoid Sabrina as much as possible. But I didn't want to leave Celeste. She was important to me.

"Are we meeting the others later?" Chloe asked, as Nix gave us the grand tour.

It wasn't anything special. But it was a fresh start,

somewhere to make brand new memories. Good memories.

They walked ahead and Nix snagged my hand, pulling me into an empty bedroom. He pushed me up against the wall, closing the door and locking it.

"Nix." Laughter spilled out of me. "We're supposed to be giving them the tour."

"They'll survive." He caged me in with his arms, leaning in until we were nose to nose. "So what do you think?"

"About what?"

"Your room." He glanced back at the light and airy space.

"Nix…" I swallowed over the lump in my throat.

"Just hear me out, okay? It doesn't have to be official; it doesn't even have to be a big deal. But we want it to be yours. Even if you want to stay in my room, which I really fucking hope you do, we want you to have a place you can call your own. A safe place."

Tears welled in my eyes. "What happens if we break up?"

My heart ached just thinking about it.

"Number one: never going to happen." He didn't even look pissed off, as if the thought was simply too preposterous to acknowledge. "Number two: even if we did ever break up, and we won't, you'd still be my best friend. That will never change. And number three: I think Jessa would kick me out first before she ever kicked you out." He grinned and damn him, I found myself grinning back.

"You don't even have to stay here; it can be for emergencies only."

"Emergencies, huh? And what about the mill? I kind of love that place."

"We can still go there." He ran his nose along my cheek, kissing the corner of my mouth as I wound my arms around his neck. "It's off the grid. No one will hear you scream my name out there."

My heart fluttered at his words, at the dark promise in them.

"You've really got this all figured out, haven't you?"

"The way I see it is, it's simple. I love you, B. I want you in my life, in my space, in my bed…"

"Hey, this is my room. No boys allowed."

"Does that mean you're saying yes?"

"It means, I'll think about it."

"Hey, assholes, unlock the door," Kye bellowed.

"We'd better go back out there before he breaks something." I went to move around Nix, but he pushed his body flush against mine, trapping me there.

"It's always been you, B," he breathed, his eyes dark and intense as he gazed at me. "I love you."

"I love you too, Nix."

I always have.

34

NIX

"Here he is," Hench hollered as I walked into the locker room.

It was my first day back at school after a week off at the insistence of Coach and Principal Marston. But between visiting Jessa, getting the new place ready, and spending time with Harleigh, it had flown by.

News traveled fast about my old man and Vince Colombo and there wasn't a single soul in The Row who didn't know about what had gone down, though people didn't ask too many questions. And if they did, Zane or Kye usually told them to shut the fuck up.

I was Joe Wilder's kid—always would be. But I was finally free of his bullshit, and it felt good.

"Wilder, my office," Coach bellowed, and I made my way across the room, my teammates all greeting me as I passed them.

"What's up, Coach?"

"Sit," he said, motioning to the empty chair. "You look a damn sight better than when I saw you last."

"I'm a quick healer, sir."

"Quick healer or not, I don't want you anywhere near practice for at least another week, and then it's light duties only."

"Come on, Coach, I'm fi—"

"I swear to God, Nix, if you tell me you're fine one more time, I will blow a damn gasket." His eyes shuttered as he inhaled a ragged breath.

"Coach?"

"I'm sorry, son. I'm just having a real hard time reconciling the fact I didn't do more."

His words hung between us, and I managed to choke out, "I'm not your responsibility, Coach."

"That's where you're wrong, Nix." He sat back and ran a hand over his stubble. "You're my star player, one of my guys, I should have— fuck. It's going to take some time to process it all, son. But I'm glad to see you back, we all are."

"Thanks, Coach."

"Now I know you won't be in Friday's line up, but it's Homecoming and I'd really like you to be present."

"Ugh, school dances aren't my thing, Coach, you know that."

"What if I told you I spoke to Darrah O'Keefe up at Albany and he as good as gave me the green light."

"No shit?" I sat up straighter, hardly able to believe my ears.

"They're talking about locking you into an early commitment if you're interested. But they want you to head up to Albany the weekend after next when we have a bye week."

"That's…" *Holy shit.* "I don't know what to say."

"I think the answer you're looking for is 'Hell yes,' son."

"Hell yes, Coach. It's real?" I asked. "They really want me… even after what happened?"

"They want you *because* of what happened, Nix. Your tenacity and resilience are two of your biggest strengths. When I think about the life you've had, what you've had to face… I'm proud to call you a Hawk, Nix."

A strange emotion tumbled in my chest. "Thanks, Coach. That means a lot."

"Are you and Jessa all settled in the new place?"

"We are. We still need to get a few bits of furniture but it's coming together." She'd officially left the hospital two days ago and had spent every second cleaning and organizing, despite the doctor's order to take it easy.

She was like a whole new person, and it only confirmed what I already knew. We'd made the right decision letting Michael help us.

"Good, that's real good, son. If you need anything, you just let me know, okay?"

"Thanks, Coach."

"And Miss Maguire? Will we be seeing her back in the halls of DHH anytime soon?"

"I'm not sure."

Harleigh was still deciding where her future lay. Things at her father's house were tense, but she didn't want to leave Celeste, and I knew she had reservations about staying with me and Jessa. Which was fucking stupid if you asked me, given the fact she'd been in my bed every night since I'd moved in.

It meant I had to get up early to drive her to school but it was worth it.

So fucking worth it.

It was also worth it just to see Denby's face every morning when I kissed the shit out of my girl before she headed for class. Now Michael knew about us, there wasn't a damn thing Marc Denby and his friends could do to Harleigh, not without feeling Michael Rowe's wrath.

It wasn't quite as good as beating the shit out of his pretty boy face but it was enough.

"You should invite her to Homecoming, celebrate together."

Oh, I planned on celebrating with her, just not the way Coach had in mind.

"Keep your head down this week and stay out of trouble, okay? And don't let me see you anywhere near the gym."

"You got it, Coach."

"Good, get out of here." I got up and moved to the door, but he called after me. "And Nix?"

"Yeah?"

"I'm proud of you, son. Real damn proud."

I nodded, my throat too clogged to reply and slipped out of his office.

Kye and Zane met me outside the door. "So, what did he want?"

"He spoke to Albany."

"And..." Kye's eyes widened.

"They want me. They—"

They both jumped on me, hooting and hollering, and laughter rumbled in my chest as I soaked up their excitement.

"I fucking knew it. I knew you'd be a Falcon one day. Fuck yes!"

"Congrats, man," Zane said. "You deserve this."

"I still can't believe it."

"Well believe it, Nix, because come next fall, you and B will be living it up in Albany."

"That's the dream."

But I hadn't brought it up again, not while she was still deciding what to do about everything. I wanted her to pick me and Jessa, to choose to transfer back to Darling Hill High, of course I did. But it had to be her decision.

Zane caught my eye and gripped my shoulder. "It's you and her, Nix. Always has been." He gave me a rare smile. "Always will be."

"Stay," I rolled Harleigh underneath me and nuzzled her neck, grazing her soft skin with my teeth.

"Nix, I have to go..." She made a feeble attempt to shove me away but ended up pulling me closer. "God, Nix..."

My hand found its way between our bodies, and I pressed two fingers inside her.

"Again?" she breathed, still flushed and breathless from her last two orgasms.

"I can't get enough of you, B." My lips crashed down on hers, swallowing her whimpers and moans. She arched into my touch, riding my hand, her body knowing exactly what to do, even if she was still too shy to ask for it.

I gently collared her throat, licking and nipping at her mouth, teasing her into submission.

"You don't play fair," she moaned. "Jessa won't be home yet, right?"

"Relax, she's out for the evening."

"Thank… *God.*" It came out breathy as I dragged my thumb over her clit. "Celeste is going to be here any second."

"Then she'll have to wait." I worked my fingers and thumb together just how I knew she liked it. Until she was clutching my arm begging me for more. "Come for me, B." I kissed her. "I want to see you fly."

Hooking my fingers, I rubbed that spot deep inside her and her legs trembled around me.

"God, Nix… *God…*" She came quietly, pressing herself into me and riding the intense waves I felt moving through her.

When she finally opened her eyes, I grinned. "I'm hungry." I brought my fingers to my mouth and sucked them clean, tasting her. "It's a shame you have to leave so early, or I could have eaten *you* for dessert."

Harleigh narrowed her eyes, but I saw the laughter there. "It's a good thing I love you." She leaned over and gave me one last kiss before climbing out of bed and pulling on her clothes. "See you tomorrow, okay?"

"It's been almost two weeks, you know. You're going to have to make a decision eventually."

Pick me, I wanted to say. *Choose me.*

"I know." She smiled, her eyes twinkling.

Something had changed. I couldn't quite put my finger on it, but Harleigh was different.

"Text me later. I love you."

"Love you," I murmured, and she threw me a parting look that said, 'Poor baby.'

But for as much as I wanted it to be her choice, I also wanted her to put me out of my misery.

THE WEEK WENT SURPRISINGLY FAST. I settled back into classes, helping Jessa out in the evenings I didn't have work at Buster's. Harleigh came by most nights afterwards, and we all hung out, watching old movies and binging on Jessa's cookies. It was nice. It was everything I'd never had.

A safe family home.

But still, Harleigh hadn't made any decisions and I was starting to get impatient.

"Remind me why we have to do this again?" Zane grumbled as we finished getting ready. If Coach wanted me there tonight, there was no way I was letting Zane and Kye get out of it.

"Team spirit, Z. You scrub up pretty good." The black jeans and black shirt gave him an edge. Even if he had rolled his sleeves up and left his top button undone. I, on the other hand, had gone all out in a magenta shirt, black jeans, and a black skinny tie. It was Jessa's doing and I hadn't wanted to ruin her fun. Besides, I looked damn good.

"Shit, is that the time?" I said, checking my cell. "We need to go." Because the sooner we made an appearance at Homecoming, the sooner we could head to the real party at Miller's house.

He'd invited us all over to celebrate his birthday. It was the perfect excuse to leave Homecoming. Besides, Harleigh was going to be there.

"Oh my." Jessa stood the second we entered the living room. "Don't you all look handsome."

"Don't think I've ever been called handsome before," Kye said, tugging at the collar on his crisp white shirt.

"Line up for me, I want to get some photos."

"Seriously? We're doing—"

I elbowed Zane in the ribs. "Humor the lady," I hissed.

"Sure thing," he grunted, moving into position beside me.

We posed for a few photographs, and then Zane and Kye headed out to the car, giving me a moment alone with Jessa.

"Oh, Nix, you look so dashing, sweetheart. I want you to enjoy tonight, okay? You've earned it."

"Thanks, for everything."

"Come here." Jessa pulled me into her slim arms and held me tight. "I'm proud of you, Nix. More than you'll ever know."

We broke away and I cleared my throat, attempting to dislodge the ball of emotion stuck there. "We need to go," I said.

"Of course." She waved me off. "Have fun and say hi to Harleigh for me."

It wasn't until I was almost at the car, I realized what she'd said.

THE SCHOOL GYMNASIUM looked like a dollar-store wedding with its magenta and black streamers and half-deflated balloons. But when you were organizing a school dance on a shoestring budget, you had to work with what you had.

"This is fucking depressing," Zane grumbled as we watched our classmates dance and grind up on each other to the two-bit local band who had been asked to play.

"Hench seems to be enjoying himself," Kye motioned to where Cherri was giving him a lap dance at their table.

"Real classy." I shook my head.

"That could have been you, Nix."

I shuddered at the thought. Cherri had given me a wide berth since the party, and if she knew what was good for her, she would keep it that way.

Checking my cell phone, I let out a frustrated sigh. Ninety minutes. I only had to get through ninety more minutes and then we could leave and head to Nate's house.

"Well, since we're here, I might as well check out the offerings." Kye rubbed his hands together, homing in on a group of girls on the edge of the dance floor. "Zane, can I interest—"

"I hope your dick falls off."

"That sounds an awful lot like jealousy, my friend." Kye grinned before stalking off toward the girls.

"How's your gran?" I changed the subject.

"She has her good and bad days."

"If you need anything—"

"I appreciate it," Zane said. "But I can handle it."

"You know, Celeste will be there later."

"So?" He shrugged, casting me a sideways glance.

"Just thought you might want to know."

"Well, I don't."

"Okay. Forget I said anything. I just think—"

I noticed a shift in the air. Everyone was looking at me. Not at me, *past* me.

What—

I turned slowly, and my heart almost burst out of my chest when I spotted her.

"Holy shit," Zane breathed. "She looks—"

"Incredible." The black dress clung to Harleigh's curves like a second skin, the delicate magenta flower pinned in her long glossy waves, the exact color of my shirt—my team.

She looked... *fuck.*

I couldn't think, let alone form words.

Harleigh approached me, but stopped just short of touching distance. And holy shit, did I want to touch her.

"What do you think?" Slowly, she rotated in a full circle.

"You look... fuck." I inched closer, needing to be near her. "Is this real?"

"I'm pretty sure I'm about to have a heart attack." She

grabbed my hand and pressed it right over the curve of her chest.

"You came…"

"I did. I wanted to be here to watch you crowned Homecoming King. And I wanted to get all the rumors and gossip over before I transfer back."

My heart stuttered in my chest. "What did you say?"

"You heard me." Harleigh gave me a coy smile.

"For real? You're transferring back?"

She nodded. "I don't belong at DA. I never did."

"But it's a good school. You can—"

"Too late. Michael already signed off on all the paperwork. As of Monday, I am officially a senior at Darling Hill High again."

I picked her up and spun her around, her laughter better than any music to my ears. "I can't believe you go here."

"From Monday." She chuckled as I lowered her back to the floor. "Technically, I'm gate-crashing right now."

"What did Celeste say?"

Harleigh's eyes flickered over to where Chloe and Celeste were busy talking to Kye, Zane, and some of the other players from the teams.

"He can't take his eyes off her," she murmured.

"Just because he thinks she's hot doesn't mean he'll act on it."

"It's probably best he doesn't."

"You're here." I cupped her face, aware that people were staring. "Do you want to get out of here? I don't care about a stupid fucking crown." *I only care about you.*

"Let them stare, Nix. I want the world to know that Phoenix Wilder is mine."

"Say that again." The grin on my face spread.

"I want the world—"

"No, the part about me being yours."

"You are, you know?" She laced her arms around my neck and leaned in close. "All mine."

"And you're mine," I said.

"I am. Every last bit. Even the broken parts."

"Perfect is overrated anyway. I happen to like you just the way you are." I kissed the end of her nose and then lifted her wrist to my mouth, kissing the puckered skin there. "Your scars make you beautiful, Birdie."

Emotion glittered in her eyes, but she smirked and said, "Yours make you kind of hot."

"You think?"

"Oh, I know so." She pressed closer, erasing the sliver of space between us, and fisted my shirt.

I liked this Harleigh. Playful and a little bit naughty.

But then, I liked all versions of her.

I always had.

And I always would.

Because love didn't come with limitations. It was unconditional. Endless. To love her was to love all of her. Even the parts I didn't fully understand yet. The parts I might never truly understand. But that was okay because we had time.

We had all the time in the world.

Starting from right now.

EPILOGUE

HARLEIGH

"Harleigh," Sabrina greeted me with a strained smile as she ushered me into the house.

"Hi," I said, hitching my bag up my shoulder.

"Will today be the last of it?"

"I think so."

God, this was awkward.

In the six weeks since everything had happened, things between me and Sabrina had been difficult to say the least. But somehow, I got through it.

We both did.

A whole lot of avoidance on both our parts helped, not to mention my weekly sessions with Dr. Matthews, my new therapist.

"Well, if you need anything…" The empty offer of help didn't upset me. She was trying, at least, in her own cold and detached way.

Sabrina didn't like me. Maybe she never would. But

the feeling was mutual and Dr. Matthews said that it wasn't always about trying to change things. Sometimes it was about acknowledging them and letting them exist. We could dislike one another but act civilly around our family.

"I'm sure I'll manage." I smiled. I had a lot to smile about these days. "But thank you."

"Harleigh, you're early." Celeste appeared at the end of the hall and her presence instantly lifted the oppressive atmosphere.

Sabrina excused herself and Celeste bounded over. "I can't believe it's finally here." She pouted. "I'm so sad you won't be staying here anymore."

"I barely stay here anyway."

"I know but you still *lived* here. It'll be different now."

"I'll still visit and we'll see each other all the time."

Almost a month had passed since I'd left DA and transferred back to Darling Hill High. But she was right, I had still been around. Splitting my time between Nix's place and here. I was eighteen tomorrow though, and I'd decided it was time to make it official.

I was moving in with my boyfriend... and his stepmom.

But Jessa was barely around since she'd met Colt at the bar just out of town, where she'd been working for the past month. He was a good guy. Hardworking. Solid. Dependable. And he treated her like a freaking princess, which after Joe was exactly what she needed. Colt had a cabin on the edge of the Hudson River, so they spent a lot of time out there. Which meant Nix and I got to play house a lot.

Sometimes we invited everyone over and hung out. But sometimes we locked everyone out and laid in the dark, making plans for the future. It still terrified me, looking too far ahead, but I was working on it.

Baby steps, Dr. Matthews liked to remind me.

"Yeah." The sadness in Celeste's voice pulled me back into the moment.

"Come here," I said, pulling her into my arms. "I love you, Celeste. You're my best friend. Me moving out won't change that."

"Good." She eased back to look at me. "Because I know where you live and I'm not afraid to turn up on your doorstep on an evening armed with ice cream and cheesy movies."

"There's always a spare bed for you, you know that." I hadn't used my room at Nix's in weeks. Jessa didn't care if we shared a room. She only cared that we were safe and happy.

"Are you excited about the party tomorrow?"

"It's not a party," I said.

"Chloe said—"

"Chloe needs to butt out. It's a small gathering."

Celeste's brow lifted with amusement. "If you say so."

"I do."

The last thing I wanted was a party. I hated being the center of attention. Besides, I didn't have enough friends to make up a party.

No, the gathering at Strike One would be close friends and family only. Something small, intimate, and unnecessary if you asked me. But Jessa had insisted and I couldn't say no to her. She was so strong and resilient, I was in awe of her. But I guess the attention of a good man helped.

"Come on then." Celeste took my hand. "I left Max packing up the last of your things."

"You owe me," Max said an hour later once Celeste's Range Rover was loaded.

"How about I'll buy you a drink tomorrow at the party?"

"Yeah, okay then," he mocked, and I rolled my eyes.

"How's it going at Buster's?"

"Shit, Harleigh, say it a little louder won't you?" He glanced over his shoulder as if Michael and Sabrina might appear at any moment.

"Relax, they don't know anything."

"Yeah, well, I want to keep it that way. See you tomorrow." He stalked off back toward the house.

"How is he?" I asked her.

"He's... Max. I'm beginning to wonder if maybe he should go to therapy."

"Hey!"

"Joke." She chuckled. "Did you think about what Dr. Matthews said about having a session with Dad?"

My brows furrowed. "Yeah, but I'm not sure. I mean, I know he's trying but it feels too much too soon."

Things with Michael were complicated. He'd done something so amazing for Jessa and Nix but it didn't negate the years of heartache and abandonment I'd felt at his hands. Not to mention all the lies and betrayal between us. Our relationship—if you could call it that—was a work in progress. And that was okay. If he genuinely wanted to repair things with me, he would wait.

"I'm so proud of you, you know?" Celeste said.

"You're not going to cry are you?" I tried to lighten the mood.

"Ugh, it's just I've loved having a sister around. Someone who gets me. You're going to leave a big hole, Harleigh Wren Maguire." She pouted again, and I grabbed her hand.

"We're sisters," I whispered, a little choked up. "Time or distance won't change that, Celeste. Because we're family."

The kind of family you chose.

NIX

"Happy birthday, Birdie." I trailed my lips over her collarbone, letting my hand drift over her hip. She gave a sleepy moan, wiggling closer to me, her ass brushing my morning wood.

Waking up next to Harleigh was one of my favorite things, and I had a lot where she was concerned. And now I got to do it every single morning.

I was a lucky fucker.

"Open your eyes, B," I whispered. "Look at me."

They fluttered open and I tumbled into her deep green irises.

"Hey." She smiled around a yawn. "What time is it?"

"Birthday time." I grinned. "Wait right here, I have your present—"

"No, wait." She wrapped herself around me. "Let me enjoy this."

I couldn't deny her, no matter how excited I was to give her the gift sitting in the bottom drawer. It had cost me a small fortune but she was worth it, and Bryson had given me a nice little bonus for all the new business I was bringing his way.

A soft sigh slipped from Harleigh's lips as she laid her head on my chest, tracing our names on my stomach. "I can't believe I live here now."

"I can't believe you finally said yes."

Harleigh had taken her sweet time deciding to finally make the permanent move here. But I'd been patient, letting her arrive at the decision herself.

If she'd have chosen to keep a room at her father's estate, I would have accepted it. I would have hated it, sure, but I would have accepted it. Because every second with this girl—this strong, brave, courageous girl—was a fucking blessing.

She peered up at me and smiled. "You're stuck with me now, Wilder."

"I can think of worse places to be." I smirked, leaning down to kiss her.

"You said something about presents."

Rolling my eyes, I slipped out of my bed and went to retrieve the jewelry box.

"What do you have there?" Harleigh leaned up on one elbow as I sat on the edge of the bed and slid the box toward her.

"Happy birthday, B."

She worked the box open and stared down at the contents. "It's beautiful," she said.

"Here, let me put it on." I plucked the bracelet off its cushion and unclasped it. Harleigh lifted her wrist, letting me fasten it in place.

"Is that a semicolon?" she asked, inspecting the flat silver charm laying in the middle of the delicate chain.

"It is. Do you know what it represents?" She nodded, tears brimming in her eyes. "Your story isn't over, Harleigh." I ran my thumb over the charm, letting it brush the scar underneath. "And I want you to know that wherever your journey takes you, I promise I'll be there. Right by your side. Always."

"I love you, Phoenix Wilder. So much it terrifies me."

"Then we can be scared together." I leaned in, touching my head to hers, breathing her in.

My heart.

My hope.

My home.

***

"Happy birthday, B." Kye pulled Harleigh in for a hug. "I hope this idiot got you something nice."

"He did." Her eyes flashed to mine, love and understanding shining there.

"Is everyone here?" I asked, and he nodded.

"Everyone is present and accounted for."

A bolt of nerves went through me. I'd either got it

right tonight or I'd fucked everything up. But there was only one way to find out.

"Come on," I said, placing my hand on her lower back. "Everyone's inside."

"I hope you know what you're doing," Kye whispered as I passed him, and he clapped me on the shoulder.

The manager had agreed to close to the general public for us. I didn't have the sway to make that happen, but the man standing at the bar, watching his daughter drink in the magenta and black decorations, did.

"Tell me you didn't invite him," she whisper-hissed.

"He wanted to be here. I thought we should give him the benefit of the doubt."

"Is Sabrina—"

"No, she didn't come."

Harleigh's expression softened. "Well, I guess that's something."

Our friends swarmed us, all wanting to wish my girl a happy birthday. I stepped back, giving her, Celeste, and Chloe some space.

"This is… impressive," Zane said, pretending not to track Celeste's every move. I had no fucking idea what was going on there. He refused to talk about it and as far as I knew Celeste had told Harleigh there was nothing to tell, even though she'd called things off with Mulligan right after Homecoming.

I called bullshit. Being around them was like waiting for lightning to strike. You knew it would come, you just didn't know when it would hit or how bad the damage would be.

"It was all Jessa and Michael," I replied. "I just had to get her here."

"Nah, you did a hell of a lot more than that, Nix. Look at her. She looks happy."

"Yeah." My chest tightened. She did look happy. She *was* happy. And I knew it wasn't all on me but it didn't feel bad at all knowing I'd had a hand in helping her find herself again.

"Is that new jewelry I spy?" he asked.

"Yeah."

Zane snorted. "Well at least it isn't a fucking ring. I know you think she's your endgame but you're still young. Things change."

"Nah," I said right as Harleigh looked at me.

"Lovesick fool," he grumbled, heading for the bar.

Harleigh excused herself and came over to me, sliding her arms around my waist. "Let me guess, he was worried you got me a ring?"

"Something like that." I chuckled, dropping a kiss on her head. "What do you think?"

"It's… a lot." She scanned the room, the friends and family that gathered to celebrate with us. Celeste, Max, and Michael. Jessa and Colt. Kye, Chloe, and their mom. Zane, Nate, and Miles. Even old Mrs. Feeley had made the trip.

Because she was loved.

Harleigh was loved even when she didn't believe it.

She let out a contented sigh. "But I think I love it."

"Yeah?"

"Yeah. I wouldn't want to do it all the time, but it's

nice." She tucked herself into my side and laid her head on my shoulder.

"Harleigh," Michael approached us, a small gift in his hand.

"Hi."

"Happy birthday. You look beautiful."

"Thanks."

"This is for you." He handed her the gift. "It isn't much, but I didn't want to come empty-handed."

"You didn't have to—" I nudged her gently and she forced a smile. "Thank you."

He nodded stiffly. "Well, I'll let you enjoy your party. If you ever want to talk, you know where to find me."

She pursed her lips, discomfort rolling off her in waves. I smoothed my thumb over her hip offering my silent support.

"Nix." He gave me a small smile and disappeared back into the small crowd of people.

"He's making it very hard for me to hate him," she whispered, the words strained.

"You can hate him and still want to know him. The two aren't mutually exclusive."

"When did you get so wise?" Harleigh turned into me and laid her hands on my chest.

Fuck.

When she looked at me like that, I felt ten feet tall.

"Well, there was this girl who told me I was worth something..."

"Yeah, she sounds kind of special." Her lips quirked, humor dancing in her eyes.

"Oh, she's very special." I leaned in, brushing my lips along her jaw. "So special I think I'll keep her."

"Lucky girl." She smiled against my mouth, a shiver going through her.

"No, B." I breathed. My heart so fucking full of love for her. "He's the lucky one."

Thank you for reading Nix and Harleigh's story.

Zane and Celeste's story, *These Defiant Souls*, is coming later this year. Available now to pre-order.

PLAYLIST

Heal – Tom Odell
Moth To A Flame – Swedish House Mafia, The Weeknd
Fade Into You – Mazzy Star
Drop Dead – Holly Humberstone
Running Up The Hill – Meg Myers
Drown – Boy In Space
Peru – Fireboy DML, Ed Sheeran
Best Friends – The Weeknd
I Fall Apart – Post Malone
Mad At You – Noah Cyrus, Gallant
Die For You – LEON
Contaminated – BANKS
Gone – Blake Rose
Love Runs Out – Martin Garrix, G-Eazy, Sasha Alex
Sloan
To Die For – Sam Smith
Fake It – Bastille
Fix You – Coldplay

Yours – Ella Henderson
Get You The Moon – Kina, Snow

While Nix and Harleigh's story is fiction, their experiences are reality for so many.

For anyone affected by the themes in this story, you can find support at:

The National Suicide Prevention Helpline (US)
1-800-273-8255

Domestic Violence Support (US)
1-800-799-7233

The Samaritans (UK)
116 123

Refuge (UK)
0808 2000 247

ACKNOWLEDGMENTS

Those who know me, know I'm not an overly emotional person. But there was something about Nix and Harleigh's story that deeply touched me. The adversity they overcame made their HEA so much sweeter, and I can't wait to watch them blossom throughout the series (yes, Zane IS getting a book!!!).

As always, I am surrounded by people who help me get to this point. Andrea, Darlene, Athena, Tracy, Jade, Candi Kane PR, and my ARC and promo teams, I couldn't do this without your help and support - thank you!

And my endless gratitude to the readers who continue to support my work. I hope you'll stick around for the ride. I have so many more stories to tell.

Until next time,
Lianne

Angsty. Edgy. Addictive Romance

USA Today and *Wall Street Journal* bestselling author of over forty mature young adult and new adult novels, L. A. is happiest writing the kind of books she loves to read: addictive stories full of teenage angst, tension, twists and turns.

Home is a small town in the middle of England where she currently juggles being a full-time writer with being a mother/referee to two little people. In her spare time (and when she's not camped out in front of the laptop) you'll most likcly find L. A. immersed in a book, escaping the chaos that is life.

L. A. loves connecting with readers.

The best places to find her are:
www.lacotton.com